A BAND OF STROLLING PLAYERS

A BAND OF STROLLING PLAYERS

Joe Neil Steward

Library of Congress Number:		2001117603
ISBN #:	Hardcover	1-4010-1929-3
	Softcover	1-4010-1928-5

This book was printed in the United States of America.

To order additional copies of this book, contact:
Xlibris Corporation
1-888-7-XLIBRIS
www.Xlibris.com
Orders@Xlibris.com

CONTENTS

11064-STEW

ACKNOWLEDGEMENTS

To Marita Weaver Steward–whose engagement sent this plowboy from the farm to the University to the theater to the West Coast to enjoy and endure his acting career. Also my loving thanks for putting up with a writer.

To Dr. Christian Moe—maybe I should have listened to him.

To Dr. Sherwin Abrams—who taught me how to take a scene at will.

CHAPTER ONE

Corvettes are Fast

We had just gotten back on the freeway after twenty miles of detour, when a new, red 1960 Corvette pulled up beside us; the driver laughed and thumbed his nose at us.

Bart didn't even shift down into third, he just 'stood-on-it' in fourth. The Bonneville, running at seventy-five in fourth, chirped its tires, and we shot away from the Corvette. The guy in the Corvette had a surprised look on his face as we left him behind. He started to pour the coal to the Corvette, but we kept gaining, one hundred, one fifteen, we hit one-twenty before the Corvette started to gain. It must have had a higher rear end—he sure didn't have the raw power.

I swiveled my head around from watching the guy in the vett behind us, and the thought flashed into my mind, there's a cop somewhere—I have always had a sixth sense about ambushes. My eyes flicked across both edges of the lanes ahead—nothing on the right verge. I switched my eyes to the six-foot high growth of horseweeds that clogged the center divider almost unbroken for miles ahead. We hit a bit of a rise, and I caught a flash of sun off of something red. My yell was out before I thought about it. "There's a cop!"

The needle was just kissing one hundred thirty-five as Bart jammed on the brakes. The Corvette shot by us, the guy's head whipping around in open-mouthed surprise. Bart had to fight to keep from putting his foot back down—he hated to see the guy go by him. He hadn't seen any cop—my yell caused him to back off. If I were wrong—there certainly was no sign of a cop anywhere. I decided to ride the hunch, I said, "He's in the weeds on the left, up ahead."

Bart and Jim's eyes were glued to the center divider. The Corvette was still leaving us, when the black and white 'land shark' tore its way out of the horseweeds with his Christmas tree lit. His tires screamed, and his whooper was singing the kind of music that makes your guts roll up, as the cop stood on it and ran right up the back of that vett.

The Corvette put his flashers on and pulled over to the right shoulder with the nose of that Golden Commando Intercepter right behind him. The Commando's strobes flicked our eyeballs as we approached. We waved to the guy in the Corvette as we went by. I bet he thought we were shills for the cop, but the vett had challenged us.

Bart looked at me and wiggled his eyebrows and said, "Thanks!"

Jim said, "How in the world did you know he was there?"

"We went over a hump, and I caught a gleam off his red lights—I just had a hunch."

Bart shook his head. "He sure was hid."

The red Corvette and the strobes took a couple of miles to fade from the center mirror. I lay my head back. My mind began to sort and file my seventeenth summer.

***

The weather had conspired with school being let out—to my disgust it was perfect for plowing. The blues, the postpartum blues brought on by not having an identity anymore after graduation, like to have drove me nuts—the first three or four days I hadn't been fit to shoot. The tractor didn't mind what kind of a mood I was in. If I put gas and oil in, and didn't try to make it climb trees, the tractor was fine.

Again this year, we had rented the place next door—the 'old Mack place.' Around and around the fields I go, turning over furrow after furrow of brown earth that looks like large pans of brownies.

The hours turn into days, the days into weeks, the weeks into a month and a half. Six weeks I've gone around in circles—ever smaller circles. I have the plowing to myself this year—Dad isn't working a shift at the hospital and then another shift at home in the fields like he did last year. I had left the Mack place till last, and I was finishing up their field, had maybe five or six rounds to go, when nature picked now, right this minute, to demand that I remove myself to the hedgerow to make a contribution to the future fertility of the hedgerow.

I was just finishing up the—well, in this case, the leaf work, when I heard voices. I peeked out from behind the leafy screen. Two very tall strangers were coming across the plowed ground.

I thought, *Who the Sam Hill, are they, and what are they doing here? I wonder if the Macks have sold this place, and all this plowing is for someone else?* I kept watching the two guys as I hurriedly pulled my jeans up. As they came closer, there was something about the blond one on the right, the way he set his feet, that tugged at memory. The thought hovered at the edge of recognition. Finally, I said out loud, "That one looks like Jimmy Hook, but Jimmy Hook is smaller than I am." This guy was well over six feet, three or four inches over.

I stepped out of the fencerow. The two guys saw me, and the blond one waved. "Hey, Bo," he yelled. *Sure as God put a pointed nose on woodpeckers, it was Jimmy.*

We shook hands, and I liked to have got a crick in my neck from trying to look up at Jimmy. He said, "This is my cousin, Bart Nelson from Kankakee."

I said, "What are you guys up to?"

Jimmy said, "We're here to get you. You're goin' back with us to Kankakee."

I opened my mouth, and Jimmy cut in, "It's all settled, Bo; we talked to your Dad and Mom before we came out to get you. Your mom' s packing your clothes right now."

I blinked and almost forgot to close my mouth while the two of them laughed at my expression; finally I said, "I've only got five more rounds to go, you guys go on back to the pond and have a swim. I'll meet you at the pond to clean up as soon as I finish." They chatted for a few more minutes and then turned and walked back towards the pond.

I finished the plowing and drove to the pond. They were swimming and diving like large otters. I shut the tractor off, stripped to my shorts, and climbed the ladder to the diving board. I bounced too hard and the board threw me slightly off, and I made a sort of a crippled swan dive that stung when I hit. Never show pain; I challenged them to an across the pond race. They might be as big as horses, but I could still out swim them. Those summer evening swims after work had given me an edge.

Finally, Bart said, "We ought to get started as soon as possible, so we won't be all night getting home."

I said, "Righty-ho," and pulled on my jeans, stepped into my shoes without socks and gathered up the rest of my stuff, and climbed on the tractor. When the tractor is this hot—you barely have to touch the starter button. At the barn, I just lowered the plows and shut it off and left the tractor in the hallway of the barn.

The car in the driveway was a brand, new, 1960 Pontiac Bonneville, a two-door hardtop, with white sidewalls. It had several coats of lacquer over metal-flake—a huckleberry would have been jealous of the color.

Mom had my suitcase packed and clean clothes laid out on the family room daybed. Dad asked, "How much is left to plow?"

As I changed, I told him, "I stayed and finished it before I came in."

He nodded and said, "I'll get started on the disking." He looked at mom and said, "You can go up to Jim's for a week. You'll come back on the train."

Mom said, "You call and let us know what time the train will be in."

Dad turned to me and said, "Your Aunt Maude wants you to stay with her the last two days you're up there."

Aunt Maude had never married, so she had no children of her own. She was a schoolteacher, and for some reason, I was her favorite nephew—she had come down several times in past years and taken me fishing, but I wasn't as thrilled about this idea of staying with her as I should have been—I would have rather spent the whole time with Jim.

Mom came in, handed me twenty dollars, and said, "If the train costs more, let me know." She knew I still had some of last year's crop money left. She said, "This is a sort of graduation present from us."

I looked at them, smiled and said, "Thanks, you two," and hugged them.

Jimmy and Bart were leaning on the Pontiac when I came out with my suitcase, and Bart opened the trunk to put it in. There was enough room in that trunk for a small third world family to live, if they didn't snore too badly. Bart shoved the two cases that were in there over and settled mine in, too, slammed the lid, removed the keys, tossed them over his shoulder, caught them out of the air as they came down in front, and slipped into the driver's seat. Jim motioned with his hand for me to get in the middle. Short guys always wind up in the middle. It was a change of place for Jim and me. The last time I saw Jim, he was the short guy. He hadn't just shot up; he had spread out, too. His shoulders were as wide as mine. It looks like we would wear the same shirt size, except for sleeve length. Bart was even bigger. They were the same height, but Bart was heavier by fifteen pounds.

I looked at Jim and asked, "How tall are you?"

Jim smiled and said, "Six-four."

I shook my head and said, "Man-o-live, last time I saw you, you were shorter than I am."

He smiled and answered, "I stayed that way until last year—I kind of just shot up."

I grinned and said, "I'll say."

We drove out our road to the highway. I asked Bart, "You plannin' to go up fifty-seven?"

"Yeah."

"Turn left. It's about a quarter mile down there."

The power of that Bonneville was something. When we had pulled up the on ramp to enter fifty-seven, Bart put his foot in it. The seat slammed you in the back, and held you there like a bug on the windshield. He ran it up to over a hundred before he let off and dropped back to seventy-five.

"How fast will this thing go?"

Bart smiled and said, "I don't know. I've only had it up to a hundred and twenty, I never had a chance to open it up on a long run and see what it will do." Bart switched on the radio, and music blasted conversation out of existence. We cruised along; the miles were eaten under the Pontiac's tires like the white lines on the road. Somewhere in the middle of the state, we ran out of freeway. We had to detour on a two-lane blacktop around the construction. This was an example of local Illinois politics at work. Some tin-pot political machine had held up the construction on that section for several years. The twenty or so miles took longer to cover than the last fifty on the freeway, but as the Bible says, "This too shall pass." Finally it was over, and we pulled back on the freeway to be challenged by the Vett.

Once the cop's strobes had faded, Bart turned the music down softer, and we settled down for the ride—the only trouble, it left me free to think, and my poor mind wandered into an area that was a personal minefield. Meggan's wedding was this week. Maybe God is still on his throne. This trip came at a time I was not equipped to live through without help. If I had been left to ferment, I might have blown her life, and for sure mine, apart. I might have all the good intentions in the world, but as they say "The road to hell is paved with good intentions." I just don't know if I could have stood it if I had been there at home, knowing that this was it, her marriage in the sight of God and the law was final. I don't know what I could have or would have done. Several things had run through my mind in the last few weeks; some of them I was shocked that I was capable of even entertaining the idea. Well, I was being removed from temptation.

Bart only made one pit stop, at a hamburger joint, to drain and refill the necessary compartments of the body.

We pulled into Kankakee at around ten at night. Bart set our suitcases out, shook hands, and took off for home.

Jim's Mother fixed bacon and eggs, we ate, and his mother made arrangements for sleeping. There were twelve kids in Jim's family, all but the oldest sister who was married, were still at home. Jim's brother got shuffled off to the couch, and I bunked in Jim's room. We turned in around eleven. Jim was starting a new job in the morning, so he had to get up early.

CHAPTER TWO

Learning to Plow with Water-Skis

Jim was gone when I was awakened. Jim had a sister who had just turned thirteen. When I woke up, she was climbing into bed fully dressed except for shoes—I don't know what she had in mind. I just reached out and whipped the arm she was leaning on out from under her so she fell fiat on her face. Then I jerked her by the arm until she was across my lap. At least her maximus glutimus—her buns were across my lap, and I spanked them soundly. Tanned her hide good and turned her loose in such away she couldn't retaliate upon my person, pointed to the door and hissed, "Out! Young ladies should not attempt to remove the covers from sleeping young men. The next time you come in here, knock first, I might have been undressed." She giggled and ran. She stuck her head back around the door and said, "Maybe next time I'll have better luck." She ducked out before I could reply.

I don't know what it is, but for some reason too-young young ladies have a passion for sharpening their claws on my hide. Where are they when they are old enough to be of some interest?"

I dressed quickly, not wishing to hold Mrs. Hook up in her daily routine, and presented myself downstairs. Mrs. Hook asked me, "What would be your first choice for breakfast?"

"I'm easy, whatever everyone else is having."

"Bacon and eggs, ok?"

"Fine."

Mom always taught me to eat whatever was set before me when I was visiting, so when she set two eggs with runny yokes down in front of me, I had to swallow a couple extra times before even starting to eat. Runny yokes make me want to whoops when that slippery stuff starts to slither down my throat. I don't much like eggs at all, but if I 'has' to eat 'em—I 'wants' them fried hard enough to resole a boot and the yokes broken. The sulfur in the yokes gives me the burps—I relive eggs till noon. Oddly enough, hardboiled I can handle. I have learned to talk to someone and not look at my plate if there is something that doesn't agree with me on my plate. Those runny yokes got sopped up with lots and lots of bread, and Mrs. Hook got far more conversation than she would have otherwise.

It was nine 'o' clock when the last bite slithered home. Jim didn't get off work until three-thirty, so there was a bit of time to kill on my own. I got out and walked for several hours.

Being a country boy, I travel by landmarks rather than street names and numbers. The sun was my first reference point, a big building in one direction, and a bit of a hill with a flagpole in another, as long as those were visible, no problem. Several hours slipped by unnoticed. My growling tummy brought the passage of time to my attention. My watch said fifteen till two. There was a hotdog stand beside a playground. The prices were shocking! At home a hot dog was a quarter; here a hot dog was six bits. Well, when in Kankakee, pay as the Kankakeeians pay. It knocked my hunger down to a quiet roar.

The one thing that impressed me was the affluence that was everywhere I looked. This country mouse was impressed.

My watch said two-thirty; time to start my perambulations for home. I found the hill with the flagpole and lined out on it. Thirty minutes of fast walking brought me into familiar country. On the way out, the sun had been on my right. There was a tree that looked familiar. At that tree with the sun on my left I made a right turn, walked over two blocks, turned left, and went down two doors on the right, and presto—the wrong house.

My steps were easy to retrace. The tree wasn't hard to find. A good look at it proved to me that it wasn't the same tree. The trouble was, there wasn't another tree that even resembled this one—that stumped me.

The main street seemed to be the best bet to me—keep on walking down this street toward that flagpole. The country mouse kept getting 'loster and loster.' The thing that saved me; Jim came by on his way home from work and recognized me and gave me a ride. Like a cat that slips on a waxed floor will go over and smell the piano as though that was what it had in mind all along, I never let on that I was lost, just was glad to see Jim.

We had an hour before Mrs. Hook called us to supper. Captain Hook, Jim's dad, arrived just as it was time to eat. He would come from one job, eat, and run to his other job. He did body work and resprays at night after his main job and on the weekends as well. He had been a full time body man when I had known him back home. His doctor told him to cut back on exposure to the chemicals used in bodywork, so he only did it for a couple of hours a night and Saturday and Sunday. I guess, to him, that was cutting back, he used to do it sixteen hours a day, seven days a week.

The 'captain' was not a rank—just a natural result of being named Hook. His real name was James, Sr., and Jim was James, Jr. Captain had done the lacquer job on Bart's Bonneville. Captain rented a double garage across town where he did all his extra stuff.

Captain had never said two dozen words to me all the time we lived next door. I had just been one of the many kids underfoot—there were so many, you had to have a scorecard to tell them apart—Captain Hook never bothered. If he tripped over you, you got yelled at, if not, you got ignored. Captain was short like me and built like me. Jim towered over him. Now that Jim was the biggest thing around, Captain took more notice of him.

We ate in shifts—there wasn't enough room for all the kids to eat at once. Captain, Jim, his brother Dave, and I had the first shift. I felt strange, me eating with little kids watching every bite I took, but there wasn't anything I could do to change things, so, I just ate and kept quiet.

Captain pushed back from the table and asked, "Jim, are you going to work at the shop tonight?"

"We'll be by so that Bo can see it, but we want to see some of Kankakee tonight."

Captain nodded and got ready to go. Jim and I left about the same time. We just combed our hair, grabbed our wallets and split in the fifty-seven Ford two-door Jim had. We started looking for girls. Our luck ran about like it does in hunting season; the Dears disappeared just like the deer do.

Jim had bragged about the beauty and availability of the Nazerine girls. Their folks were so strict that they couldn't dance, go to movies, bowl, swim in mixed company, or wear makeup. The only thing left to do was sit around in cars and neck. Wouldn't you know it; we picked the one-week they were all off at their church camp. The streets, like Mother Hubbard's cupboard, were bare. The only young ladies we saw were working girls—no, not that kind of work. These working girls worked in department stores, drugstores and A&P stores.

In desperation Jim took me into a department store and introduced me to a girl who worked there. She was thrilled over what she called my southern accent. When I would say something, she would giggle and say, "Say it again, Bo."

The way Jim was acting, I couldn't tell if she was something special to him—so flirting and kidding was as far as it went; besides she didn't get off work until 10:30 P. M., and Jim had to get up and go to work in the morning.

We drove down a street eight lanes wide. Jim said, "When it snows, the heavy traffic packs the snow into a thin smooth layer of ice. Three o'clock in the morning on Saturday night when most cars are home and their drivers asleep; me and my buddies drive down the center of the eight lanes at fifty, slam on the brakes, cut the wheels, and see who could do the most brodies."

"Yeah," I said, "We do the same thing down home when the lakes freeze hard enough to support a car."

We came into an area that seemed to have more girls around to the casual glance, but up close it became apparent that they were hovering on the edge of puberty with maybe one or two that had just fallen over the edge.

We pulled up at a house, and Jim got out, so I got out. There were two girls who needed or thought they needed training bras. Jim went up to the door and knocked, an older lady came to the door. Jim said something, and she shook her head, and then she said something and looked at her watch.

I was sitting on the front fender of Jim's car watching Jim. The next thing I know I'm sandwiched between two girls that are too little to keep. The feisty, scrappy kind, that will be keepers in a couple of years if they don't get caught and fried to a crisp first.

Jim came back to the car. "Her two older sisters," he nodded to the one nibbling on my neck, "are gone for the rest of the week."

Why do I draw the kittens that are just learning to unsheathe their claws? Why do they find my hide perfect for scratching? Keeper or not, this one had been peeking through keyholes and was making most of the right moves. Parts of me that are not controlled by logic were saying *yes, oh yesss!* The mind at the same time was saying *you gots to be kiddin' me, Kingfish.* She moved around to a full lip-lock. I said to Jim, "Uh, mfhmmph—Jim don't you have to get to work? What time is it getting to be?" Jim watched and grinned as she attacked again.

I rolled one eye around to accuse him, and Jim grinned and said, "Oh no, I've got plenty of time, Bo, before we've got to go." When she pushed me over backwards into the car seat and climbed in to do further close combat, Jim took pity on me and grabbed her by the waist and hauled her out and said, "Scoot, we've got to go."

As we drove away, he laughed, "You're lucky her older sisters weren't home, you would have been a sack lunch."

As I tried to recover from the effects of close combat, I found myself wishing she had sent her older sisters, so I wouldn't feel so silly. We drove around for a while; there was no action anywhere, at least anywhere we were. I was wondering what a sack lunch felt like. I felt like a run over Twinkie.

The next day was Saturday, Jim called in sick—Mary, his older sister, and her husband came over and got us and took us out on their boat. The Kankakee River, at least the part we were on, was about fifty yards wide and four feet deep and as the old saying goes, "Too thick to drink and too thin to plow," a tad muddy.

I had never water-skied, when they found this out, there was nothing for it, but "I had to learn to ski." Well, why not! I'm game. In a twinkling of an eye I'm over the side, skis on my feet, rope stretched between them to the boat. I gave the high sign; the boat took up the slack and pulled me up and right out of the skis—I didn't know if you lost the skis, you were supposed to let go of the rope. In any new endeavor there is always some little thing they forget to tell the first timer. I held on and with my head down, the angle of my body planed me right straight to the bottom where I bounced along digging up great gouts of foul tasting mud. I only let go when I ran out of air. My person had shoveled enough muck to start a small truck farm. You could have planted prize-sized cabbages in various nooks and crannies of my body. Air never tasted sweeter, although once the oxygen quota was restored to my starved lungs, my olfactory glands went into overdrive. The smell of river bottom muck perfumed my person, and it was hard to get rid of. My olfactory glands relived it periodically throughout the afternoon.

The second run was much better. After some belated advice, the kid was able to get up and ski, until the wake of a passing boat stripped off one ski. I skied on doing fine until I looked down about fifty yards later. Looking down finished me; down I went to plow another furrow, but just a short one this time. The water was so shallow that you had to let go the rope before you hit the water or be transformed into a dredge.

Jim's brother-in-law had us back to their place for a cookout. The evening lasted so late, there was no use even trying the fleshpots, so we went home and crashed. Worn out by my aquatic workout, sleep overtook me and overcame me with no fight what so ever.

CHAPTER THREE

No One Under 21 Allowed!

My Aunt Maude drove over from where she lived the next day after Mass. She was the only Catholic in a family of rampant Baptists. As a young woman, Grandpa had made her life so miserable, she had rebelled against the religion of her father and become the thing he hated most, a Catholic.

Grandpa had ignored and repeatedly violated the Scriptural injunction against provoking your child to wrath. None of his daughters had any respect or liking for their father. He used to run off any young man who came to court any of his daughters. My Dad's oldest sister married a man who was a gentle soul, but when Grandpa tried to run him off, he just laughed and said, "Go ahead run me off. I'll be back again, and again until you get tired." Then he walked over to my aunt and took her by the hand and said, "Come with me. If he won't let you come home again, I'll marry you tonight." They walked out the door, and Grandpa sat there and glared, but he never said another word or made a move to stop them.

Aunt Maude wasn't so fortunate with her beaus, they all ran away when Granddad growled—Aunt Maude never married. As she grew older, she put on weight. She was resigned to being without external beauty and unloved, she was resigned to her lot, but her love for children never died; she transferred it to teaching other people's children. She was the only one in the family who went to college, and she'd gotten several degrees, but she never let on she had them.

Even though, I had all the usual lack of couth of a teenage male, for some reason, she wished I had been her son—why I don't know. As we drove to her home, I was polite, but wishing I could have spent my whole week with Jim. Family duty was thrust upon me, and like the mostly dutiful son I am, I gave in gracefully. I won't say I enjoyed my stay, for it was too circumspect and lacking in spice for my taste. I was raised to be mannerly, and being mannerly came naturally to me, so mannerly I was. I opened doors, pulled out chairs, and said yes ma'am, all the things that were sorely missing from Aunt Maude's life. There was nothing to be gained by it for me. It was simply a selfless giving of one's self to another human being.

The Bible says, "Train up a child in the way he should go and when he is old he will not depart from it." The bonds of childhood—I found I didn't care to break them—my choice not someone else's. Those bonds had made my parents people I not only loved, I respected. I wanted to be like my dad more than any other person.

My time with Aunt Maude seemed to go on forever, but finally drew down to my leaving. I was to ride a train, something I had never done. Aunt Maude embarrassed me by going to the conductor and telling him, "It's his first trip—would you keep an eye on him?"

Gus, the conductor, turned out to be a fount of information about the towns we passed through, but his greatest kindness was when there was a layover in the middle of the night, he took me into what seemed to be the seediest sort of a dive with some of the roughest people I had ever seen. There was a big sign on the door.

> "NO ONE UNDER 21 ALLOWED! WE CHECK IDS!"

I stopped when I saw the sign. Gus smiled and said, "It's all right, son, you're with me. I eat here every trip. The food's good, and they'll let you alone if I say so.

We walked in and the bartender said, "Good morning, Gus." His eves narrowed when he saw me.

Gus jerked his thumb over his shoulder at me and said, "The kid's with me."

The bartender smiled, and said; "All right, Gus, but I don't want no trouble."

Gus whispered, "Stay with me kid." We washed up and came back and had the best chili-melt hamburger, with onions, and bacon and a big order of fries, with coffee as a chaser. Pie if you had room—I did.

The yard crew was breaking down the train. I was worried about my suitcase—Gus had locked it in the caboose. "Gus, you think my suitcase'll be all right?"

He said, "Don't worry, they'll get it knuckled on to the right train, son."

After an hour, we paid our bills and went back. Sure enough we found the caboose hooked onto the tail of the southbound headed for New Orleans with a scheduled stop in Anna. I was supposed to call ahead, but as it was the middle of the night, I didn't want to wake the folks. I figured I'd get a chance later.

Gus went dead at four in the morning. Going dead is what railroaders call running out of operating time. A dog catch crew was brought out, and Gus' crew taken to a hotel to rest.

The train got into Anna at 7:30 in the morning. I called home and told Mom, "I'm in Anna."

She said, "Well, go get something to eat, I won't have time to cook."

I had to lug my suitcase four blocks to a cafe. A cinnamon roll, the size of a tire, made my day. I didn't drink coffee often, but I had only napped and not much of that, so coffee filled in for sleep. After paying my bill and lugging my suitcase four blocks back to the station, there was still a ten-minute wait for Mom.

Mom drove up and got out to open the trunk. I put the suitcase in, and we hugged, and she asked, "Well, how was your trip, Worrywart?

I might be seventeen, but I hadn't proved anything to her yet. Worrywart, I had been—Worrywart I still was to her. She started to call me Worrywart as a little kid, when I started to fidget around whenever I had to sit still in public. I dropped her off at work, and she said, "Don't forget to come back and get me this afternoon, Worrywart."

It was a mixed blessing to be home. It was a place where I was loved, but it was also the site of my first defeat. While I was gone, Meggan became a married woman. She was truly lost and gone forever. Not a single thought of her had troubled me for the last three days. The familiar sights, sounds, and smells, had brought her crashing back, tossing everything else aside. The wave of helpless rage that engulfed me wasted the day—rage, not at another human being, but at God for taking the one person I loved away from me. I blamed God for taking her away from me. In my anger my own shortcomings didn't count. I was the one who didn't ask her out, but that didn't count. I was the one who acted like a little kid, but that didn't count. I was the one who was afraid to be her friend, but that didn't count. No, God didn't stop me from my stupidity! That counted! That and only that.

CHAPTER FOUR

The Carmen Miranda of Horses

Dad had the planting done, the weeds hadn't gotten a good start yet, the hay wasn't ready to cut, and I didn't feel like cutting wood. When I asked, Dad said, "Yeah, it's all right with me if you go for a ride tomorrow."

I planned to ride over toward Lick Creek and visit a kid named Max Colter. Max was in the FFA and had a horse, too. I called Max on the phone and told him my plans.

The ride, as planned, would be over twenty miles; the farthest Smokey had been ridden since he broke his leg. Mom made me a large lunch to carry along. Everything was ready for my trip before bedtime.

Dad woke me up at six, and my chores were done, breakfast eaten, and Smokey saddled and ready to go by eight. I took my lunch out of the freezer the last thing before I left—Mom had frozen my lunch so the sandwiches wouldn't spoil. A hot horse on a hot day could spoil meat in a couple of hours. The frozen package felt good as I slipped it into the saddlebags. I took a long drink before mounting.

Smokey was ready to travel, he wanted to run right off, but the day was too hot, so, much to his chagrin, he got held in on a tight rein. That made him twitchy—a dangerous tuft of grass could make him do his 'Oh my-oh dear' dance across the road and back. It also made his guts squelch-squelch—I hate that sound. We went past the pond, through the Mack place, and turned on the road to Charley Hawk's place. We turned off that onto the road to Cash Creek and crossed at the bridge, then followed the road on through the Cash Creek bottoms until we hit the Lick Creek Road.

I could have taken the freeway and ridden down the center divider, that worked fine except at the underpasses, there you had to cross on the pavement bridges, That gets a little hairy—there are so many nuts out there that love to scare a horse. If I have to ride along the freeway for a short distance, at the underpass I ride down the bank to the road below, cross it, and lunge Smokey up the bank to the other side.

The only trouble with the Cash Creek Road, you have to watch out for snakes around the water. Smokey found one; I never did see it, but the smell of fresh-cut, ripe cucumber was rank. Smokey had a dancing fit, but evidently the snake had moved out. Spooky feeling, being close enough to smell one, but not be able to see where it was.

A couple of miles after we got on the Lick Creek Road, we turned off on the county graveled road that led to Max's place. Max was waiting with his horse saddled at the barn.

He waved and said, "Howdy, Bo."

"Hello, Max, you mind if I get a drink?" I swung down and tied Smokey by Max's horse. He led the way to the pump in the yard where I took on a good bate of cold water and wet down my hat. Smokey had watered in a ditch a mile or so back.

Max told his Mom, "We're leavin', Mom."

She handed him a lunch—it was only about a quarter to eleven, too early to eat yet.

We walked to where our horses were in the process of sniffing hello. Max's horse was a stocky palomino mare—a racing quarter horse. From the time Max swung on board, that horse was in constant motion, fidgeting, fighting the bit, wanting to run. It looked like trying to ride a roller skate that had wheels that spin around in circles as well as roll. That horse was doing four steps in place for every step that Smokey took. The mare's twitchy antics were making Smokey jumpy as well.

Max said, "Well, I'd better run her a ways or she'll never settle." I nodded, he loosed his reins, and that horse sprang from a fidgety walk to a dead run. Smokey was two lengths behind before he ever started. By the time we had gone a hundred yards, we were five lengths behind and losing ground rapidly. We ran a half mile, Smokey was thirty yards behind, and it wasn't getting any better. Max tried to pull up, but it took him another hundred yards to stop that mare.

Max said with a grin, "She loves to run." The mare was standing in one place dancing because she was being held. The run hadn't improved the ride any. She was still just as antsy as when we started. Her front feet were running all the time. She was sort of the Carmen Miranda of horses, except she didn't wear funny hats.

When I exclaimed, "That horse is fast."

Max asked, "Why don't you ride her, Bo?" When I swung up on the mare, I noticed the cantle of his saddle was broken and only the seat leather held it in place. As soon as I loosened the reins and said the, "Git-" part of "Getup," that horse shot out from between my legs, only my quick grab at the saddle horn kept me from going over on my butt. The mare had me stretched out on my tummy, feet and legs flapping like flags in a high wind. I pulled myself back up into the saddle by main-strength and awkwardness. That horse was awesome! I understood why the cantle of Max's saddle was broken.

We ran for another half mile, and then it took me over a hundred yards to pull her back to a walk. Walk is a misnomer; she jigged in place. It felt like riding one of those wind-up mechanical monkeys with its head against the wall and it's feet going a mile a minute. We rode on for about a mile, and the constant jigging was starting to affect my vision. Finally, I said,

"Max, if you don't mind, let's trade back. I have enjoyed about all of this I can stand. This is some horse. I've never seen the like." I finally got the motorized mare to stand still long enough for me to get off. It took me a couple of seconds to get used to standing on something that wasn't in motion. Max looked down from Smokey's back and chuckled.

Smokey had covered a lot more miles than the mare, the mile we had run had put a lather on him, and I still had many a mile to cover to get home. It was close enough to lunch to satisfy me. We came to a shaded creek, and I suggested to Max, "Let's eat and let my horse rest."

Max was agreeable, so we swung the horses in under the trees by the water and tied them so they could eat, but not get to the water.

My sandwiches were thawed out real nice, no hard spots, but still cool.

Max asked, "What are your plans now that you've graduated."

"Max, I haven't got a clue. Look for work I guess. I can't stay on the home place, it isn't big enough to support two families if I ever found a woman I wanted—that was dumb enough to marry me—big if."

Max just smiled around his sandwich. The subject of marriage wasn't one I wanted to stumble around in; it brought thoughts that were too hard to handle. I switched the subject around to going on to school. Max listened with a sort of disbelieving curiosity to my talk of wanting to study acting. That was as far outside of his field of interest as learning to speak Chinese.

All he could say about my not being able to go to Chicago to the Goodman School of the Theatre because of a lack of money was, "That's too bad, Bo."

After lunch we led the horses over and let them drink and retightened the cinches. Then I thought about all the miles that Smokey had left yet to travel to get me back home. I pulled the saddle off and took a handful of grass, scrubbed his back, checked his feet, made sure the blanket had no wrinkles in it, and resaddled. We rode on for a couple of miles more; Max's mare was still off to the Camptown Races.

We came to a connecting road, and Max said, "Take this road, it will come out at Cash Creek, turn west at the creek, and you'll come out at the bridge."

"Thanks, Max."

"See you around, Bo."

Max turned the mare toward home and let her go. The last I saw of them, it looked as though he was winning. "Man-o-man, that horse could move."

I was glad I didn't have to ride the mare home. Smokey picked up into a lope; his gate was like sitting in Grandma's rocker. The only fly in the ointment was my saddle was too small—it was a youth model. Sometime when I wasn't looking my butt had done gone and got bigger; and the bigger was rubbing on the back of the saddle. This was the first time in a long time I had put fifteen plus miles in the saddle. The pain caused by the rubbing became the focal point for my mind. I found a bunch of elder berry bushes. Elder berry leaves have a healing effect on places where the sun-don't-shine, that get raw. I packed my shorts with elder leaves. I must have stuffed about ten pounds of leaves in there trying to cushion as well as help it heal. It worked fairly well, but when I got home I found I had picked up a mess of chiggers from the leaves. The next few days, till they wore off, were just wonderful.

About a mile from home, Smokey started to limp. I got off and led him. He was putting weight on his bad leg, but favoring it. The vet had said the last time he looked at Smokey's leg, "There is a ringbone buildup in that cannon, he may limp a little if you ride a long distance. Let him rest a couple of days and rub him down with liniment, he should be fine."

I was one tired cookie by the time we got to the pond. That water looked so inviting, we went down there. Smokey got a long drink, and ol' Bo got a swim. A deep dive got me down to where the water was cold and ol' Bo got a drink, too.

The next morning, Smokey came when I made the feed bucket sing its siren song. The limp was mostly stiffness. Smokey sniffed at the smell of liniment, curled his upper lip, and whuffed a couple of times. He was moving well so he got a pat and was turned loose.

At breakfast Dad suggested that I spend some time cutting wood, i.e., trimming Sassafras out of the fencerows. Sally, my beagle came and jumped in the truck when I called her. I drove to the fencerow where I had quit last year and unloaded my saw. Sally piled out, glad to be of service—she inspected the fencerow for dangerous rogue rabbits. She threaded in and out back to front through the place where I planned to work, and declared it clear. She decided to check further afield and trotted off, in that rear slewed trot dogs travel in, for a hundred yards or so. She heard me start the saw and by the time I had it running properly, she was back to flop in the shade of the pickup. Tree after tree dropped—I usually manage to drop them so they clear the one beside it. When I have ten or so down I come back and begin to limb. As soon as I finished limbing, I shut the saw off and begin to pile the limbs into brush piles. By noon I'd cleared fifty yards of fencerow and made three brush piles where they could be burned later in the fall.

Sally has gone off somewhere on doggy business—so, just me and the saw go in for lunch. Mom and Dad are both working days. Now that I'm out of school I don't need a baby sitter, so they get to have a more normal married life. They had worked opposite shifts all the time I was in school, so there was always one of them home with me. Checks and balances for morals and manners. They needn't have bothered, Meggan was the only girl I was interested in, and she couldn't see me for beans.

Mom had left me a half-pound hamburger ready to fry. That was easy, throw it in the pan, and whack off a brutal slice of onion. For some reason the onions we raised could make a strong man weep, vicious dogs run from your breath, and turn you socially repulsive for an afternoon; but my, they were good! Add Velveeta and enough lettuce to feed a small herd of gerbils, and you had a meal fit to make me lay on my back and wiggle my toes.

When I finished, I started to clean up. Mom didn't like grease poured into her sink, so I got a handful I of pages from an old newspaper to clean out the pan. When I finished cleaning the pan and set it in the rack to dry, I turned to put the rest of the newspapers away. The page lying next up was the hatches and matches page (birth and weddings page) from a few months ago, Meggan's picture lay there smiling up at me with the caption announcing that Mr. and Mrs. Fournier are pleased to announce the marriage of their daughter Meggan to—. I grabbed it and ran into the family room, rammed it into the stove and fumbled for a match with hands that were trembling so badly it took four matches before I got one to stay lit long enough to get the paper burning. I slammed the stove lid and stormed out of the house, grabbed the chainsaw from the back of the truck and slammed my way to the barn, clamped the bar of the chainsaw in the vise, and with rough violent strokes of the file, began to sharpen the chain. In my blind heedlessness, I cut my hand on the tang of the file—sucking the wound, I reached with my other hand for the black electrical tape; the black tape stopped the bleeding. I finished the sharpening and filled the gas and oil, stalked to the truck and tossed the saw into the back. My mind wasn't on the cutting; the second tree I attempted to cut, pinched the bar. Anger had made my patience about as long as the hair on Yul Brinner's head. I jerked it hard, it didn't move, so I jerked it again and again. The third time it came out—I had the trigger depressed, the lugged down engine snarled to life just as the momentum of my pull brought the chain into contact with my jeans. The hissing chain grabbed up the denim and pulled it between the chain and the housing of the motor and killed the saw, but my leg was laid bare from knee to cuff. The leg of my jeans hung in tatters around my unmarked leg.

I set the saw on the tailgate of the truck and started to dig around in the glovebox for a screwdriver to dig the shreds of cloth out from under the chain. Realization hit me and the shakes came—only the grace of God had spared me from an injury or perhaps death as a result of my stupidity. Maybe fifteen minutes passed before the shaking finished. I bowed my head and thanked God for his mercy and went back to work with a tad more caution. By five I had cleared fifty more yards of fencerow, stacked three more brush piles, and ricked all the poles to dry. Time for a swim.

CHAPTER FIVE

What No Flowers, Bo?

It clouded up to rain. The lightning played tic-tac-paddy-wac, get the dog with the bone, across the sky. It must have hit the phone wire; the bells of our crank phone rang and blue fire jumped from one bell to the other. It was time to leave for church. We made it to the car, before it started to drown the world a second time. I would say it poured, but that doesn't describe what it did. Someone kicked over Heaven's water bucket, and it dumped. There we sat in the car the motor running, not moving, the wipers couldn't clear the windshield. Our driveway, what little I could see through the little circle I kept clear with my hanky, was a maelstrom as runoff poured from everywhere. It deluged for twenty minutes solid. Then, the sun cut through, the rain stopped, the earth steamed, the frog-strangling rain was over, and we were late for Sunday school. It was time to dismiss from general assembly when we arrived. A lot of other people hadn't made it either. Barbara Ann had played as usual—not being there I'm guessing—but this I do know, Baptists start on time if there is one person there besides the speaker.

There were four people there besides the leader, therefore, I supposed they had done the whole nine yards.

Barbara Ann, leaving the piano to go to her class, brought to mind a Sunday afternoon a few weeks ago, I had run into her while Harold and I were riding. I had taken Barbara Ann for a ride on Smokey. When I lifted her down, there had been a silent promise of more to come between us, before Harold's whining intruded. The problem with that was me—I was still bleeding inside over Meggan, even though she is now married. I wasn't in the mood to keep the promise for more. The wound kept pulling apart. It would seem all healed up and something as simple as having Meggan's picture smiling up from an old newspaper would rip the newly formed scar one more time.

Barbara Ann waited to speak to me. "Hello Bo, I didn't see you last Sunday."

Last week in Kankakee I was as bold as a London pickpocket, cheeky and perky saying outrageous things and having a heck of a time, now, suddenly I was so shy I looked everywhere but her face. I stammered, "Yeah, I was out of town. That was some storm we had, made us late. I'd better get to my class." The teacher wasn't even there yet, but I brushed past Barbara Ann and left her standing there—that was the last time she ever made a move to be personal with me. She was always correct in her behavior, but there never again was a hint of personal warmth. As I walked away, I had the strangest feeling that I had just thrown a rather large chunk of coal on the fires of my own personal Hades.

That afternoon I got a phone call from Mark, the man who's orchard I had worked in last summer, he asked, "Bo can you come tomorrow at eight and work in the shed again? The crop's small this year, a late frost killed half the blossoms."

"Yeah, I can work for you. How long do you think you will need me?"

"I think about a week at the most. Is your Dad there?"

I gave the phone to Dad. Dad listened to Mark and answered, "Mark, thanks but I can't spare the time this year. Yeah, well, thanks for thinking of me." Dad hung up and said, "Well, you've got some work son. Not as much as last year, but the money will come in handy." He looked at me crossways of his nose, with a smile playing around his mouth. Something was coming, that look was a sure sign that he was going to rib me about something. He said, "Bo, if those two nieces of Mark's show up this year, go for the younger one. She's gonna be a looker, and she's worth the most of the two. The older one is surly and greedy, also if she doesn't watch herself, she'll wind up the size of an Angus heifer across the rear, and I don't think that I'd trust her as far as I'd trust your dog not to chase rabbits, either. Whoever gets that girl, his life is gonna be real interesting. Now the young one, she's something else."

I just shook my head and grinned, hoping he'd let up, but he shifted gears on me.

He said real serious like, "Son, how are you doing?"

That stopped me cold. I didn't have a truthful answer that I wanted to give him. I couldn't look at him, but I said, "Oh, I'm fine."

He looked at me a long time, then he said, "I hope so, Bo, I hope so.

He spoke as though he had a way of looking into my mind that I didn't know about. It left me feeling angry—well, not really angry, just sort of miffed that my defenses were not as effective as I'd thought. I hate to be read like an open book.

The mugginess that came after the rain made sleeping something that had to be worked at—six-o'clock came far too soon. Dad came to the foot of the stairs and in a singsong voice sang, "I've got to get up, up, up, and go to work, work, work." He hadn't done that for quite sometime—attempted humor at dawn with no blindfold.

My groan upon attempting to rise was merely my camel Clyde protesting his load, so that a heavier load wouldn't be thrust upon him tomorrow. On second try, third groan, the vertical was managed. Then the slippers, flashlight—flashlight? Where, oh where, is my little flashlight? The silly thing has rolled under the bed again. Groaning in protest is allowed under these conditions. The third try rakes the flashlight to hand.

By seven-fifteen my chores are done, I'm fed; nature has been appeased, with lunch in hand, I'm off to work in the peach orchard. I'm so thrilled I could just whimper! Some of life's treasured experiences, peachfuzz, hard work, and no time for anything else.

It's five of eight when I arrive at the grader shed. This year wiser at the start, I have gloves—my hands hurt for days last year because I tried to do without them.

Mark is in the shed when I got there. I nodded and said, "Hello Mark, it's good to see you."

He looked up around his cigarette, nodded, and shook hands. "How have you been Bo? It's good to have you back."

"Where do you want me?"

He gestures with his cigarette at the lidder loader station. *Well, that's a relief, less fuzzy, less bulk of peaches to handle.*

He said, "This year the crop ain't hardly worth foolin' with and the market's down, but we'll do the best we can."

Letty came out of the house across the road—well, I thought to myself, they're still together. I had wondered when she said what she had said about, "Bobby Mack being so sexy." Wish she hadn't told me that, it puts a load on the way I act around her.

The lids and liners are stacked against one wall, so I grabbed as many as I could carry at one time and arranged them. The value of gloves was quickly impressed in my fingers—collected a splinter from one of the lids, it took three tries with my teeth to remove it—I put the gloves on. The rest of the crew has come in by the time I get the splinter out. The two nieces are standing at their stations with Letty. Mona is easy to spot, there is a heck of a lot more to her stern view, and seen in profile, her bow-sprint has added heft to it, too.

Well, well, Dad was right about that, she could be a prize winning Angus.

Sarah turned around, and my heart nearly stopped. That's another thing Dad was right about. Sarah is a woman! She's no little kid anymore. She's so beautiful it hurt to quit looking at her. When I come to myself, my mouth has been open long enough to trap every fly in the place. My mind can't absorb just what all has changed about Sarah, but the overall effect is stunning.

Mark hits the master switch; the grader hums to life. The conveyer belts begin their endless journey around and around.

There are twenty or so crates of peaches stacked on the dock—the first fruits of the year. One of the tackles of the football team is the dumper. I just hope he lasts longer than the football player who was dumping last year.

At ten o'clock, Mark shuts the grader off for a break. As soon as the thing stops, ol' Bo, is over to Sarah's station. As she turns to step down, I hold out my hand to help her down, she reaches for it automatically—then sees it's me. She stops and looks at me and drops her hand to her side and steps down. I ignore the slight, except for that unruly left eyebrow of mine; it shoots up to its full height of arch like a semaphore.

"Well, hello Sarah. It's good to see you again." I have the eyebrow still raised, and I smile, too.

The corner of her mouth twitches. "Bo." She steps around me and goes to get a drink.

Letty looks at me, her eyebrow is up. She smiles and says "Hello Bo," paused and looked after Sarah, then she says, "You should have listened to me last year."

I grinned self-consciously and nodded. "Yeah, I can see that now!"

She chuckled. "She's going to lead you quite a dance; if you ever get anywhere with her at all. Pity, she was yours for the taking last year, and you wouldn't even look at her."

Sarah timed her return to the second with Mark's turning on the grader. My poor mind was spinning. Maybe if I say this—or maybe if I say that. Well, it made the time pass, noon was there before I was ready. Nothing I could think of to say seemed to be just the right thing to say. I decided to talk to Letty, she'd been right before.

I walked over to Sarah and took her by the hand as she stepped down. She tried to pull her hand away, but I held on and said, "Have a nice lunch, Sarah." Gave her a smile and walked away. As Letty got ready to go to lunch I said, "I think I need to talk to you—I think I need help."

She said, "My boy, I don't think that I can help you now—if you had listened—."

I cut in, "I didn't! And all I've got is now, so what do I do now?"

She sighed and said, "Let me think about it over lunch."

My lunch was in the truck—the truck was hotter than a tin roof. My food had a funny taste to it; I ate it anyway. I felt queasy from the first few bites. It got worse, so I drank a lot of water. Finally, I had to go to the honey bucket and stick my finger down my throat. The whoops helped except for the bile taste, rinsing my mouth out and eating a peach cut the taste, but I was still hollow from lack of food. I didn't dare eat too many peaches or yours truly would have to camp-out in the honey bucket.

There wasn't enough time to go to town and get something to eat—I would just have to tuff it out. Ok, tuff it out I will, but it didn't help my attitude.

Letty came back from lunch early—she said, "Bo, I don't think you will do what I'm going to tell you to do."

"What's that?"

She smiled and said, "Get her some flowers and write her a note. Apologize for hurting her so badly last year. Give them to her here, in public." I stood there with my stunned expression so long, Letty said, "You can close your mouth now, Bo."

"That means that I would have to declare myself a suitor in front of God and everybody."

She nodded. "Right you are, young-feller-me-lad."

"What if she turns me down? I'm going to look silly."

She raised that eyebrow of hers again and said, “You asked me. Anyway you ought to be used to feeling silly by now, what’s one more time. You hurt her in public, acknowledge her as a desirable woman in public.”

When I didn’t say anything, she shrugged, “Your choice, Bo.”

The idea totally bumfuzzeled my mind.

At three o’clock, the football player quit. Mark took over from me at the lidder loader slot. I knew the easy job was too good to be true.

At six when we quit, Mark asked, “Bo, do you know anybody who would want to work?”

I thought of Jim Buckley, but that meant that I would have to leave home twenty minutes early to go and get him. Also it meant that I’d be stuck at dumper. Jim just wasn’t big enough yet to handle the orchard crates all day. But I knew that Jim needed the money, and Mark needed the help. I said, “I have a buddy, but I would have to go and get him every day.”

Mark said, “Bo, I’ll pay you an extra hour a day to get him and take him home.

I wrote Jim’s number on a page of Mark’s note pad.

Mark said, “Thanks Bo, I’ll call him tonight, and I’ll let you know one way or the other.”

He called at eight o’clock. When I answered the phone I could hear the clicks down the line as eight of the twelve people on our party line picked up their receivers to evesdrop. Mark said, “Jim wants to work, can you pick him up?”

“Sure thing, Mark.”

“Thanks, Bo.”

That night in bed I thought about flowers, whether to get some for Sarah or not. It seemed silly—I decided not to.

I had set my alarm for five thirty, an hour when not even the angels are awake, or if they are, they’re probably grumpy. I just wanted to roll over and pretend that this was a dream—a bad one. Duty called, rather it yelled. There is something in my nature that once I have given my word, compels me to unreasonable lengths to keep it. The older I get, the more I try to avoid ever giving it—that way I don't have to keep it.

One leg is out of bed—two legs are out. Thank God there aren't any more. The body ain't gonna be easy. Supreme effort, the body is now sitting. The mind is not with us yet. Ok, all together now, amazing what can be accomplished with the mind absent, I am now standing. Big yawn, my jaw cracks, have to work it around to get it to feel right—now for the slippers. "Oh great! I kicked the flashlight under the bed again. Mumblefratz, come here you silly turkey." Ok, now down the stairs.

I go schlepping out to the hogpen. *Ah ha! I've beaten the oinkers up—free throw at the trough. I wish I had a picture of that, the trough brim full and not an oinker in sight.*

The chickens aren't even up. They're going to think that it rained corn from heaven. For once that silly rooster isn't strutting around cackling with suspicion that I'm the Sunday chicken strangler come to whisk one of his flock off to doom, and a crisp brown coating. He just crowed—the sound of the corn must have waked him up.

Mom was just starting breakfast. "What are you doing up so early?"

"Well, the football player Mark hired as a dumper quit at four yesterday. Mark asked me 'If I knew any one who would work.' I told him about Jim Buckley, and Mark hired him and is paying me to go and get him, and take him home." She looked unimpressed, but she didn't say anything. She put the first two pancakes on my plate. I slathered them with peanut butter, butter, and Karo syrup and made quick work of them.

Mom brought me my lunch. *Gloves? Oh, I left them in the truck.* As I'm running to the truck, nature woke up and called rather loudly. *Fine! I will answer your ill-timed and strident request posthaste, forthwith, etc. etc.* Nature appeased once more, I again ran to the truck.

At the highway I cut over to the Dongola blacktop and turned off at the Big Creek road. Jim was sitting on the front porch drinking coffee. I yelled out the window, "You got any gloves?"

He held them up, along with his lunch. Sometimes I think the boy is smarter than me. Jim piles in, and we leave in a cloud of dust. We are running a little ahead of time, so a temperate rate of speed will do, just fast enough to kick the tail out on the corners.

At Highway 51, a right turn heads us toward Anna, and a head on crash with deja vu. As we pass Meggan's folks' place, I can barely see the road. Deja vu don't sit on your back quietly, oh no—it's spurring and fanning. *Oh, God, won't it ever let up*? This for sure ain't the way to start the day bright eyed and bushy tailed. By the time we got to the shed I felt as solemn as a snockered owl. The prospect of being the dumper for the rest of the peach harvest didn't do anything to lighten my load either.

Jim and I went over to Mark. "Mark, this is Jim Buckley."

"Hello, Jim." They shook hands. "Thanks for coming to work on such short notice." Mark looked from me to Jim, "Jim, I'm going to have you put the lids on and load the truck."

I had known that was the way it would have to be, but still it was a downer to have it carved in stone, so to speak. It was five till eight—an idle mind is a nasty place to be—I just don't know if I can drive past Meggan's old home as many times as peach harvest is going to take. Mona and Sarah came in, and that took my mind off of old troubles and put it on my new ones. Not much improvement, but at least a change. Mona is sporting a stone on her finger. I hadn't noticed that yesterday. Poor bugger, she's gonna be a hat-full of trouble. Something had changed about her—she no longer radiated sex appeal indiscriminately to every male who came within range of her aura. It was as if she had turned off her bug light and no longer attracted moths to her flame. Sarah, on the other hand, had blossomed. She wasn't, as Mona had been, broadcasting musk into the air—no, Sarah didn't make you want to tear your clothes off wherever you chanced to find her. With Sarah, you wanted to be the one to take care of her. It was a gentler response Sarah invoked—one that you wanted to last forever.

I went over and said, "Good morning, Sarah."

Her eyes flicked over me, "Bo." She turned and stepped up onto her station and stood with her back to me.

I decided to throw my hat in the door to see if anyone would shoot at it. I said, "Sarah, turn around I'd like to talk to you." She stiffened, but she turned halfway and glanced at me. I said, "Sarah, I'm sorry if I hurt you last summer, will you forgive me?" Her mouth dropped open, but she didn't say anything, so I said, "Is that a yes or a no, Sarah?"

She said without turning, "I don't know what you mean. Whatever gave you the idea that I was hurt?"

"The way you're acting made me think that. You used to come and talk to me, now you won't even speak to me except to say my name if I say good morning, that makes me think that I've hurt you. I'm sorry, Sarah. I'd like to take you out—will you go?"

There was a long pause. She didn't turn, she just shook her head in a quick shake and said, "No."

"Fine! I'm sorry." I turned and walked away. Well, I'd done it. I had made a royal fool out of myself. The only trouble was I was a year late in doing it. I couldn't see Sarah's face from the dumping station, all I could see was that long blond hair and the curve of her left hip, and nice as that curve was, it couldn't tell me what her mind was thinking.

Mark hit the switch and brought the sleeping giant to life, and I had to feed the sucker. I had forgotten how bad peach fuzz makes me feel. It was going to be a long day.

I could see Jim from where I worked, he seemed to be doing fine. At the ten o'clock break, I went to the truck and brought our lunches in so they wouldn't spoil. One day in a row was enough of that. When I had put the lunches in the shade, I looked over at Sarah, she was looking at me; she looked away and spoke to Mona. I wanted to go over and stick my oar in again, but I just didn't have the heart or the guts to do it. One rejection per day is my standard fix; I don't want to become addicted.

Mark started the grader; the hum of it soon numbed the

mind. The routine of turn, bend, lift, turn, and dump became a place to hide until it stopped.

At noon, when Mark shut it down, Sarah came by my station on her way to the house, my station was in the way if you wanted to go to the house. Sarah came by with her eyes avoiding mine. That's a switch, it's usually me that does that.

I was still leaning up against the dump station when Letty came by. She asked, "What was that all about?"

"I don't know. I apologized to her and she said, 'What makes you think that I was hurt?' and I said, the way you used to talk to me and now you won't. Then I asked her to go out with me and she said, 'No.'"

Letty listened and then she asked, "No flowers"

I shook my head.

Then she said, "Women love foolish things—like flo
things that don't make sense to most men, things that mo
couldn't be bothered with. Women are different than m

I looked at her and grinned.

She raised an eyebrow and said, "Different in oth
the merely obvious ones. Most men have no idea
cries, or feels loving, or hates. They just stumble
and the results surprise the heck out of them. M
the way things work or the shortest way to get
deal in the way things make them feel. D
wanted for more than her body? Does sh
liked?" She stopped, looked closely at m
flowers, Bo."

I shook my head, "No. I feel like

Letty looked at me—there w
shrugged and went to lunch.

Jim came over, and we ate o
find us. The peach fuzz was st
time I could think it away, h
itself known, and how!

Jim asked, "Who's t

"Which one?"

"The one you were talking to."

"Sarah. Her granddad owns the orchard, and Mark is her uncle. She and Mona, her big sister, come down in the summer to make money."

He chewed a bit, then he asked, "What's between you two?"

"What do you mean?"

Jim took another bite, chewed and said, "Well, it seemed that you two have known each other before."

"Yeah, I worked here last year."

"Oh." He bit off a bite and looked at me quizzically.

He didn't say anything, but I could feel him thinking, so I said, "Last summer she was"—I stopped—"younger, well, a little kid. She has grown up quite a bit this last year . . . She would follow me around and talk to me, but I was hooked on her sister and didn't want anything to do with the kid. I asked Mona out, and Sarah was standing right behind me—didn't know she was anywhere around. Mona turned me down, and then Bobby Mack came in and Mona took one look and went ape over Bobby the vay women do. She liked to wore Bobby out three nights in a w until Bobby couldn't take anymore and never came back. rah heard me ask her sister out, she was hurt, and she hasn't a dozen words to me since. Now she's the prettiest thing I've seen." Jim didn't say anything—he just nodded. We finished n in silence.

Vhen Letty came back from lunch, I asked, "Did Sarah say ng?"

ty smiled ruefully, "I asked her what was going on between and she said, 'I don't want to talk about it.'" Letty walked o her station.

ht Mark looking at Letty as she walked away. Something vonder if that speech about flowers she made to me wished she could make to Mark, or more likely she didn't need to make it, he would just know it and

The rest of the day was just time to be endured through. My mind was trashed to the limit, the unaccustomed work was hurting places that hadn't hurt since last year, and the peach fuzz was killing me.

Quitting time was ten hours late. Jim was bushed, too; so we didn't talk. I just drove him home and went on across on the Big Creek road. When we had driven past Meggan's old home, it hurt, but I was too numb to get serious about it. Deja vu was loosing its hold—I hope.

The week passed in numb sameness. Saturday, we were winding down, the crop, what there was, would be finished today. The pickers were going back over the orchard to get the peaches that were too green the first time through. The peaches were slow to come into the shed. We had shut down for an extra break at eleven—the wagon rolled in at eleven fifteen. Mark started the grader. Sarah had gone to the house for something. She came back by the dumping station, and a sprocket that turned the conveyer belt caught the tail of her shirt and was pulling her into the machine. I saw it happen, but had a crate in my hands. I upended the crate, and then threw it to get it out of the way and tried to get around the end of the grader. It was too far—Jim was closer, he got there first. He grabbed the shirttail with one hand and the chain with the other and stalled the chain for a second and pulled the shirt free. I hit the switch and stopped the grader when I saw what he was trying to do.

She was scared; tears were shimmering in her eyes. Jim let go of her shirt and stepped back.

Sarah said, "Thank you for saving my uncle' s shirt." She said it over and over again. We all knew that he had saved more than that. I turned and went back to the dumping station.

Mark came over and checked to make sure she was all right before he restarted the grader. At twelve, Mark shut it down for lunch.

I turned to get our lunch sacks down from where I had stashed them. Jim came over to get his, and as I turned to give him his,

Sarah came up and thanked him again on her way to lunch. This time she kissed him on the cheek and said, "Jim, you remind me of a boyfriend that I used to have."

Jim didn't know whether to whistle or to try and wind my watch, he didn't have one of his own. He knew how I felt about Sarah. There wasn't any way for him to follow up with her if he wanted to, and she was leaving tomorrow to go back up north to somewhere around Chicago.

If I didn't know better—I mean she was bearly sixteen, I would think I had been given the slickest jab of a woman's needle I'll ever get. Maybe I shoulda got the flowers.

Jim had a hard time looking at me while we ate.

Five more hours, then it will be history. Any day you can walk away from ain't as bad as it could have been.

When the people came back from lunch, I was sitting in the breeze on a stack of lids. Jim was off somewhere. Sarah came and went to her station, dug her gloves out, and carried them to where Mona had gone to sit. I was sitting sort of quartering away as though I was looking out at the road, but my peripheral vision is quite good—I was watching her, although, I appeared not to be. Sarah turned and saw me looking away, and she stood there thoughtfully watching me. I knew if I turned and caught her watching me, it would be over, so I stayed as I was and watched her watching me. She finally turned abruptly and swung her gloves against her thigh in an angry manner. "What did that mean?" Ol Bo has enough tooth and claw marks on his hide. Whatever it means I'll leave it to some other gentleman to puzzle on.

Letty came in, she looked at me and said, "Bo, you should have brought the flowers."

I shrugged and said, "Letty, I just don't care anymore."

"Pity!"

I grimaced and said, "Oh, I don't know, I got away with only a few claw marks this time, they'll heal, and soon I won't feel the pain unless it snows."

When we started up again, I buried myself in the numbing routine.

At six we finished, and Mark went to the house and brought out all the pay envelopes. With the five extra hours for driving Jim, I had made forty-eight seventy-five for a six-day week. Not bad! Mark asked me to stick around until he had paid all the others.

When he had finished, I walked over and he said, "Bo, would you work a couple of days, say Monday and Tuesday, helping me to clean things up?"

"Sure, be glad to. Thanks for the work."

"Bo, if there is work here, you have work."

"Thanks, Mark."

Jim was waiting in the truck. "Any thing you want while we're in town"

He said, "No."

I started the truck and pulled out to Fifty-one. As we drove by Meggan's old home, the feeling was down to—well, feeling like the air in my lungs was too thin to do the job, it just didn't seem to satisfy. I don't know if I'll ever pass that section of Fifty-one again without some kind of a pang.

When I pulled up at Jim's, I shut the truck off, and we just sat there, neither of us said anything for a minute or so. Finally, I said, "You gonna take her out? I mean you've got my blessing if you do."

"No, I've got no way. Bo?"

"Yeah?"

"You know that wasn't none of my doing?"

"Yeah—no problem."

"You going to town tonight?"

I shook my head, "No, I'm not going anywhere if I can help it."

"Right. You're not mad?"

I smiled and said, "No, why should I be?" I almost added, *I think she played you off against me to get even with me, but there was no use stirring that up.*

Jim opened his door and got out; before he closed it, he said, "I'd hate for this to come between us as friends."

"I looked over at him and grinned, "It won't. Goodnight, Jim."

He nodded, "Goodnight Bo," and slammed the door.

I started the truck and whipped around into the road. I didn't feel like driving fast, so I just moped along and tried to keep my mind blank, and I made it for three minutes. Then the circus parade, I call a life, started running the elephants and the clowns through my mind, by the time the calliope arrived with its whistles and wheezes, there I was again thinking about Meggan.

This year, just since Christmas, I had lost her and found out that I couldn't afford to go to the Goodman School of the Theatre to study to become an actor as I had desperately hoped. Then at graduation came this awful sense of loss of the identity that being a student had given me. Now Sarah is gone, and I don't have a full time job. I don' have a clue as to what to do with the rest of my life. It looks as though I'm finished around here, but where do I go?"

Anyway I can't leave until I'm eighteen and that won't be until the end of December. Lord God, you seem to be stirring around in my life with a big stick, I just wish I could make sense of it.

I fed the hogs first, then carried feed to the chickens. I looked at Smokey in the pasture, but I didn't feel like going for a ride—I'm just too tired. The folks are working, so I'm left to my own devices. I felt like going for a swim, so I did.

Floating on my back was soothing to both soul and bod. The hurt from strained muscles eased out, and like the dirt from the outside, the warm currents carried them both away.

The swim lasted so long that the stars came spreading out—the smear of the Milky Way, the dippers, both big and little. So vast, so close, so far away. "God's handiwork through out the universe displayed." That verse of an old hymn kept running through my mind, and not able to make sense of what was happening to me, I prayed "Lord God, show me what you want, so that I can get on with my life." Hunger intruded, so food became the next order of the day, and pronto-mushi mushi-post haste-avanti-or as Teddy Roosevelt said, "Hasten forward quickly there."

CHAPTER SIX

Is There Room Under the Porch for the Truck?

Barbara Ann, as usual, played extremely well. However, toward me, she was aloof. When she saw me, there was a hauteur that slid over her like a protective screen. No moving parts, no visible physical change. I think it was in the eyes, suddenly there was a cold fire quickly covered by the lids, so I wasn't sure what I had or had not seen. The shape I was in after Sarah, I could care less. If Barbara Ann wanted to look disdainfully in my direction, that would be just fine!

Gene Pass asked, "Are you coming over after church?"

I don't have any clothes to change into."

"I think we can fix you up."

I told the folks, "I'm going over to Gene's after church, if that's all right."

Dad nodded. I think they were agreeable because it gave them a chance to be alone, something that had been in short supply all the years I was in high school, when they had to work opposite shifts so there would always be one of them home for me.

The preacher's sermon title was, "How to Know God's Will for Your Life." A timely subject, given my condition.

"Basically," he said, "it boils down to, know what God's written word says, and have your life in line with God's written word, and then do whatever you want to do. Because if your life is in accord with God's written word, you will want to do what is God's will, providing, of course, that you are a Christian. People often confuse being religious with being a Christian. The two are not necessarily the same. One who is a Christian will be, to some degree, religious. But one can be religious—even believe in God, and still not be a Christian. A biblical Christian is one who's Lord is Jesus Christ. People who claim to have Christ for a savior, but he is not their Lord, are not Christians, they are merely religious."

The message clung tenaciously in my mind after the service was over—and it came back to stir the ashes from time to time through the day.

We ate lunch and fooled around at the barn until enough time had passed to be safe, then we went for a swim at Diller's pond.

Gene couldn't swim as well as I; to compensate, he used fins—with them, he gave me a real workout to try and keep up with him. We swam till it was time to go eat and go back to church. We had driven over in his old black Chevy. On the way home, Gene asked me, "Bo, what are you doing for work?"

"Well, I worked all week in the orchard I worked in last year, and Monday and Tuesday I'm going back there to clean up the shed and orchard. Why?"

As he turned off the road into their drive he said, "Well, I heard about a job building a grain elevator down in the river bottoms back of Ware. It's a non-union job, and it pays in cash—a dollar an hour. They need two or three more guys. The foreman is Charlie Markus. Daddy worked as a painter on a job that Charlie was a carpenter on. He lives over at Lick Creek, at the edge of town. You could run out there tomorrow after work and talk to Charlie. Daddy said you could use his name."

"Thanks, I'll do that." When we came into the kitchen—Paul, Gene's dad, was eating a piece of pie.

"Thanks for the recommendation, Paul."

"That's all right, Bo. Glad to help."

We ate supper, and Gene drove us back to church in time for BTU—Baptist Training Union. Barbara Ann had a new beau with her. She seemed to take pleasure in having me see her with him.

Well, whatever. My poor heart didn't need another feminine foot stomping that sucker flat. I guess I'm supposed to be like a car-chasing dog, when a car goes by, I'm supposed to chase it. Lady, I'm too tired to do more than growl. So, y'all have a good time now. Y'hear?

After the evening service, Mrs. Willis, who had been my Sunday school teacher when I was a little kid, stopped me and asked, "Bo, what are your plans for college?"

"Mrs. Willis, I don't have any plans for college."

She listened, then she asked, "Bo, what do you plan to do with your life?"

I looked at her and wished she would ask me a question that I knew the answer to. Then I said, "I haven't got the slightest idea," hoping that she would let it drop. I couldn't be rude to her because I knew that she really cared about me. She had always wished, when I was little, that I had been her own son.

She nodded and then asked, "Bo, what would you want to do if you could do anything you wanted to do?"

I didn't even have to think—I just came back with, "Mrs. Willis, I want to be an actor. I had planned to go to the Goodman School of the Theatre in Chicago. I wrote to them and got their information. The tuition was over three thousand dollars a year, my folks just can't afford to send me."

She was silent, then she said, "Well, Bo, I'll pray about it."

"Thank you, Mrs. Willis."

I went out to the car and sat in the driver's seat, waiting for the folks, feeling lower than a toad's belt buckle.

Monday morning, I parked in the shade, Mark came from the house; his after coffee cigarette leaving a trail of smoke like a train. He ground it out under a boot heel. "Morning, Bo."

"Good morning, Mark."

He seemed in a good mood this fine day. "Well," he said, "let's get the shed straightened up first."

We stacked empty crates all the way to the roof and straightened the stacks so they stood straight with no slumps in the stacks. Next, we brought in a hose with a high-pressure tip and washed the grader off. He backed the pickup over to the discard pile. Mark and I had to tie rags over our nose and mouth to keep from sucking in gnats as we breathed. There was a huge pile of spoiled peaches. We scooped them into the truck, pulled off about a hundred yards from the house, piled them in a ditch and came back and washed out the truck. Then I took the hose and blasted the goop where the pile had been, so it wouldn't draw gnats and flies.

Mark looked at his watch and said, "It's close enough to noon, let's eat."

I went over to the truck and reached in for my lunch.

Mark said, "Come on over to the house. It's cooler there."

I took my lunch and tea jug and followed him to the house.

Letty was gone, shopping I guess, she had pulled out around ten or so. Mark turned the burner on under the coffeepot and got his lunch out of the fridge—Letty had fixed a plate and wrapped it. I wondered how they were getting along? I hate knowing, or at least, thinking that I know something that I'm not supposed to know about people. I have to tip toe around trying not to stick my foot in my mouth. When the coffee was hot, he got a cup and looked at me. I shook my head and held up my tea.

He sat back down and asked, "What are your plans, Bo? You're out of school now—this was your last year?"

"Yeah, I graduated in May. As for plans, I'm going out Lickcreek tonight and talk to a guy named Charlie Markus—the foreman on a construction job. They're building a grain elevator around Ware or Wolflake somewhere.

"When will the job start?"

"I don't know. I don't know much about it, just the guy's name."

"Well, if he needs you tomorrow let me know. I can fool around by myself if I have to."

"Thanks. If you don't hear otherwise from me tonight, I'll be here tomorrow."

He finished off his plate and lit up. "Letty told me you like my niece. How did that go?"

"It didn't! She didn't want to have anything to do with me."

"That's funny, she asked me all kinds of questions about you."

I sat there with my mouth open staring at him, finally I asked, "When was this?"

"When she first got here this summer, before we started to work." He paused, then he asked, "What happened?"

"I don't know. Well, I do, but I don't understand it. Last year I wanted to take Mona out, but a friend of mine came in and when he's around women go ape. He took Mona out, right after I had asked her out, and she told me she was going steady. Sarah had been hanging around underfoot for two weeks. But as far as I was concerned She was just a little kid. I thought she was gone when I asked Mona out, but she was standing right behind me and overheard the whole thing. She acted like a whipped puppy. I was too dumb to know what to do. This year she had grown up—she's the prettiest thing I've ever seen. She doesn't want to have anything to do with me."

He smiled and said, "Women, there ain't no way to live without them, and there's no way to tell what they want."

I thought of Letty's comments; she'd tried to help me—I think I'll try to help back. I said, "I knew I didn't have a clue as to what to do about Sarah, so I asked Letty. She said, 'What I ought to do, is go get Sarah some flowers, that women love for men to do silly things that show they care, like flowers. She told me, 'I had hurt Sarah in public, apologize in public, and make her feel like a desirable woman.' Well, I didn't have the nerve to bring her flowers, I felt too much like a fool just apologizing. I couldn't bring myself to go get flowers and walk in here in front of God and everybody. Anyway, she stayed mad at me. I don't know, maybe I should have gotten the flowers. It's too late now."

Mark's eyes got hooded; I couldn't tell what he was thinking. Finally, he ground out his cigarette. "Well, Bo, let's get back to work."

We spent till four o'clock trimming dead limbs out of the orchard, cutting them up for firewood, and stacking it on the back porch.

At four, Mark said, "Let's quit for today. See you tomorrow, Bo, unless I hear from you."

I nodded and said, "Goodnight."

I drove out to Fifty-one and took it to the edge of Anna by the Bunny Bread factory and turned east on One-forty-six and turned off for Lickcreek.

Charlie Markus' place was hard to find—I had to ask twice. Finally found this grown over lane that didn't look like a driveway and bounced along it for three-quarters of a mile, to a rundown, weed grown place that looked like a mechanical elephants' graveyard—the place where all the old machines go to die.

The porch looked like a real leg breaker; rotted boards, knotholes popped out, and loose boards with nails sticking up.

There were two of the scroungyest, meanest looking hounds. Well at least one of them looked like a hound. Well, actually both of them did until you got a good look at the one's tail. One of the dogs had the longhaired tail of a Collie, the body of a Blue-tick, and the face of a Bloodhound or Basset. That must have been one heck of a party the night that dog became a twinkle in his mamma's eye. I just sat in the truck and waited, surely, as much racket those two were making, if there was anybody home, they couldn't hear themselves think, so somebody would come out to shush the dogs. Sure enough the lady of the house came out. She had a voice that could clabber milk, cause or cure warts, and kick the hens into overdrive. Her vocabulary was rank—in essence she told those hounds "Your ancestors cohabited without benefit of the clergy and your-bleeping—mother didn't have any idea, which of her forty-eight suitors was your—bleeping—father. And would you kindly shut the beep beep up?"

Then she looked at me, and in the same tone of voice said, "Now, what do you want?" I was ready to run under the porch too, but I didn't think the truck would fit and there was no way that I was going to get out of the truck with those two hounds loose.

I blinked and swallowed a couple of times and said, "I'm looking for Charlie Markus."

She said, "Well, he ain't here. What did you want with him anyway?"

I said, "I was told he is the foreman on a grain elevator they're building around Ware. Paul Pass said he was looking to hire help."

She looked up beyond the truck and said, "Well, he's a'commin' yonder, talk to him about it."

She turned around and went in the house. I wonder if Charlie's ever brought that lady flowers? Somehow, I kinda doubt it. The two dogs started sounding off again and ran out wagging their tails

Surprisingly, Charlie was driving a brand new pickup. It shown like a new dime except for the tailgate, which had a U shaped dent in it where he had dropped a big timber. He got out of his truck and said, "What can I do for you young feller?"

I didn't know Charlie; from the size of his wife I was expecting somebody the size of "Olaf the Norwegian tree killer," instead he was short and potbellied with three day's growth of whiskers. He wore overalls, one strap of which, was safty-pinned, a kaki shirt that had needed to be buried ten days ago. His smell was strong enough to see. I said, "I heard, from, Paul Pass, the painter, that you're hiring guys to work on a grain elevator you're building around Ware."

He scratched his nether regions, stuck his hand in the vent of his overalls, and caught something, brought it out to where he could look and see what it was, and crushed it between thumbnail and fore finger. He asked, "Got any experience?"

"Not much, I live on a farm and I helped Dad build a barn and hog houses."

He said, "Hog houses?" He scratched some more. "Well, we're shut down right now, waiting for lumber. We'll start Thursday at seven."

"How do I get to the job?"

"You can ride with me, meet me out at the Lickcreek junction on 146 at six-thirty Thursday, and bring a hammer and a lunch. There ain't no place to eat around there."

"Thank you sir. I'll see you Thursday at six-thirty at the Lickcreek junction."

I turned the truck around, pointed it toward the road and bounced out to the Lick Creek Blacktop.

Just a short way out of Lick Creek, I got on Hwy 57, it put me home a lot quicker than going back to Anna. I thought, What have I gotten myself into? I just hope I don't catch a load of what ever Charlie was killing, from riding in his truck, and I hope his day to change clothes this month comes on Thursday.

Tuesday, Mark was slow about coming from the house. I sat in the truck until eight, then got out and walked over to the house.

When I knocked on the door there was no answer. As I stood on the porch waiting, I looked around; their truck and the car were both there. "Odd! What now?" While I was trying to make up my mind what to do, I heard the door open behind me. Turning brought a sight that had my eyes bugged out on their stems. Mark was standing there with Letty draped—no, that's not strong enough—wound all over him like a vine. Mark's back was turned to me, Letty looked over his shoulder at me and winked. She had a single yellow rose with ferns and other leaves in one hand. I blinked several times and turned my back to give them privacy.

After what seemed like several minutes, Mark said, "Good morning, Bo."

I turned back and they were just standing there, she with the rose held to her face, he just looking at her fondly. He reached out and took her face in his hands and kissed her.

I shuffled my feet and said, "I can come hack in an hour if you want."

They both cracked up. When he finished laughing, he wiggled his eyebrows and said, "You want to?"

She said, "No, that's not enough time.

He turned to me and said, "Bo, can you come back tomorrow?"

I was three steps down the stairs, before their laughter stopped me. "Bo." He called, "We'll just have to quit early today."

I turned and smiled. "I'll be over at the shed."

Mark came over in about five minutes; he was still smiling. It was the first time I had seen him smile unless there was a joke, just smiling because he was happy.

We greased the grader so the pulleys wouldn't rust. Mark turned the grader on to work the grease all around.

He had grass seed, we went out into the orchard and smoothed some areas that were torn up by the tractor wheels, then resowed them.

We padded with rags and bound with wire the crotches of the trees that showed signs of splitting from the weight of their limbs and put props under some limbs. We spent a couple of hours doing some careful trimming to bring trees into balance—removed the limbs that stuck out into driving lanes. Some of the green limbs we cut to length to serve as props; others were cut up for firewood and stacked by the shed to dry.

It was one o'clock and Mark said, "Bo, let's call it good, come on over to the house and I'll get you your money." He led the way into the kitchen; Letty looked up as we came in. There was a light in her eyes that had been missing all the time I had known them.

When Mark went to get his wallet, she came over to me and put her hand on my arm. "Thanks, Bo."

"For what?"

She smiled and said, "For the Flower. This morning he told me what you said yesterday when he gave me the rose."

I nodded. Mark came back with his wallet and handed me a twenty-dollar bill. I said, "I don't know if I can change that." And started to dig for my wallet.

Mark put his hand over mine and said, "There is no change, Bo. You've earned it all. See you next year."

"Well, thanks, both of you." I had the feeling that the best thanks I could give them, was to get the heck out of there. Sometimes three is fifty percent too much—I had a real strong hunch that this was one of those times.

CHAPTER SEVEN

You Got any Kids, Bo?

Six-thirty meant five-thirty, rise and shine time. I set the alarm to let my folks sleep the extra half-hour. By the time they were up and around, I had nature satisfied and the hogs fed. By the time I had the chickens fed and watered, Mom had side meat and grits with onions frying. Before I came in to eat, the hammer, gloves and water jug were in the pickup.

As I left for work Mom said, "You ate too fast, you didn't swallow, you just inhaled it—brush your teeth!"

"Already did."

I took my lunch and was on the road by six-ten. By six twenty-five I was parked and waiting at the Lick Creek junction. Charlie pulled up at six-thirty, and I hopped in with my stuff.

Charlie said, "Good morning, young feller."

"Good mornin', Charlie." I sniffed and smelled fresh soap.

Charlie had the radio on. He said, "I want to get the market report—I'm fixin' to ship some hogs."

The radio was playing a zippy git-tar number with a lot of bass notes and the rumble of a Ford V-8 being wound through the gears—its glass-packs were chewing the air to pieces. Sounded so real I could close my eves and see the taillights fade as the Ford pulled away. I loved that song. I had tried over and over to find out what it was called and who did the picking—I wish I had a record of it. The song faded out, and the announcer came on reading in nasal tones the prices of pork bellies, feeder pigs, boars, and aged sows. I had tried to get a job at WRAJ. At the interview, the manager had me read a news report that had a lot of words like intercontinental ballistic missiles in it—I didn't get the job. The market report clattered to an end—I hope Charlie got the price he was looking for.

We went through Anna-Jonesboro, and on out the other side on Route 146 toward Ware, and turned off on a side road and wound and twisted around on that for several miles through the river bottoms. Where the road crossed the railroad tracks out in the middle of nowhere, Charlie pulled over by the ribs of the elevator he was building. There was a tower at one end made of metal beams. The feet of the beams were bolted to an eight-foot square concrete base. The tower stood about seventy feet tall and was held by four guy-wires anchored to concrete blocks set thirty feet from the base. Even with the turnbuckles cranked as tight as a man could hand turn them, the tower swayed when the wind blew.

I asked, "Charlie, what do you want me to do?"

"Just wait up till the rest of the crew gets here. Get your stuff out of the truck, I may have to do some runnin' around."

At five till Seven, two pickups and a car pulled in. Charlie introduced us all around. "This is Earl, this is Paulie, but we call him Speed, and Jeff." Earl was stocky and wearing overalls. Speed was lean and nervous, quick moving. Jeff was a tall handsome fellow who spoke with a drawl. Earl and Jeff wore their hair Ivy-league, short, but combed over with a part. Speed wore his long and greased back, and combed it every five minutes or so, if it needed it or not.

Charlie got around to me, and said, "This is Bo. Earl, you take Bo with you and show him the ropes. Bo, you fetch and carry for Earl."

Earl led the way to a sort of ticky-tacky scaffold that poked up about twenty feet on the sidewall. I figured right then, that me and the ladder to that thing were going to become very familiar to one another before the day was done. By noon I had made about sixty trips up and down that ladder, carrying everything from a box of nails, to several 2 x 10's, twelve feet long. The legs were going to be sore—no wonder this job had opened up. I needed work, so I just had to grit and go, pain or no pain. When noon sauntered around, food had great appeal for me.

Earl said, "Bo, the next time you come back up could you go to my pickup and bring my lunch back with you? There's a nice breeze up here, and I'm going to eat right here."

Well, Charlie had told me to fetch and carry for Earl, but I wasn't all that sure that he meant getting his lunch for him so he didn't have to get down and get it himself. But whatever, anything to keep peace on earth, good will toward men. The next trip, I brought his lunch, and mine.

He was right about the breeze, and there was a heck of a view. We ate lunch, and then Earl walked to the edge of the scaffold and cut loose with a whizz. He seemed to get a buzz whizzing from that high up, kept trying to see how far out he could force the flow.

He came back and sat down and asked, "Bo, you married?"

When I shook my head, he said, "Well I am, been married nigh on five year. Ain't got no kids . . . can't have any, so, me and my wife are going to try to adopt. Had our name in over a year now."

I nodded, and he continued, "The reason I can't have no kids, when I'se twelve, I'se walkin' acrosst a barn loft, the floor planks was just laid loose on the rafters. One of the planks had worked back and wasn't on the rafters anymore. It was covered with hay, and I stepped on that loose plank, it tipped, and I fell astraddle of the rafter and mashed my privates all to pulp—they don't work no more."

This was more than I wanted to know about his personal life, but he seemed to think for some reason, I ought to know. He continued, "I may not be able to have kids, but I shore can tickle my old lady."

I thought, *fine! But why are you telling me? I don't know you from Adam.*

"Yes sir, I can tickle my ol' lady for hours at a time—can' t feel nothin', but I shore can tickle her. I hope we can get that kid soon . . . She wants one, bad—she'd like to have one of her own, but I can't have one. Shore do hope we get one soon."

He got up then and climbed down the ladder and went over to his truck and listened to the radio for the rest of lunch. I couldn't figure out why he had told me all this personal stuff.

I finished my tea and climbed down and put my jug in Charlie's truck. Charlie was sitting in his truck asleep. I woke him when I opened the door. He stretched and yawned and looked at his watch, groaned, got out, and yelled, "Ok boys, let's hit it."

The afternoon wasn't so bad, evidently we had enough stuff on the scaffold to keep Earl and me busy for the afternoon. Earl had me hold one end of a timber while he marked it for holes, and then stand on it while he drilled the holes. One by one, the planks went up.

About two we took a break. Out of the blue, Earl asked, "Bo, yuh got any kids?"

"I said, "I'm not married."

"I didn't ask you if you was married; I asked if you got any kids?"

"I don't think so."

Pretty soon he said, "You're a good looking, clean cut kid. Do you think you could give a woman a child?"

I was scared that I knew where this conversation was headed. I wasn't real sure this ol' boy was wired right, and here I am working twenty feet off the ground with him. I studied on his question and said, "Yeah, I probably could."

"Would you want to try?"

I said, "Earl, there is no way, I would ever touch another man's wife. I couldn't live with myself before God if I did." Held my breath to see what his reaction would be.

He just nodded and never said another word the whole afternoon, except what he had to say for us to work. He never brought the subject up again.

We quit at Three-thirty, having only taken a half-hour lunch.

When Charlie let me out at my truck, he said, "Think you can find your own way, now?"

"Yes."

"Fine, see you there."

I set my alarm for Five-thirty. I'd give myself a little more time to find my way to the job site. If I have time to spare this morning, I'll split the difference tomorrow—half the time to sleep and half to allow for wrong turns, or whatever. Even with two wrong turns, I arrived at six forty-five. I'll sleep an extra ten minutes tomorrow.

At five of Seven, two pickups and a car rolled in like they were tied together with twine. Charlie pulled in at seven-o-three. Well, he's the boss.

Earl's wife had brought him—I felt funny meeting the lady who had been the unwitting subject of conversation between her husband and me. She was a plain to pretty woman about thirty. She looked a little sad—the quiet smile didn't quite go all the way to the eyes. The eves looked as though they might be more used to sadness than gaiety. I hadn't allowed the conversation to quite get there, but I felt sure that it was headed towards my making her pregnant. Earl loved his wife. She desperately wanted a child—he was afraid that if she didn't get one, he might lose her. They weren't having much luck adopting; she really wanted one of her own, but women have a way of falling in love with men they make love to, so he picked on me—I guess he figured that the age difference would prevent that. The process began to make sense once I had thought it through. It was a relief; I had been worried about working so high off the ground with someone as strange as Earl had seemed. Maybe there was more to him than I had thought.

I was fetching and carrying up the ladder again. The soreness made the first ten trips up the ladder pure anguish—then the muscles loosened up and began to work without complaint. By the time noon tardily made its appearance, I was feeling fine.

On one of my trips down, I asked, “Earl, you want your lunch brought up?”

He said, “Yeah, it’s over there by the truck door in the shade.”

On my return trip, I carried it, along with the sack of nuts and bolts.

Earl hadn’t said two words other than what he had to say for us to work. I didn’t figure he would miss me if I ate on the ground with Speed and Jeff. I reminded myself not to sit where Earl was likely to try to set a New World’s record for distance whizzing.

At twelve straight up, everybody quit as though a whistle had blown. Speed and Jeff headed for a spot of shade cast by a section of scaffold at one corner, where there was a stack of lumber to sit on. Speed, whipped back the covering tarp, and whapped the stack of lumber with his hammer seven or eight times.

I asked, “Why are you doing that?”

He grinned and said, “Snakes! You got to watch out for the sneaky buggers. The first day I’se here, I had one crawl out of the stack I’se sittin’ on. It crawled right over my boot before I saw it. I had to sit there and not move till it got out of biting range, it got back in the stack a’fore I could get a stick and kill it.” He eyed the stack and sat down, leaned back, stretched, and then looked into his sack. He took out a sandwich, unwrapped it, peeked into it, and muttered something under his breath.

I said, “What?”

He turned to me and said, “I said, my sister has no imagination at all—none whatsoever! Would you look at that?” He held the sandwich out for inspection. Then he said, “Looky there, two slices of white bread, one slice of 'baloney', and a lettuce leaf. That's it! No pickle, no onion, no cheese, and no mayonnaise or mustard. Drier to eat than a popcorn fart. She does it every day. Day, after day, after blasted day."

I asked, "Why don't you tell her about it?"

He took a bite and sat there chewing and chewing, finally he gave up and poured some coffee and washed it down. Then he said, "I just moved here from Terre Haute. I ain't got enough money to get my own place yet. My sister's husband ain't real thrilled about havin' me stay at their place, so I don't dare make any waves and get her on my case. If'en I could afford it, I would buy my lunch ready made, but I've got to save ever' dime to get my own place."

Speed and Jeff were both fast car enthusiasts. Their conversation quickly got over my head, I just drove them, I had no idea what made them work, and could care less. I sort of tuned out of the conversation. It intruded into my nap later—Speed had gotten loud over some point. I came to, to hear him say, "I had this Caddy I would have put up agin your Pontiac in a drag race from here to Terre Haute any time."

Jeff was laughing at Speed, and came back with, "That would have been the world's longest drag race. What is it from here to Terre Haute, four hundred miles?"

Speed, was taken sort of off stride, but he said, "Well, we wuz talkin' about whichin' of them cars was better; an' I say you run them two cars at top speed from here to Terre Haute an' we'll just see whichin' is blowin' smoke when you finally get there. I'll bet it's your blamed ol' Pontiac." He was quiet for a second, then he said, "You run a car that hard and that far an' it's gotta be the better car—just pure an' simple got to be."

Charlie woke up from his nap and yelled, "Ok boys, let's hit it."

I made fourteen more trips up that ladder in the afternoon. The first five were pure torture. My legs had stiffened up during lunch. At last, they limbered up, and I could move without wanting to wet my pants.

Earl's wife came back for him at about a quarter after three. She got out of the car and walked around and looked at what we were doing. I tried to keep from seeming too interested. Earl had put me in a strange position, and I didn't know how to handle it. I just pretended that nothing had ever been said.

Quitting time! The hour of the day that we were all looking for, and I felt might never come.

Mrs. Earl, I didn't know her given name, or his last one, had parked next to my truck. She smiled as I came out.

I nodded and said, "Ma'am." Driving home, I kept thinking how embarrassed she would be if she knew of the conversation between her husband and me. Those poor, unhappy people—it must be sheer desperation that pushed him to approach a stranger for that purpose.

The days blended together in an unremarkable chain, like beads in a plastic rosary. As my body toughened, the soreness of the first few days fell away. I hammered my memories under unrewarding brute labor. Using the mindless physical tasks to beat down any dreams that might float up from somewhere. Fancy words to say that I just didn't give a rip anymore.

A three hundred-pound electric motor had to be installed on top of the seventy-foot tower. The tower without its sheathing was so limber that the top swayed in a three-foot arc as I climbed up the first time. Charlie wasn't offering to pay any extra, just our usual one-dollar per hour, but I had volunteered to help install the motor. Speed had no head for heights; Earl didn't want to fool around with the three hundred-pound motor, that high in the air. Jeff said, "Why not?"

Jeff and I worked all morning to get the motor brackets bolted in place at the top of the tower. When we broke for lunch, Jeff and I ate lunch together. There is a bond between men who risk their lives together. You want to know as much as you can about this guy you're going to share danger with. You need to know—is he going to be there if I need him?

Jeff told me about being an over-the-road, long haul trucker. He said, "I've got tickets that have gone to warrants in seven states. I have to drive on several licenses so they don't grab me at the border. One time, I jumped the border in Arkansas, the border guard knew me by sight there, so I hit the striped pole at fifty, smashed through it and kept the hammer down. The Green Weenie in the box came running out and jumped in his unmarked car and put a flasher on top and came tearin' up behind me. By that time I was running on a built up road across a swamp—I had kept him from passing by flicking my trailer at him like a whip. When we got out in the middle of this fill, with water on both sides, I let him come up along side. When he got to the middle of my rig, I just eased over and crowded him right over the edge; left him on his top with all four wheels stickin' out of the water. I drove on twenty miles and stopped at a truck stop, and phoned in an attempted highjacking, told them where, and gave them a phony name, and truck I.D. I was five miles down the line when I met the highway patrol—lights aflashin'—headed back the way I had come. That cleaned the fuzzies off the road so I put the hammer down."

It turned out that he knew some of the Anna ladies that I knew. He told me which ones would, in his words, put out, and which ones wouldn't—some of both surprised me.

Jeff said, "I was racing a guy from Dongola to Anna, when the sheriff's car picked us up on radar. The sheriff was headed the wrong direction and by the time he got turned around, I had close to a mile lead."

At this point, Charlie yelled, "Let's hit it."

Jeff and I put our stuff in our rigs, and walked over and started to climb the tower again. We got to the top, and had to sit there while the rest of the crew pulled the motor up the side with a block and tackle.

Jeff and I are sitting up there with the tower swinging back and forth, so to pass the time I said, "Finish that story about the Anna cops chasing you."

He thought for a second, and then he said, "I got far enough ahead to turn off on a side road. It was a dirt road, and I left a rooster-tail of dust, thirty feet high. I couldn't see behind me for the dust, but I heard the siren turn off the highway and come after me." He paused and looked to see what was going on below.

I said, "What happened?"

"Well, I didn't know the road at all, and I went into a curve too fast and lost it, rolled, and landed on my top in the ditch. When I felt myself going over, I throwed my hands up on the top to keep from banging my head. As soon as I stopped, I reached up, switched off the engine and killed the lights. I just lay there with the lights off and let the cop go right on by me—the dust was so bad he never saw me there in the ditch. I waited till I couldn't hear his siren any more and got out and walked to a house and paid the farmer twenty bucks to come and pull me out with his tractor. The car was a write off, but at least I didn't get my license pulled."

The motor was coming up to where we sat. I crawled outside the tower's frame and tied myself off with a short length of rope. The tower was going nuts. The swing wasn't much bigger, but our movements and the weight of the motor swinging on the lines had speeded up the time it took to go through the cycle. When the tower reached the end of its arc, it returned in the other direction with a snap. When the motor got high enough to clear the mounting seat, I put my shoulder under it and lifted, while Jeff pulled from the other side; inch, by inch, it slowly slid into place. Sitting there hugging a loose three hundred pound motor, trying to bolt it to holes in a bracket that is trying to imitate Chubby Checker can get your pump started, and keep your natural functions urge at a peak that is only defeated by Pucker Factor Nine. (Pucker Factor Ten is the point where a sixteen-penny nail can't be forcibly inserted where the sun don't shine, without bending.)

I wrapped my legs around the strut, put my chest against the motor, and reached across and grabbed the strut on the side and pulled for all I was worth. Jeff was over there grunting as the tower slammed into his chest at the end of each arc. He was trying to get a bolt started through the motor mount and a matching hole in the mounting bracket on the tower.

He whispered, "Just a half inch more, Bo."

I shoved until the blood was roaring in my ears. At last, the whip of the tower worked for us, the motor slid over a rough spot on the bracket. Jeff slammed the bolt through. Now, all he had to do was reach in a pocket and get a lock washer and nut and get them started on the bolt. When they were in place we could rest. He dropped the washer; it pinged down through the tower. Funny how far down I could watch that washer fall.

I said, "Forget the lock washer, put the nut on, the other three will have lock washers, just get the nut on."

He said, "Yeah, right." He worked in sightless concentration. Finally, he said, "I've got it started, Bo." A couple of seconds later he said, "There, it's finger tight."

We both let go of the motor and eased our bodies, trying to work the kinks out.

Charlie yelled up, "How are you boys, doin'?"

I yelled, "We got one bolt in."

After we rested, the second hole was almost lined up, but the motor was just enough off center that Jeff couldn't get the bolt to slide through. I got the tip of a large Phillips screwdriver through both holes and pried. I really had to reef on the screwdriver to move three hundred pounds. Finally, it moved enough that Jeff could drop in a second bolt. He handed me a nut and washer. I crouched down to hold the washer in place while I started the nut. I just turned it finger tight—some times you need to be able to move things just a tad. "Jeff, hand me the last two bolts one at a time." I had to wiggle the bolt to get it to go, but it went. Jeff handed me the last bolt, I had to wiggle it even more, but finally it went. The washers and nut went on without a hitch. All four bolts were finger tight. I got a crescent wrench from my back pocket and tightened the two nuts on my side. Jeff reached over and got the wrench from me. The tower slammed just as he reached for the first nut—his hand hit the tower strut and the wrench went flying.

We both yelled, "Look out below." The wrench clanged its way down through the tower. The three men were running because you never know which way something that hits cockeyed will bounce. It hit thirty feet from the tower.

Jeff grinned, "I ain't seen Charlie run that fast in years." He felt around and said, "I got a pair of Vicegrips here somewhere. Yeah, here they are. If I can get them out of my back pocket." He wiggled like a bump and grind dancer, trying to hold on, and get at the Vicegrips, at the same time. At last he grunted, "I got them." He swung around and began working the thumbscrew on the grips. I heard him clamp them on a nut, grunt four or five times, and release, and clamp again. He grunted three times and said, "Bo, I think we are done here."

I said, "Halalujah!"

The knots I was tied off with had worked themselves tighter than I had intended. It took several minutes of picking to get them loose. We started down that tower like "hongry squirrels." The ground felt good after two and a half hours on that whippy-tippy tower.

Jeff and I went over and sat down on the pile of lumber. Jeff lit a smoke, and we sat there till he finished it.

Charlie came over and said, "Well, boys, we got the hard part done now—let's knock off early and get out of here."

It was Saturday—pay day! Charlie had our pay envelopes ready for us. Six days, forty-eight bucks.

We had at least another month building it, and rumor was that the guys who built it would have first shots at jobs running it once it was built,

A steady job would be great. I was making more money on a regular basis than I ever had. Maybe I could save up and buy the Mack place and build a home. As I drove home, visions of sugarplums danced in my head—I was starting to dream again.

CHAPTER EIGHT

My Buddy, Gene, the Rocket Scientist

The folks got home around five. I had fed the hogs and chickens and then taken clean clothes with me down to the pond for a swim. When I got back to the house, Dad was milking Maude. Bobbie, the mean little Jersey, hadn't taken the first time we had her over to visit the bull, and we hadn't caught it, the second time she came in. She finally got in a family way, but wasn't due for six weeks or so yet—so Dad only had the one cow to milk. He was just finishing up as I came back from a long refreshing swim. I was crossing the yard to the house when he came out of the barn with the milk.

He called, "Bo." Hearing my name, I turned. "Wait up." He came carrying the milk with his rolling walk. As he walked up to me, he said, "We got a call at work from Mrs. Willis, she seemed really excited." Mrs. Willis had been my Sunday school teacher when I was eight through ten. I was trying to think why she would have called my folks at work and why she had been excited. Something flickered around the back of my mind. "A month or so ago she had asked me something after church . . . What was it? School! She asked me if I was going on to school."

Dad said, "She had to go to Carbondale to a teacher's meeting at the University for three days this week. While she was there, she checked on the Theatre Department. She talked to some other teachers from other states that were there for the meeting. It turns out that they have one of the best Theatre Departments in the country—it is widely known and highly thought of all over the country. She signed you up. She took the time to fill out all the paperwork, because school starts in a week, and there's just one session of entrance exams left, and it's Tuesday. She registered you for that session. She said, 'I got one of the last seats open.' She told us what the tuition and book fees are. They are low enough that we can afford them. She said, 'You would have to drive back and forth to classes because all the dorm rooms are spoken for.'"

By this time, my head was spinning. "School? I didn't even know if I wanted to go. I didn't even know if I was smart enough for them to let me in. I had thought that only the really smart kids went to college. I didn't know if they would let someone like me in. Some teacher's opinion that the Theatre Department was good, what did that mean? Besides, I've got a job. I'm making money, if I save it I can buy a place of my own. I don't want to go through all this testing, just to see if they'll let me in." My mind was racing around like a mouse in a round silo, looking for a corner to pee in.

When I didn't make any response, Dad said, "We'll have to let her know tomorrow what you want to do, son."

"My life is being jerked around, I'm not real happy with my life as it is, but these aren't my choices either; they are being thrust upon me, unlooked for. I don't know if I want them or not."

Dad listened as I dithered, then he said, "Son, she also said, ' It would be a shame for you to waste your life.' I think she loves you, and wishes you were the son she never had. She's gone so far out of her way to find out all this stuff and fill out the forms for registration, and she paid the fee for the test. Son, you've got to try, at least try."

There wasn't any answer for that. I nodded and said "All right, Dad; I'll take the test."

He looked a little sad at my lack of enthusiasm, but all he said was, "Let's go in Son, I think your mother has supper ready."

During supper, Mom was quiet, a sort of disapproving quiet.

After we finished eating, I called Mrs. Howell, the speech teacher for the Anna High School. She was wildly enthusiastic about the theatre department at Southern Illinois University. She said, "The only problem I can see is your lack of experience as an actor—you will have to compete against some very professional people for parts. I recommended Goodman because they will take you as a beginner and train you. In the University, you will have to compete for parts, just like in the legitimate theatre." She urged me, "If you can, go for it! Just don't be disappointed if you don't get any parts for a year or two. Just hang in there and keep trying!"

Somewhere in that phone conversation, desire was kindled. The only thing left to overcome was my fear that this, too, would be snatched away from me—that I wasn't smart enough to get in or good enough to compete.

Dad picked up on the tiny flame of hope in my eyes after the call. He sat there listening to me enthuse, I think he was praying a prayer of thanksgiving that his only son had found something to live for.

Sunday morning, Mrs. Willis gave me a list of times, which building I was to go to, how much money to take, and which fees had to be paid by Tuesday evening. She had worked up an itinerary that led me step by step through the process of registration, testing, lunch, fee paying, and on the Carbondale campus, the most important item of all, parking. In my callow way I don't think I even thanked her properly. It simply did not occur to me to do so.

After church, I went home with Gene Pass. Gene is currently building and launching rockets. This sounds very worth while, as though we have a budding space-man on our hands. In truth, it was a life-threatening, house-wrecking, cow-frightening, menace to life, liberty, and the pursuit of a good time—at least the way Gene went about it.

I had found the formula for crude homemade black powder in a book I'd read. I shared the formula with Gene; I mean what are best friends for? Gene had mixed up a large batch and was gluing together a giant-sized rocket kit. We painstakingly put together a portable, wooden launch ramp and installed it by Gene's bedroom window.

By the time Gene had assembled the rocket, waited for the glue to set up to full strength, drilled the right sized hole with his pocket knife in the base, found his mother's funnel from her iron, filled the giant sized rocket with black powder, filled the paper soda straw with black powder to use as fuse, got the rocket set up on the portable launching ramp, got the stuck window in his bedroom pried open, and re-aimed the rocket three times because of an overhanging branch; it was almost sundown and the cows were coming home to the barn.

Gene lit the soda straw and got his field glasses to watch the rocket's extended flight. We crouched by his bed listening to the hiss of the burning fuse/straw. Hissssssssss—it quit. "Now what?"

I said, "Gene, changing the angle of the launch ramp made the powder separate. The fuse no longer has contact with the powder in the rocket."

Gene got up from his observation post and picked up the rocket. This movement caused some powder to sift down into the straw, where there was a tiny glow yet. As they say in the movies, "Contact! Houston we have ignition!"

Gene had it in his hand looking at the fuse, when ignition took place. He got his eyes closed, but the thrust from the rocket burned off his eyebrows and lashes and gave him a set of black freckles all over his forehead. The rocket shot out of his hand, hit the bedroom ceiling, glanced off, set the curtains on fire, bounced off the window sill and left in a spinning loop-the-loop flight—wailing like the souls of the damned. It homed in on the homecoming cows, and belching forth a contrail of fire and purple smoke, as the plastic of the rocket overheated and began to melt; it made one shrieking pass over the line of placid cows, looped over and came back at them again. The startled herd did a bolt upright about face. They retreated back the way they had come, holding their tails straight up in the air, running to the accompaniment of a sort of a jazzed-up version of the William Tell overture, played on the lead cow's bell, all the while emitting loud frightened bellows, punctuated by rude noises, as they ejected near-liquid, green spurts of—well—politicians are known for dispensing large amounts of this uncontrolled substance.

Gene was banned from the house and environs with his experiments. He also was grounded for a week and had to buy new curtains for his room.

I don't want Gene to be made to sound like a complete idiot. Prior to this one minor disaster, he had made several successful launches. I would have to come to Gene's defense and list him as an incomplete idiot, especially after the loss of his hirsute facial adornment. With the loss of his lashes and eyebrows, he wore a perpetual surprised look for about six weeks until they grew back.

We spent the rest of Sunday afternoon in his room, listening to his Everly Brothers collection—he had one Everly Brothers' record—I think we listened to **Wake up Little Suzy** eighteen times while he lay with an ice pack on his face.

Gene lost his commitment to active participation in the space program that afternoon. Perhaps it's just as well, Cape Canaveral might have become known as Cape-hole-in-the-ground, the former site of our space program.

I didn't mention to Gene that I was going to take the entrance exam to try to get into the University. I was scared my test results might be as much a debacle as his rocket launch. If I didn't make it, I didn't want anyone to know.

***

I had to be at the SIU lecture hall at eight o'clock, Tuesday morning, to take the entrance exams. Up at five-thirty as usual, I was stiff from yesterday's exertion. It had been my last day of construction work—at least, I hoped so.

I had told Charlie first thing Monday morning. He was a far more caring man than his outward appearance would lead one to suspect.

He said, "Young feller, I sure hope it works out for you." He paused and sort of sucked on the leftovers in his back teeth, then he said, "Bo, if it don't work out for you, you come and see me. You're a good hand."

I had toted planks up the ladder all day long. A month ago, I would have died. I had skinned both shoulders. I had to change positions as I drove to Carbondale. The muscles warmed as I drove, and the ache eased off.

I had only been through Carbondale on my way to show a hog at the State Fair last summer. I found the campus and got snarled up trying to park where, professors only, are allowed to park. I got told where to go by the campus police, politely-sort of. At long last, I found the parking lot where they let people of my rank park. Put my ticket on the inside of the windshield, made my way—by asking twice, to the lecture hall. I signed in and was assigned a row and seat. This lecture hall had as many seats as the high school gym. The steps were steeper. It was like being in a square bowl. Each seat had a view of the speaker's podium. The place was packed; they even had kids who showed up late sitting on the steps.

Somebody came out on the platform and said, "Welcome, to SIU! There will be people coming down the stairs to pass things out to you, take one of each item and pass the rest on."

There were four sections to the test. When they had passed them all out to us, the fellow at the podium said, "You have three hours. If you can't do a section, skip it and go on to something you can do." He looked at his watch and said, "All right, begin!"

Most of the stuff wasn't too hard. I skipped the section on chemistry. I had had no chemistry, so I just skipped it. The advanced math section, I skipped, too. The vocabulary section was easy and took very little time. I knew all of them. English, I felt I did fair to middling. History, I felt good about. Geography, well, at least I knew which countries, all but one of the cities named, belonged to. By the time an hour and a half had passed, I had filled out all of the parts I knew. I had even gone back to the higher math section and worked my way through two of the exercises. In the chemistry section, there were two things that I knew the answer to simply from my reading.

After I had done all that I could do, I got up and worked my way out of the row and went up and turned in my test. The people up there were kind of surprised. It was so soon that no one else had finished, but I had done all I could do and sitting and staring at the papers wasn't going to help. I began to feel that maybe I wasn't smart enough to go to this place after all.

I went outside and took out the itinerary Mrs. Willis had given me and found I was to pay tuition next. I had no idea how to find the building. I asked a guy going by with a beanie on his head with the letters S.I.U. on it. I figured he must be an employee if he wore a hat with the school name on it.

I said, "Excuse me, do you work here?"

He said, "What?"

I said "Well, I saw your hat with the school name on it, and I thought maybe you worked here."

He stared at me for a second then he said, "No, I'm a freshman. They make me wear this dumb beanie because I'm a freshman."

"I'm trying to find the place where you pay the tuition, do you know where I should go?"

He pointed off across the way to a street, and said, "Turn left, and go up to the end of that street, and the building's on the right at the end. You can't miss it. The line is about a block long."

"Thanks." He ran off holding that silly hat on.

I went over and found the line and got in it. I didn't think I had done too well on the test, but since I was here I might as well go through the motions.

A cute girl with raven black hair came up and asked, "Is this the tuition line?"

I said, "I sure hope so." She raised an eyebrow at my accent and my attempted humor. She was from back east somewhere. I could tell by the attempted culture and her stiff manner of speech. I grinned at her and said, "Yes, Ma'am, I was only teasing."

Well, she just didn't know what to make of this uncouth person who attempted humor without being introduced. One does not do that. No indeedy, one, does not!

I kept up a running conversation. When I said, "I'm here to study Theatre," her eyes opened, and she said, "I'm also here to study Thea-tuh." I could read her mind—*this uncouth person was planning to stain the purity of the Thea-tuh with his low vaudeville humor. Well!*

There is one thing about standing in a long line, it gets harder and harder to maintain a pose, also standing in line soon forces one to lower one's social standards. By the time we had shuffled our way to the pay window, it was Bo and Elvie.

I waited until she had finished at the window, and asked, "Would you care to join me for lunch?"

We ate at the Student Union. As we were both theatre people, all of our stops on this merry-go-round were the same, so we spent the afternoon together.

There was a little old man, who said he was our advisor, and told us, "You are signed up for this class and this class and this class. You will need this book and this book and this other book."

We thanked him and moved forward on the treadmill one slot, to the library and got in yet another line. We finished at five-thirty.

I still didn't know if I had passed any of the tests. The possibility of standing in all these lines and then be told, "Sorry, you didn't make it" and have to go through the whole merry-go-round in reverse—Well, I didn't even want to think about it.

As we finished the last line I said, "Elvie, I have a car. Would you care for a lift somewhere?"

Her eyes lit up—she was staying at a women's housing unit a mile off campus. It wasn't a dorm; it was a private house that had been knocked together into a barracks, with a tribal kitchen. She had no transport, except there was a tram once in the morning and once in the evening, or call a taxi.

She asked, "Bo, what are your plans for the evening?"

I kind of perked up at that—it turns out she needed a ride to a party—I was to go feed myself and come back at seven to take her to this off-campus party at a private home. I had some time to kill, so I drove over to the Baptist men's dorm and ate at their dining room. After supper, I went into the office and asked the lady there, "Do you have any rooms."

She liked to have hurt herself laughing. "We've been fully booked for six months."

I said, "Well, Ma'am would you put me down anyway? I figure that all these other people who are on your list have found other places, but I'm commuting from home, thirty-two miles one way. If someone cancels, just let me know, and I'll move in. Everybody that signed up hasn't showed up, have they?"

She smiled at that and said, "No. There are three or four that haven't claimed their rooms, but I'll have to hold their rooms for two weeks or until I get written cancellations."

"Yes, Ma'am, that will be fine. My name is Beaulieu Rogers. My number is Anna rural telephone line number five and our ring there is two longs and three shorts."

She laughed and said, "You sure are from way back in the sticks. I haven't seen a number like that in years."

"Yes, Ma'am, we are a fur piece back in the hills."

I walked around and looked the place over; at a quarter to seven, I left to go get Elvie. I picked her up and drove according to a map she had that was drawn on a placemat. When we got to the place and went in, we didn't get in the door good until Elvie was into the booze. Within fifteen minutes, she was sloshed out of her gourd. At Ten, I tried to get her to leave. She was a sloppy, loud drunk, not a happy drunk. The drunker she got, the farther back under the porch she crawled and the more she bared her fangs. If she hadn't been too drunk to run, I do believe she would have chased cars and howled at the moon.

She turned on me, laughed raucously and yelled, "Hey, everybody come see the hayseed who's gonna become an actor."

That was the point in time that I bowed out—I turned to the hostess and said, "Will you see that she gets home?"

She said, "She can crash here."

"Whatever! Goodnight." College sure was different.

CHAPTER NINE

Just About Orientated to Death

To my surprise, SIU sent me a letter stating I was accepted for enrollment. Further stating, to my further surprise, my scores on the entrance exams placed me in the top one third of the freshman class. They requested—I took it as a demand, my presence for the necessary procedure of performing orientation upon it. The procedure was to commence at eight o'clock sharp on Friday morning.

On the morning the University had summoned me to Freshman Orientation, I was running late. Thirty-two miles lay between me and being an "orientated" freshman. It was Seven-o-five. Two towns with 25-mph speed limits along the 32-mile trip, plus Carbondale itself, add to that, the time consuming necessity for finding a parking place on campus, you could see how fifty-five minutes could dwindle away. To compensate for the aforemtentioned speed retardations, (retardations—whoa, I'm already sounding like a college man), I drove fast, but under control—taking the curves at an average of eighteen mph over the posted speed. This caused the tail to lay out, but not too badly. The trip was proceeding well, until I came to a long straight stretch that while straight, dipped between two hills about three miles apart. The road dipped down one hill in a long swag and then ran up the next. I overtook a fellow in a Ford. The Ford was dogging along at about forty, until I tried to pass. He stomped that sucker and ran it up to seventy-five just to keep me from passing. I had a good head of steam up, but the Ford had a large V-8. I just couldn't get clear of him to pull back in my lane. It didn't bother me, because there was no one else on the road in either direction. We were running neck and neck at seventy-five, he was looking over at me, laughing—he wasn't watching the road at all. I was pushing that six-cylinder Plymouth as hard as it would go; I knew if I gave up and dropped back, he would slow down to a crawl and hold me back as long as he could. I could tell by the way he was smirking, as he punched that Ford, what he had in mind. He was having a high old time laughing at my efforts to get by him.

Something happened that I never would have thought of in a million years. The steep cut-bank to our left had a woods running along the top of it. There was no sign of a road or driveway. An old farmer in a 1927, bugeyed—lights-out-on-stems pickup drove out of the woods, slid down over the bank, bounced through the ditch, and turned to meet me head on in my lane at one hundred feet!

"I can't stop in time! There is no shoulder to go around him, and I can't get over because the fool in the Ford doesn't even know the pickup is there." I did something, that looked at later, seemed totally mad. I down shifted that six-cylinder to second with the gas held to the floor. When I released the clutch, that screaming engine jumped me ahead of the Ford, and before he could react, I lay the wheel over hard, hit the horn and flipped the wheel straight again—cleared the pickup's bumper by less than three feet. I didn't have time to look, but I think if the Ford had had thicker chrome, I would have nicked his bumper.

The Plymouth went up on two wheels and tried to roll. I caught it at the balance point, held it up on two wheels, and managed to keep it from going on over onto its top. When it came down, it was going to go looking at roadside real estate I didn't want to see. As sure as organic apples have worms, it crossed the road from ditch to ditch more times than a hen in love. The guy in the Ford finally woke up, smelled the coffee, and got on his brakes. That gave me some space as I fought the car back to a nose forward mode of travel. One half mile later, the reaction set in—started shaking so bad, I had to pull over and park. I was so scared, my lungs could only get about half a load of air. Some people talk about, "Messin' their pants," but my sphincter was puckered tight. I turned the motor off and sat there shaking. The muscles in my lower back spasmed in waves further inhibiting my ability to breathe.

The guy in the Ford came by slow and mouthed, "I'm sorry."

I nodded and under my breath said, "May your coffin leak."

What I remembered most vividly was the old farmer's eyes and knuckles. His eyes were as big as silver dollars, and his knuckles were as white as the keys to an old piano.

I think my guardian angel went totally gray that morning. I remain firmly convinced that there was more than just mortal mainstrength and awkwardness that did what was done. If I tried for a week, I could not stand that car up on two wheels and let it down without crashing, much less timing it to fit it between two other vehicles at that speed.

The Plymouth didn't run quite right after that; it used oil from then on. I think I spun a bearing on the crank or something.

I arrived only five minutes late for orientation. Orientation was about helpful things, like how to find Thompson Point by auto, which had most of the class laughing, because students were not allowed cars.

The guide slipped in a modicum of attempted humor at this point. "The path to Thompson Point is lighted by lights set on ankle height standards every few yards. Freshmen men, in past years, have been told if they wished more romantic lighting when wooing a date, just kick the nearest light, and it would go off. This misinformation has resulted in freshmen men in walking casts."

The guide next stated, "There is a virulent strain of poison oak, a low growing plant, and each year many freshmen girls could be seen vigorously scratching their backs after visiting Thompson Point Woods."

Our orientation group came upon the campus cannon during our perambulations around the campus. Our guide said, "Attention, you young men. This campus legend might save your life. The legend states that if a virgin ever walks in front of the cannon, it will go off." He paused a few seconds and said, "The last time it went off was ten years ago." A titter ran through the group. "At that time a group of frat guys loaded it with black powder and rocks and touched it off at three o'clock in the morning. The blast lurched the cannon off its mount and broke several windows. The campus authorities filled it with concrete. Now a days, the most dangerous thing that happens with the cannon is during Frat Hell Week—some group or other will try to paint the cannon—sometimes they are caught by the police and fined. Other times the cannon shows their ingenuity and taste—or lack of it."

Somehow I felt cheated. The sum total I obtained from being orientated was the location ofThompson Point, a few improbable legends, and a few other useful facts and or opinions. I had wasted the better part of a day and nearly killed myself for a handful of information that could have been mailed to me on a well thought out post card—sometimes higher education doesn't make sense.

The daily commute, to and from Carbondale over the twisted and hilly Hwy 51, made studying sketchy at best.

At seventeen, after weeks of hard work, the physical side made few demands on my resources. My patience had never been a vast resource, though. I drove faster than I should have because it seemed that time spent in the car was wasted time. The weather was at its best; the hazards of winter driving hadn't intruded yet.

The grind of driving to and fro had made me wonder how I would be able to manage to find the time it would take, if I did get a part in a play.

When I got home Monday evening of the third week of school, Mom and Dad were at work. There was a note that a Mrs. Brown had called. It was a Carbondale number. I had no idea who Mrs. Brown was or what she wanted. I decided to wait to call her till the next day.

After my eleven o'clock class, I went into the office at the Theatre and asked to use the phone. When a woman answered, I said, "Mrs. Brown, please."

"Speaking."

I still had no idea who or what she was. "Mrs. Brown, this is Bo Rogers, I'm returning your call."

"Yes, Mr. Rogers, we have a room."

"Room?"

"Yes." She said as though I should know all about it. "Two weeks ago you requested to be put on the waiting list at the Baptist Dorm."

Light sprang into my fevered brain. I had forgotten the name of the kind lady I had talked to at the dorm. I said, "I'm right up the street, I'll be right down. Thank you so much!"

"Well, a room!"

It was a four-minute walk from the Theatre to Doyle Dorm. Mrs. Brown turned as I came in, "Oh, Mr. Rogers, have you eaten?"

I shook my head and said, "No, ma'am."

"Neither have I. Let's go down to the cafeteria in the basement, and then we can finish the paperwork after we eat."

The cafeteria and snack bar were separate from the section of the dorm basement that contained dorm rooms. There was an outside door for boys that lived there and a connecting door to the public part. We went down the public stairs, through the cafeteria, to the serving line and made our selections. A cafeteria was a new idea to me, my only experience was a family-style restaurant, where some of everything on the table was yours for one price.

Mrs. Brown handed the cashier a meal card, and a meal was punched out. I didn't have a card so the cashier totaled mine, and my bill was a bit of a shock, about ‘two dollars more than I was used to paying for a meal. The extra food I took left me stuffed to the gills as well, but the meals were better prepared and less expensive than at the Student Union. Many people who were not Baptist or even religious, had discovered the good, inexpensive food.

Mrs. Brown ate in a calm, neat manner. I ate in my usual eat it before someone grabs it manner.

The business offices were on the ground floor. I filled out the paper work up to the point where my age became a factor. Mrs. Brown said, "I will have to have your parents signature, as you are still a minor."

Mrs. Brown said, "Come with me, and I will show you to your room." Mrs. Brown opened the door into the dorm section. She yelled, "Woman on the floor."

We waited a few seconds and when no one screamed or fainted, we proceeded to the stairs. She asked, "Would you go up ahead of me and as we come to each floor call out woman on the floor?"

We went up four floors until we came out under the attic roof in an open hallway furnished with four beds and lockable lockers ranged along one wall.

She smiled and said, "This is your room, and this"—pointing to the only bare mattress—"is your bed."

There was a small dirty window that looked out into a tree and part of the University president's back yard. She pointed back down the stairs and said, "The bathroom is one floor down."

I thought, *a bed in an open hallway where everyone has to walk through and a bathroom one floor down. Well, it beats driving seventy miles a day. At home, the outhouse was one floor down and forty yards away, outside, and unheated to boot. I've seen worse. Whatever! I'm here to learn to act. I won't do much here but sleep. Praise God for it!*

The big move came on Sunday after church. There wasn't much to move, just a suitcase full of clothes, two pairs of shoes, actually one pair of shoes, and one pair of boots. I brought a winter coat, a light jacket and my guitar. I don't know why I brought that. Can't tune it, and I can only play three chords and bits and snatches I pick out by ear. I keep hoping that I'll get serious and settle down and learn to play it right.

I only ever had one lesson—that's where I learned to play the three chords. The guy who taught guitar had one of the first TV sets in the county. I was so fascinated by the TV that Dad thought that I wasn't paying attention. On the way home he was so mad that he said, "I'm not payin' five dollars for you to watch television." So, that was the only lesson.

The folks came up and saw my room; they just kind of stood around and didn't say much. They hugged me and said all the usual things like, "You be good now—be sure and get enough sleep."

Just the polite surface things. Underneath, I suppose there were the real things that they didn't say. Like, *be careful Son, the world is a rough place and there are mean people mixed in with the good ones.*

And the things they couldn't say. *My child! I'm losing my only child! Oh, God look out for him*—the kind of things you only pray.

They had to get back, there were chores to be done. We walked down the stairs, out to the car, and I watched them as they realized there was nothing more for them to do, but go. Dad stood indecisive with the stiff, hard hands that he didn't know what to do with, the massive shoulders kind of hunched, no hat, and his hair thinning and blown about. Mom, her hair getting gray, her sharp eyes moist, sort of huddled into the cloth-coat she'd made herself. At the end, as she kissed me through the open car window, she said, "You be good, Worry Wart." Dad started the car, and they drove away.

I stood there and watched them out of sight—out of the center of my life. Then I turned and ran up the four flights of stairs to my room under the eves.

Being in the theatre department kept me out of night classes, but the Eight o' clocks were forced on to my plate instead. I would be up till ten-thirty or eleven working at the theatre—night was when our work was done. Then home to the dorm to go to the bathroom to study until twelve, up at seven-thirty for an eight o'clock. Yes, I said go to the bathroom to study. It was the one place the lights were left on. My room—hallway had no desks, and after the others were asleep, no lights to study by.

Howard, my hallmate was from St. Louis. We had one class together. It was an early evening class that ran from six to seven, seven being the latest class that could be forced on me as a member of the theatre Department.

Most theatre programs began at eight, there had to be enough time for costume and makeup calls before show time.

Howard and I used to eat together and walk over to the class. We sat together at the back of the class. Health ed was one of those classes that the powers that be throw in, that are useful to a student with a heavy load, the reading wasn't heavy, and if you listened in class you had an easy credit.

It wasn't going to make or break your academic career, but it could give you some breathing space, if you were short on time, like I was.

This particular night we were discussing dating. Howard and I huddled in our back row seats hoping that we wouldn't he seen and called upon.

The instructor was a jovial, white haired man with a round pleasant face, about forty, laid-back, and a pipe smoker.

The subject was one where everyone's opinion was as valid as the president's. The instructor was reading the sports page as he shepherded the class through an evening of shared ignorance. He called on me, "Mr. Rogers, what is your approach to selecting a date?"

I sat there wondering what to say, and said the first thing that fell into my mind. I drawled, "Well, my Daddy always told me not to date any one I wouldn't want to marry . . . I might have to."

The paper the instructor was hiding behind began to shake. From the slight angle he sat to me, I could see his jaw muscles bulge as he bit down on his pipe to keep from laughing out loud. His face was red and getting redder as he held the laugh. The rest of the class was deadly silent. The kind of silence that is so loud that you can feel it like a wet blanket. The boys were afraid to laugh from fear of offending the young ladies. The young ladies were afraid to laugh for fear of being thought unladylike.

Howard stepped into the breach with his loud infectious laughter. It boomed out into the deadly silence of the room and saved the instructor from an aneurysm from holding in his laughter. The instructor also was saved from having to buy a new pipe; he got to laugh just before he bit through the stem. The girls started to titter softly. The boys seeing the girls laughing started to laugh. It grew like Topsy until it filled the room and spilled out into the hall. Passers by peeked in to see the source of such unbridled mirth. Howard saved me from being a pariah on the order of one who loudly passes gas in church. Oddly enough, I never was called on to answer in that class again.

The second week after I had moved into the dorm, a notice was posted on the corkboard in the theatre.

***

Open reading tryouts for the children's play,
The Golden Mask
will be held on Thursday evening of this week.
The tryouts are open to all members of Faculty,
Staff, and student body.

***

I read and reread the notice. Members of the student body. Yours truly is a card carrying, paid up member of the student body. Yours truly will he there with bells on.

The next day a second notice appeared announcing:

* TRYOUTS *
FOR
Thorton Wilder's
* TRYOUTS * * TRYOUTS *
OUR TOWN
* TRYOUTS *

The tryouts are open to all members of faculty, staff, and student body.

Yours truly will attend that one as well.

Everyone who wished to tryout was given a card to fill out.

Name:	*Beaulieu Rogers*	*Age:*	*17*
Height:	*5'8"*	*Weight:*	*148#*
Hair:	*Brown*	*Eyes:*	*Blue*
Experience			*None*
Address:			*Doyle Dorm*

That line about experience was a real heart stopper for me, but about halfway through the lineup, my name was called. I left the comfort and safety of my seat halfway back in the darkened house and walked to the front and mounted the steps to a brightly-lit stage for the first time in my life. Oddly enough, I wasn't afraid, it felt like home. The director asked me some questions; I suppose to set me at ease, or maybe to hear what I sounded like. I'm sure my country boy drawl was a source of amusement. Then, for the first time in my life, a script was handed to me, and I was asked to read.

The director had me read several of the parts. He paused, and then asked me to read the lead. The part of a young country boy who comes to the King's castle to find his fortune and is thrown into prison.

After I read, I returned to the darkness of the auditorium. That brief time on stage under the artificial sun had infected my soul. That stage was now my country, I would never again be happy away from it. As the line of people waiting to read crossed the stage one by one, I noticed no one else read for the boy. I began to hope, afraid to hope, but hoping just the same.

At the end, the director thanked us for coming and said, "You will be notified if you are chosen for a part."

I left the Theatre and walked the four minutes to the dorm, still not knowing, only hoping.

Sleep came, but only after the whirligig that turned and fluttered in my mind drove sleep away many times. I went through the day wondering did I have a part or not? There was no list posted at the Theatre. So harking back to the comment that Mrs. Howell made, "You might have to try out many times before you get a part." I resolved to attend tonight's open tryout for *OUR TOWN.*

I went through the whole routine again, with a different director and assistants, and filled out the same blank card.

Name:	*Beaulieu Rogers*	*Age:*	*17*
Height	*5'-8"*	*Weight:*	*148#*
Hair:	Brown	Eyes:	Blue
Experience:			*None*
Address:			*Doyle Dorm*

From the beginning, the part of the Narrator was filled by a grad student. I was too short for George and too young for the father. Finally, I was called to go back to that home of my soul with its harsh sun. The director asked me to read one line from the graveyard scene, "Aya, right smart farm." in a harsh down-east accent. He even led me through the reading phonetically. My poor little country-boy mush-mouth had the darnedest time forming itself around those foreign Yankee sounds. The director was patient and led me through the sounds two or three times until I sounded, for one line anyway, as though I had spent the bulk of my life knocking apples off a tree in Maine.

Like last time, we were thanked for coming and told that we would be notified of the results.

When I got back to the dorm there was a note to call Dr. Moe. Dr. Moe was the director of the **GOLDEN MASK.** It was too late to call him tonight—a second night of not knowing, but fervently hoping.

Now the whirligig has the music of a calliope added. Sleep had to make twice as many passes before I succumbed to its wooing.

Even though it was Saturday, I went to the Theatre. I knocked on Dr. Moe's office just on the chance he might be there. A voice told me to come in. Dr. Moe looked up over his glasses and said, "Ah, yes, you're Rogers, Beaulieu Rogers."

"Yes, sir. You left a message last night to call you. It was too late when I got home from tryouts for **Our Town.**"

He blinked at that bit of information. "You tried out for two plays?"

"Yes, sir. I came here to learn how to become an actor. One must act to learn how to act. I plan to do as much acting as I can."

"I see." Then he said, "Mr. Rogers, I would like for you to play the lead in my production of **The Golden Mask.**"

"The lead!" He nodded. "Wow! Thank you, Sir."

He tossed a script across the desk. "Here's your script, get your lines down as quickly as you can."

"Yes, Sir!"

"We will start rehearsing Monday at four."

"Where?"

He pointed to the lobby and said, "Out front. See you Monday at four."

As I went out, an assistant came out of one of the other offices and tacked the cast list for **Our Town** on the board. I scanned the list and found my name listed as second farmer in graveyard scene.

I had two parts in two plays! Or rather I had one part in each of two plays. I wanted to yell and wave my hanky and run up and down the aisle. In my rapture, I almost forgot to sign my name, to show that I had seen the list and accepted the part.

Walking two feet off the ground is hard work. Trying not to bust one's button with pride is tiring, too. I ran back to the dorm and up four flights of stairs to find no one home. Good news and no one to tell, that's got to be a torture invented by a psychologist to generate work. Down four flights of stairs to the first floor room of my buddy from Anna, Gary. Nobody home. Back up four flights so frustrated, I sat down and wrote a letter to Mrs. Howell, describing my enormous good fortune. I had tried out for two plays and won parts in both of them. The lead in one and a one liner in **Our Town**

My buddy Gary was going home, so I gave him the letter and my dirty laundry to give to mom at church.

I should have gone home myself, as this was the last free weekend I would have for over two months, but the shift from who I was trying to become, back to who I had been, was one I just didn't want to deal with. Here, I was Bo Rogers the rising young actor, there I was just Bo, our son in college.

Time passes slowly when you're young, eager, just beginning, and you have to wait. Four PM Monday took forever to arrive. When the cast and crew met in the lobby to sit around tables and read through the play, it was a bit of a letdown. I had envisioned myself on stage moving, and speaking lines, feeling the burn of the lights on my face. Instead we came in and sat around tables and introduced ourselves by our names and character.

Elvie, the girl I met in the line to the Bursar's pay-window, was playing the cook at the king's castle. She lit a cigarette, saw me looking at her and looked away. I wondered how much of that night, she could remember. It should be an interesting association if she is going to pretend that I don't exist—we had one long scene together. She was a bit artsy in speech and manner. Dr. Moe asked her to read it more simply.

The rehearsal lasted till six. I had to skip supper and go straight to Health ed. After class the food service section of the dorm was closed. I had to go to the Student Union, get a stale hotdog and pay more for it, and I was left with an un-punched square on my meal card. From now on I would have to eat before rehearsal.

The rehearsals for **Our Town** began on Tuesday evening—this one began as I had envisioned, on our feet and on stage—script in hand.

I wasn't on until the third act. I sat out in the house and watched. The grad student who was playing the Narrator had done the part before in summer stock. The part fit around him like an old sweater.

The guy playing the father was from Hollywood. He had doubled Montgomery Cliff in **From Here To Eternity**. He was back at the University to get his masters. He would finish rehearsal and go next door to the radio station and do the graveyard shift as DJ. He had one of those precise mellow voices, and Jim never makes a mistake. James T. Lash was renowned among radio people for being unflappable on the air. His coworkers had done every thing they could think of to break him up when he read the late night news. They did things like fake a teleprint, "Egypt—Moses announces new ten-point plan!" One time they had set his news-script on fire, he had to read faster and faster before it all burned up. They finally broke him up one night. They paid a huge, fat guy to come in and do a strip tease while Jim was live on the air. This humongus fat man started to do a Little Egypt imitation (she was a local belly dancer.) With each bump and grind cycle he shed another article of his clothing. He got all way the down to his jock supporter before Jim fluffed a line, but from then on, that newscast consisted of Jim's howls of laughter. This was radio, and the audience had no idea why James was shrieking with laughter.

Jim's precise control and delivery were legendary among theatre people. He held his liquor well—few ever saw Jim inebriated. Jim never got drunk, he was a seldom drinker. When he did indulge, the higher the alcohol level the more dignified Jim became. He only rarely indulged beyond his capacity to function. When he was beyond function, close friends said, "The only way you could tell—Jim would be in the middle of a story or a quote and his voice would be flowing along with the tale and one word would deteriorate to slush and then he would resume normal speech"—his friends knew then that Jim was close to passing out and they would take his car keys.

The word was around the Theatre department that there was this crazy farm kid that was doing two plays at once. I was so dumb, earnest, honest, willing, and naive that the Theatre people led by Jim adopted me as a sort of mascot.

Jim was a natural teacher. He taught me about theatre by telling stories.

I didn't know it at the time, but he was writing a play as a part of his masters program. A children's' play called, **The Wicked Wizard of Wobbly Way**. There was a character in the play that was a young, naive, over-eager, honest, and enthusiastic Wizard's apprentice. Jim studied me and wrote the character around my personality, speech patterns, and way of moving. That first rehearsal was my first exposure to the proper way things are to be done in the theatre. The lessons go down easy when you have old pros to copy. You learn without having to study, things just become a part of you, by seeing and doing. I became an actor—so to speak—by being there and watching the good ones do it.

The sum total of my part in **Our Town** was to walk out on stage, sit in a row of chairs, and say one line. It was perfect for a beginner; it left me free to watch the good ones. And they, in their generous spirit, shared their little tricks and secrets that it had taken them years to learn. The kid had found a family.

Dr. Moe had rank amateurs in most of his speaking parts. We didn't know which way to move when he gave us stage directions.

The poor man stopped rehearsal and gave a seminar on stage terms. "Ladies and gentlemen, please note these directions in your script for future reference. Upstage is toward the backwall of the set. Down stage is toward the audience. Stage left is toward the actor's left as he is facing the audience. Stage right is toward the actor's right as he is facing the audience. The apron is that portion of the stage that extends past the proscenium arch and is closest to the audience. The proscenium arch is the frame around the picture that the stage makes. The wings are the areas immediately to the left and right of the set. The flys are the area above the lines of sight over the stage. There are more technical terms and descriptions for these areas, but these will serve well enough to allow us to get on with rehearsal."

"Oh! Two more things, the items that an actor uses in the course of a play are called properties or props. Also a platform is called a riser. That should allow us to continue." We resumed the rehearsal.

Each time we came, the set was larger and more complete. The theatre crafts class was working like beavers building flats, stretching unshrunk canvas, sizing, and painting the final colors to fit into the design the set designer had envisioned.

Our castle had gates that opened, and we had a dungeon mounted on wheels. The lights would go to black and the stage crew would wheel the dungeon into place. It was then lit and the rest of the set blacked out.

The tumbling I had learned in high school PE came into its own when the guards heave the kid out of the castle gates. They gave me an airborne heave-ho, and I landed in a tumbler's roll that brought me right to the edge of the apron within inches of the front row patrons. I would sit there and weave woozily as though knocked half-silly by the fall—sometimes I wasn't acting.

After the first day's shortage of supper, before I came to rehearsal, I got the lady who ran the snack bar to make up some sandwiches of my own invention. The first time I ordered one, the lady looked at me and said, "Son, I ain't never heard of anyone eating something like that before!"

I looked at her and said, "You'll be sellin' hundreds of them before I'm gone."

It had a double burger, double cheese, ham, onion, and dill pickles. There, that doesn't sound so bad, does it? Oh, I forgot the bacon; it had two strips of bacon. Let me tell you, hot it was great! But let that sucker sit in a sack for two hours until it congealed, gobble it as fast as you could and you had something guaranteed to roll around in your gut like a stone, and generate gas for hours. It did stave off hunger though. Sometimes it did feel as though I had swallowed a brick, especially if we had to do the flying through the air bit more than once.

In health ed, Howard would cock an ear toward me and grin at the sounds of battle emanating from the perking of my internal workings as my guts quarreled over some small portion of a Bo-Burger as it was now known. They did catch on; people took to it like ducks don't have to be taught to pee in water.

At six, **Mask** rehearsal would end. I would dash over to health ed, at seven; health ed would release me to dash over to **Our Town** rehearsal. At ten of ten, **Our Town** would let out so that the female members of the cast could get to their dorms before the ten o'clock lockout. Ten minutes to get to Thompson Point. My first date was to walk a young lady home from rehearsal. I had not dated anyone all the time I was in high school. I don't know why. I suppose I had some idea of being true to Meggan. She was gone now, and there was no one to take her spot front and center in my affections. So what did it matter if I dated one or two or as many as I could find the time for?

Here the rules had changed; there weren't the invisible lines that marked off the social strata in Anna. We dressed the same here, and no one had a car. And if one turned you down, so what? There were only four or five thousand more to go. I wasn't looking to fall in love, so I wasn't as picky.

My farm background supplied most of the things I could talk about—you have to start from where you are. Each failed encounter added one more thing that I knew not to do next time. The one thing I could take encouragement from, when fishing in such a large pool of women, if you miss one there will be another one along shortly.

One young lady was accompanying me as we neared the famous cannon. In an attempt to be witty, 'swave, deboner,' and devilishly clever with sexual undertones, I said, "We mustn't walk in front of the cannon, My Dear, it might go off."

She stopped, and said in a bitter, almost teeth gritted manner, "That is one thing that you don't have to worry about, Buster!" The exchange left me feeling like I had been cut off at the lips. She never went out with me again.

Being in the theatre allowed me to get to know women without the usual fandango of the dating ritual. You were in and out of each other's pockets all the time. One didn't have to stalk up on a lady to be near them. I got to see them as they were, not as I had thought they'd be. It was as close to having sisters as an only-child could come.

We opened with **The Golden Mask** first. The children of Carbondale and the surrounding area were bussed to the theatre en-mass. The theatre seated two hundred fifty; and we had full houses for the ten-day run.

I had to tone down my performance in the dungeon scene. Dr. Moe said, "You are so realistic that some of the younger children might be hysterical." I had thought that was the idea, scare the little buggers to death.

Children are the most difficult audience an actor will ever face. The girl who was playing the princess turned up-stage and a sticky lollypop landed between her shoulders. I removed it from her dress and wagged my finger at the little fellow who had thrown it and tossed it back. The next day, as I was thrown from the castle, my wooden dagger flew out of my belt and landed in the front row. I felt it go, saw where it landed, and was wondering how the heck to get it back. The young gentlemen, who's lap it had landed in, got up and reverently placed it, with both hands, on the stage in front of me as I sat weaving as though I were knocked silly. I winked at him, and he caught his breath and walked on air back to his seat. You just never knew with kids, sometimes they were horrid, some times super.

Our Town opened next. The actor's green room was in a connecting building. We could go there to talk, drink coffee, and smoke without bothering the actors still on stage. Jim Lash was always the center of a circle of actors and crew there when he was off stage. His story telling was an art, and he was continually pressed to draw upon his deep fund of stories and regale us.

"There were these three old character actors in a scene, they had gone up—forgotten a line—they covered beautifully by adlibbing. They were doing a wonderful job of covering, the audience loved it, but the play was going nowhere. The stage manager tried to prompt from the script. From the wings-stage left, he loudly whispered the line, 'Lo, the dawn breaks.' Nothing! The three kept right on adlibbing. The stage manager thought, perhaps they didn't hear, so he went around to the wings-stage right and loudly whispered the line, 'Lo, the dawn breaks.' Nothing . . . He went upstage and whispered through the fireplace, 'Lo, the dawn breaks.' Nothing . . . So in desperation he climbed into the flies and worked his way out along the pipe that held the flies. He got right over the three actors and whispered as loud as he could, 'Lo, the dawn breaks.' Nothing. So he whispered again as loud as he could, 'Lo, the dawn breaks.' The three actors stopped and looked up and one of them said, 'We know the line, damn it! Who's is it?'"

"Supposedly during one of John Barrymore's performances of **Richard The Third,** he was being heckled by a large fat drunk in the balcony. When John came to the line, 'A horse, a horse, my Kingdome for a horse.' The drunk laughed with a loud, 'Haw haw.' Barrymore never missed a beat, he went on in an ad lib, 'And if thou can'st find a horse, hasten and saddle yon braying ass, 'twill serve just as well.'"

"There was an old character actor, who had retired, after a few years and some financial reversals he needed money, so he cabled his agent, 'Need work! Will do any part, no matter how small. Financial situation desperate!'

"A few days later he received a cable from his agent. 'Have part in new play. One line, 'Hark, me-thinks me hear the cannon roar.' Train ticket waiting at station. Open tomorrow night.'"

"The next day the old actor packed and got on the train. The train was held up by track work and he got to New York just in time to take a taxi to the theatre. All this time the actor is saying over and over to himself, 'Hark, methinks me hear the cannon roar. Hark, methinks me hear the cannon roar.' He gets to the theatre and pays the taxi off and the stage manager rushes him into makeup and costume and shoves him out on stage. The curtain goes up and there is this awful BOOM! The old actor looks wildly about and says, 'What the hell was that?'"

About this time the stage manager rushes in and yells, "Rogers! You've missed your entrance." I'm a dead talking-body, or spirit in the graveyard, I'm supposed to be in my chair on stage when the curtain goes up for the third act. I raced around through the connecting hallway, across the back of the stage, and walked out through a slit in the curtain and took my seat.

The actor who sits next to me in the scene says out of the corner of his mouth, "Glad you could come tonight, Bo."

I whispered, "Have they come to my line yet?"

"Yeah, I said it for you."

It was a good thing I had pancake makeup on, or my face would have shown like a stoplight. I got a dressing down by the director after the performance for missing an entrance. I never missed another one. I don't think the audience knew what, if anything, was wrong. Probably put my strange arrival down to creative staging—one hopes so.

We finished the run of **Our Town** on a Saturday night. The cast and crew were invited to a wrap party at the home of the head electrician. He was a grad student living off campus. The female curfew was 1:00 AM on Saturday.

I don't know what a good Baptist boy was doing at a party devoted to the worship of Baccus; I was the only non-drinker there.

Sunday afternoon, my buddy, Gary, brought my clean laundry back from home for the third time. Mom had put the clipping from the Gazette Democrat in the suitcase.

"A-J grad makes cast in two plays at SIU. Word has been received from SIU that Bo Rogers of the class of 1960 has been accepted for casts of two plays now in rehearsal at Southern Theatre."

"Bo was a member of the speech class last year at A-J and was a winner in the annual FFA speech contest. He placed second to the winning DuQuoin entry last March. Rogers' first tryout this fall at Southern was for the famous **Our Town**, which is to be the opener for the 1960-61 theatre bill there."

"Rogers said, 'He found himself in the rather frightening competition of pros from all over the Midwest. He considers himself very fortunate to secure a minor part in the cast. The part carries only a few speaking lines. It is the role of one of Emily's friends who meets her again after her death and her appearance in the village graveyard."

"In the children's play, young Rogers is to have the lead. The '**Golden Mask**' is a new play, which has never been seen as yet in this part of the country."

"Young Rogers says, 'I get the chance to bring to life a new hero of the fantasy world,' and according to the old tradition, he asks all of his former speech friends to wish him a grand and glorious flop."

When I picked up my laundry from Gary, he told me, "Rev. Bramford said, 'Tell Bo, that I think his folks are hurt because he's not coming home.'"

I hadn't been home since I moved into the dorm two months ago. That made me feel bad, but there were too many things at Anna that hurt. It didn't really have anything to do with the folks. The wounds that Meggan had opened in my life were starting to heal, but I had been thinking of Barbara Ann more often than was comfortable. I didn't need to get into a rerun of love at long distance; I had four years of that. But hurting the folks, well, I wasn't made that way. I'll go home Friday night. I'd have to hitchhike to Anna and call Gene Pass. If Gene wasn't home—leave my suitcase and walk the mile and a half out to the Hospital and get whichever vehicle the folks had at work and then come back at quitting time and get them.

After I finished reading the Gazette article, I ran down to Gary's room and read it to him—I read it to him, but he was studying for an exam, so I think I more or less read it to myself.

The rest of the week it felt strange to have evenings—to be able to eat supper like a normal person. The only trouble with that was, nobody had time to talk, so I just fooled around. Most of my classes were theatre classes and the work for those classes was done in class. With my trick memory trained by years of my family's oral tradition, if I heard it, and was paying attention, I had it. My tests were no problem. I only had two non-theatre classes, health ed and PE.

CHAPTER TEN

Poor Dumb Bull

Friday, 4:00 P.M. rolled around, health ed didn't meet on Friday, so at 4:10, I was south bound on Hwy. 51, thumb out, little sign taped to the side of my suitcase.

College Student—Need Ride to Anna

The fourteenth car that came along was an Oldsmobile; it slowed and the lady driver looked at me, but drove on by about a hundred feet to pull over. I didn't know if' she was stopping for me or not. I thought, *I'll just about get to the car, and she'll take off—well, what the heck, nothing ventured, nothing gained.*

I ran over to the car, and she put the window down about an inch and peered out at me, "Are you Bo Rogers?"

"Yes, Mrs. Miller." She unlocked the door. She was the teacher who had tried to take Meggan's scholarship from her and give it to one of the more socially correct girls. I upended my suitcase and set it between my feet. She lurched the Oldsmobile back out into traffic.

She tried to carry on a conversation and drive, but she had never quite mastered the complex thought pattern required for the exercise. As she questioned me about school, the speed would go up until we were roaring along at seventy, she would catch herself, brake, and the speed would drop off to under thirty—back and forth from one extreme to the other.

"What are you taking?" She asked.

"Theatre."

She reacted as though I had said moon walking.

I didn't know the lady personally; I had never taken any classes under her, in fact I don't even know what she taught. She was a guidance counselor, but no one had ever bothered to guide me.

All the way to Anna, she either floored it or jammed on the brakes to slow down to too slow. She could really snap your neck when she floored that big Oldsmobile. It was like a thirty-mile long bumper car ride. *Well, it was a ride; and if we didn't run over something or get hit from the rear, it beat walking.*

She let me out at the four-way in Anna, and I went into the Rexall and used the phone booth to call Gene. When Gene came on the line, I said, "Gene I'm at the Rexall by the four-way in Anna, can you come and get me?"

"I'll be right there Bo."

He was there in ten minutes. When I got in the car he said, "Where to?"

"Well, first off have you got a date tonight?"

"Yes, I do."

"Well, in that case, why don't you run me out to the hospital, and I'll get the car from Dad and go on home."

He looked at me and grinned, "I've got a surprise for you." Gene was sitting there grinning in a way that made me think the joke's going to be on me. I thought, *Now what*? "Well," he laughed as he said, "I've got orders to tell you that Sharon Spears wants a date with you the first time you come home from college." I was wondering who Sharon Spears was. Gene saw my blank look and laughed. "You can't remember who she is, can you?"

"No, I can't."

He said, "She's the girl who lives next door to us."

I looked at him like he was nuts. "You gots to be kidding me Kingfish!"

He laughed and shook his head. "Hun-uh, no sir, I ain't. She told me yesterday to tell you the first time I saw you, she wants to go out with you."

"But she's a little kid!"

He smiled and said, "She's a freshman in high school."

"That makes her all of what? Fourteen?"

"And, how old are you my man?"

"Seventeen—the same as you."

"Right! Three years difference."

"Yeah, but those three years have been hard ones. I ain't ready to play tea party dolls with some little—."

He cut in, "Wait until you see her, she's growed some since summer."

"Yeah, but what about the mind?"

He chuckled. "She's still into bubble-gum."

"Great! Just flip-flappin' great! How do I get out of this?"

He looked over at me and said, "I don't think you do—she's a friend of Sandy's. I promised Sandy I'd ask you to do it."

"So, you asked!"

"Does that mean yes?"

"I hope nobody sees me."

He repeated, "Does that mean yes?

". . . Yeah . . . I'll do it. But if anybody gives me any flack about robbing the cradle, I'm gonna give them your name and tell them that you're gonna kick their butt." He laughed, put the car in gear, and headed for the hospital.

"You mind if I ask how is this date set up, I mean how is she gonna know that I'm coming over?"

"I'll stop on my way home and tell her.

"Fine, tell her I'll be there around six-thirty."

"Will do, ol' buddy."

He's enjoying this, and after all I'd gone through to help him with his love life. Oh Lord, why is it always the ones I don't want. I'll bet she's just figured out that she's got claws. My poor old hide gets used as a sharpening post again.

We drove around the hospital grounds until I spotted Dad's car. I had my keys, so I locked my suitcase in the trunk.

"Thanks for the ride Gene." He waved and drove off. I did not thank him for the date—I was more of a mind to put Exlax in his cocoa.

I found Dad through the duty nurse and called him on the phone. "I'm in Anna, and I want to take the car." He seen real pleased to hear from me until I said, "I've got a date."

He said, "Be back here by eleven-thirty, your mother will be tired and want to go home."

"Yes sir."

On the way home, I thought over and over, Why didn't I just say no?

While I fixed supper, I heated water on the back burner, and after I ate, I scrubbed in the kitchen sink. I dressed in my second best sport coat and even put on a tie. I had left my colored shirts, fake leopard skin vest, my pocket watch and chain in Carbondale, so a plain white shirt and a tie that only had one spot on it, was the best I could do. I looked at the clock, twenty minutes to get to the Spears—ol' lead-foot made it with two minutes to spare.

When I pulled up, Sharon was out the door and in the car before I could get out—I was going to get out and open the door for her, but she was too fast for me.

Her dad—boy he's a big sucker—came out and yelled, "You be home by midnight Sharon!"

Whew-boy! A blind man could tell that somebody had gotten into the car. The scent of gardenias overpowered everything! My sinuses were vibrating under the assault. She had poured enough perfume in her hair to prepare an Egyptian mummy for burial. This was going to be a fun night. *I'll probably never be able to smell again. Oh well, I could take up skinning road-killed skunks for pocket change.* She slid over and snuggled right in there, tight—put her head on my shoulder as I drove. *This sport coat is going to be a write off for at least six months.* I asked, "Where would you like to go?"

She said, "I don't care. Where ever you want to go."

I said, "Well, let's go to the drive-in."

It was gonna be colder tonight than a witch's elbow. I would have to run the car to keep the windows clear so we could see out. I paid and drove to the back row. I really didn't want anyone to see us. I got out to hook up the speaker and asked, "Do you want anything to nibble?"

She said, "No."

I hooked up the speaker, got back in and turned around into a lip-lock. Oh my, oh dear! Oh, yes indeedy—I can feel the kitten claws scoring my hide and the show hasn't even started yet. It's gonna be a long night. She didn't know what she was doing, but she shore was trying. Like an inexperienced driver, she was giving it too much gas and had my wheels spinning all over the place—the over-revving was starting to heat me up. When the lights came on after the movie, I didn't even know what the movie was about. I heard a lot of shooting and tried to look once, but I couldn't get her turned around so I could look over her shoulder. Finally, I just 'gave up and turned the speaker down so I wouldn't hear and be curious anymore.

It was a quarter till eleven when the movie let out, and I drove her home. Her Dad's car was gone, so I parked to one side of the drive. They came home about ten minutes later, but by that time, we had the windows all steamed up, and we might have been on the backside of the moon. I had the doors locked so no one could yank a door open and say, "What's going on in here."

At twenty after eleven, I said, "I've got to go, I have to pick up my folks at eleven-thirty."

She didn't have to be in the house until midnight, and she didn't want to lose a whole half-hour. She was wound around me like a killer vine. I thought, *I'm never gonna get out of here*, so I slipped my hand under her skirt. It got clamped in a vise so fast I liked to have sprained my wrist. She came up for air, and I said, "Sharon, I've really got to go." It was now eleven-thirty.

She said, "When will I see you again?"

I said, "I don't know. I don't get home very often."

"Come and see me when you do."

"Well, I'll try."

I finally got her to her door at eleven thirty-eight. I made the goodbye a short one and drove like a maniac trying to get unlate. Wouldn't you know it, when I got to the railroad crossing in Anna, there was a train across it setting out freight cars.

Mom and Dad were standing out by the parking lot when I pulled up at five minutes to midnight. Mom got in and asked, "Where have you been?"—like I was six years old again.

Dad said, "He had a date. I can remember you making me late a couple of times, myself."

I said, "I'm sorry, there was a train across the tracks—I had to sit and wait."

Mom sniffed and looked at me. "What's that smell?"

I said, "I think it's gardenias."

She smiled and said sweetly, "Why are you wearing so much of it?"

I wasn't about to answer that, so I just said, "It seemed like a good idea at the time."

She said, "Oh, I see." She smiled and said, "Well, Worry Wart why don't you get us home before you have some more good ideas."

Barbara Ann was an ambush Sunday morning. Sunday school had started when we walked in—we had had a heifer bullin' this morning. She was missing from the pasture. I found her calmly eating grass by our neighbor's big Hereford bull. The sweat still hadn't dried on him. He was so worn out; he didn't even get up when I came to chase the heifer home; all he did was watch her go and give one sad moo. I had to cut the neighbor's fence. She had jumped in—this heifer could clear a six-foot fence when her season was upon her—but do you think that she'd jump back out, not on your life.

Barbara Ann was playing the special music when I came in. I had to stand at the back until it was finished—then the general assembly was dismissed, and I never even got to sit down. The music was wonderful, but watching the lithe rhythmic movements her woman's body made as she played were as enticing as the deliberately provocative movements others made; that and that red hair broke down all the walls I had so carefully built up around my poor heart. That blasted red hair. I felt as helpless as that poor dumb bull.

Gene came over and slyly smiled.

"To you," I said, "I ain't talkin'."

He laughed and asked, "Are you coming over?"

I shook my head. "No, I think I had better go home. I have spent exactly one hour with the folks this trip. If you want to come over that's fine, but I'd better go home."

He said, "I've got some work to do, so I got to go home and finish."

After Sunday school we sat together in our usual seats in the back row of the balcony. That seemed to upset some younger guys who had moved into our haunts while I was gone. Whatever!

When Dad went over that afternoon to pay Herman Williams for the unplanned use of his bull, I rode along. Dick Smith's dad was the manager of Herman's place, so we went to the Smith's house.

Dick was away in the Air Force; his brother, Will, was there. Will came out when we drove in. We all said, "Howdy."

Then Dad said, "Will, is your Dad home?"

Will shook his head, "No. Mom and Dad went to my sister's, she's expectin'."

Dad nodded, then he said, "Tell your, Dad that one of our cows got out and jumped into your pasture with that white-faced bull. I need to know how much to pay for your bull service charge."

Will, said, "I'll tell him; he'll probably give you a call and let you know."

Dad said, "Thanks. Be seein' you."

I said, "See you around, Will." I leaned out and yelled as Dad was turning, "Say hi to Dick, when you see him." Dad drove off and, Will waved.

The Smiths only lived five hundred yards from us, but we had to drive about five miles there and back to go see them.

As we drove back out their road, Dad asked, "How are things going for you son?"

I said, "Some ways good, real good. Some ways, I just get by."

He just drove for a minute, then he asked, "That girl still bothering you?"

"Which one?"

"The one you were so tore up over."

I said, "You mean, Meggan?"

He said, "I couldn't remember her name. The one that got married."

"Meggan. I don't know, I don't think so. I don't know what would happen if I ran into her, but most of the time, I just don' think about it."

"Then what is bothering you?" I didn't answer him. He looked at me and asked, "You can't talk about it?"

"I'd rather not. I'd rather talk to you than just about anybody, but I can't make sense of what I want."

He chuckled, "I had that problem when I was about your age."

"Does it get any better?"

"Things happen that direct the flow of your life into channels you would never pick for yourself. You fight at first, then your sense of duty takes over, and like an unbroken horse harnessed in tandem with older horses, you finally quit fighting the bit and settle down and learn to pull." He smiled, "Yeah, I know. Some men fight all their lives, tear up the things they have, that could have given them joy—never get to where what they've got satisfies. Always wantin' something they haven't got, never contented. The Bible says—well, it was the Apostle Paul, 'In whatever state I'm in, I have learned to be content. Rejoice always, and again I say, rejoice.' Son, are you giving God thanks?"

"No. Well, at least not very often."

"I didn't think so, you should!"

I nodded, but I was thinking, *all God has done is take the one thing I wanted away from me. I'm supposed to thank God for that?* I think Dad read what was in my eyes, for he looked sad, I turned away and looked out the truck window. There were a lot of ow-ees I didn't want him digging around and touching. I'd just as soon muddle along on my own.

Dad and Mom drove me back to Carbondale after church. Mom had put together enough clean clothes to last for a couple of weeks. When we pulled into the dorm, Dad gave me some money.

I said, "Thanks Dad," then kissed Mom.

Dad said, "It's late! We've got an early day tomorrow."

Mom said, "You be good, Worry Wart."

They backed out of the drive; I watched the car's tail lights out of sight, then climbed the four flights to my hall—sweet home.

CHAPTER ELEVEN

Charley Smoot's Tame Pheasant

I was still putting my clean clothes away, when a guy named, JD Hardy came through on the way to his room. The floor widened out just past my bed and from there on, there was room for both a hall and rooms. JD's was the first room. There were four guys in the room. The other three were from the same hometown, they hung out together, JD was in the room, but not of the room. The other three were ungenerous to JD every chance they got. They weren't openly hostile to him because he was on the Greco-Roman wrestling team and could jerk a knot in their tail so fast it wasn't funny.

JD stopped to talk; I had seen him and knew who he was, but I had not had any real conversations with him. He said, "I'm JD Hardy."

"Bo Rogers."

He said, "I just got back from home."

"I did, too."

JD asked, "Where do you live?"

"Anna. Well, near Anna. My folks have a farm seven miles east of Anna."

"How's the hunting there?"

"Lots of rabbits, two separate coveys of quail, and lots of squirrels. Where do you live?"

"Just north of Chester, a little town called, Ellis Grove."

"You live in town?"

"Yes, but the town's small enough that you can walk to the woods. I got five hundred ground hogs last summer. There's a fifty-cent bounty on them. They dig holes in the dykes along the Mississippi, the water follows the holes, and breaks the dykes."

I was impressed! I had killed six ground hogs in my whole life.

He said, "I hunt with a pistol." I perked my ears up at that. If he was killing groundhogs with a pistol he must be good. I had never gotten much closer than a hundred feet to a groundhog. The ones I got, I had used a rifle. He said, "I go out shooting every Saturday. You want to come with me this Saturday?"

"Yeah, I'd love to." He went on to his room. His invitation gave me something to look forward to.

Thursday was Thanksgiving. I'd be stuck here. The folks had to work. I couldn't go home, as I had a class on Friday. Thanksgiving was one of those 'taint' days, 'taint neither school nor weekend. I was going to miss being home for Thanksgiving; we always went to Granddad Rogers' for dinner and a hunt—rabbit season, but the single day off was too short to go home. All the University buildings were like an engine left to idle, not really shut down, but not really running either. Going into one of the buildings was sort of like going into a sleeping dragon's den. You know he's there, you can hear him breathing an' smell the smoke of his breath, but it ain't a real dragon's den because there's no roar, no fire, and no click of talons on the stones.

I've been in too many fairytale plays; I'm starting to think in fairytaleese.

Thanksgiving I was caught up on studying, there was nothing to do, and no one to talk to, and most of the dorm was gone. The snack bar was closed, and the dining room was closing at one. I had skipped breakfast and pigged-out at lunch, but youth and a hearty appetite drove me out around ten. Carbondale was dead. The only thing open was the drugstore part of the drugstore; even the Coke machine was empty. The off-campus walk to most anything was over a mile. I finally found a liquor store open. They had ice-cream bars; I bought half a dozen. As a Baptist boy, I felt purely sinful going into a liquor store. I shuffled home with my stash in a brown paper bag. Oh whoopee—happy Thanksgiving! Holidays are hard when you're alone, especially your first one.

JD and I had made plans to go shooting on Saturday. We met at eleven for brunch—too late for breakfast, too early for lunch. We ate and walked to the garage he rented to hide his car in. The reason we got the late start, JD worked nights cleaning the library until two AM. Most days he went short on sleep, Saturday was his day to catch a full night's sleep.

He drove to a sandpit, set up two regulation twenty-five yard targets, paced off the distance, and loaded his Smith & Wesson K-22 target model. I had never seen anyone use the regulation stance; he fired five rounds. They were all in the ten-ring except the last one, which only cut the line.

He said, "I thought I flinched on that one." He reloaded and handed me the gun.

In fast-draw, I just pointed and pulled the trigger; at ten feet or so I could come within four or five inches of where I wanted to hit. Trying to aim at a six-inch circle twenty-five yards away was harder than I had thought it would be. My first five shots didn't even hit the paper, much less the six-inch bulls-eye, and you can forget the tiny ten-ring in the center.

He smiled and said, "It's not the gun." He took a stick and drew a target on the ground. Next he sketched how the pistol's sights should look when they are in proper alignment to the target. "Now," he said, "put your sights like that and squeeze the trigger, so that you are surprised when the gun goes off."

The front sight was quivering and dancing all over the place, but my next five shots hit the paper, not the bull, but I was on the paper, not a tight group—about a nine-inch spread.

He reloaded and said, "All right, take several breaths and then take a big one and hold it, slowly let it out as you squeeze."

The next three shots were scattered around the seven ring; the last two were fliers.

He nodded as he looked at the target, "I'm going to load just one shot at a time, and then look at the target after each shot." He moved behind me where he could look over my shoulder. When I fired, the hammer snapped on an empty chamber, but the barrel jerked up as though the gun had been fired. He laughed, and said, "I thought so! You're flinching and jerking the trigger, and I think you're probably closing your eyes in anticipation."

It was such a hollow feeling to be really set for something to happen and it doesn't—my ego had taken quite a beating, my own footprints were all over it. I was humbled now and ready to learn.

JD patiently corrected my mistakes, and by the end of fifty rounds, my last five were all in the seven and eight rings, except for one flier. JD said, "Well, that's enough for one lesson, you're starting to lose your concentration."

JD set up a new target, and had me time him—so many seconds to fire so many shots. At the end of fifty rounds, he had scored a ninety-five. Most of his shots were tightly clustered in the tiny ten-ring. There are a few people whose concentration, discipline, and dedication are so above the 'normal' they become precise and machine-like in their ability to perform a skill. JD is one of those.

JD took a box of 22 short, half-power rounds and loaded six of them. He had me stick six pennies to a post with chewing gum. From fifteen feet, he made six perfect little cups out of the six pennies. I asked, "How long have you been practicing?"

"Two years."

"How much practice do you do?"

"In the summer, I shoot fifty rounds every day. During school, I shoot once or twice a week, or as often as I can."

As we drove back to school, I felt in awe at his skill, and pride that I was learning a new skill.

The week off at Christmas was a trip back into another world—the world of farm chores and sleeping in an unheated room. My room in the dorm collected the heat from four floors—I was still sleeping under just a sheet. Howard and the other two guys had long since gone to sleeping under a blanket. I take after Dad in this—he can almost sleep in the snow in his shorts. Being back home in an unheated bedroom where the thunder-mug freezes some nights is an attitude adjustment.

We went to Granddad Rogers' for Christmas. Uncle Cotton said, "Let's go hunting, Sprout!" He called the dogs and we hiked to the back forty. Granddad's dog, Jack, and Uncle Cotton's dog, Sport, are neither one worth the price of the powder it would take to blow them up. Jack sight trails, as long as he can see a rabbit he will trail it. When one leads him into the high weeds, he jumps like he's trying to clear a six-foot fence and swivels his head all around looking for the rabbit. Sport, is a short-coupled ball of fur that looks like a four and a half-pound Husky. When Jack is out of sight, Sport races around Uncle Cotton in a twenty-foot circle barking as fast as he can. Sport comes into his own when a rabbit goes into a brush pile. Sport works through brush piles slick as grease through a goose. If there is a rabbit in there, Sport will bring him scooting out.

We have jumped three rabbits so far. Cotton got the first one, we didn't see the second one until too late, and I missed the third one, which, Jack is off sight trailing now.

As we wait for Jack to either bring the rabbit around in full circle or come back alone, Uncle Cotton lights up the first cigarette of his second pack of the day. Lucky-Strikes—Uncle Cotton has smoked three packs a day for thirty some odd years. He just had his fifty-fourth birthday. I don't think I have ever seen a better, built man than Cotton. He's not handsome—his face looks like it was cut out of oak with an axe. His build looks like that statue of David, by Michael Angelo. Even at fifty-four, there's no sag to the man. His hair has always been white—hence, the name Cotton. He reminds me of one of the highland chiefs that made the Romans build a wall to keep them out of England.

He made enough money during the depression, that, had he not drank it away, he would have been a wealthy man. As a young man, he was as wild as a mustang stallion.

Jack yelps and leaps about thirty yards off to our left, the rabbit's coming back, we ready our guns.

I see it, and say, "There it goes," and swing the gun through the gray blur. As the brass front bead passes the rabbit's nose, I touch off, and the gray blur cartwheels. I run to get the rabbit before Jack does—if he gets a rabbit, he takes off in a run to eat it. If he is ever allowed to eat one, he's through hunting for the day.

You might ask, why would anyone keep such a sorry dog? The answer is, nobody knows why Granddad keeps Jack, he's just his dog, I guess. Jack comes and tries to take the rabbit from me. I have to twist away and yell at him to make him leave it alone.

Half an hour later, a hen pheasant flushes. Cotton, as startled as I am, yells, "Don't"–Boom—"shoot." Too late! My reflexes, stirred up by the heart stopping kerfluffle of the pheasant's take off, have cocked and fired the four-ten like a pistol.

Cotton picks up the bird and shakes his head, "It's one of Charley Smoot's tame ones. If Charley is over to the house while you're here, don' t say anything about the pheasant."

I said, "I've never seen one around here before."

Cotton smiled and said, "Pheasants and quail don't mix, where you find one, the other doesn't do well."

By four-thirty, it was getting on toward dusk; we walked back to the house. Cotton stopped by his truck and put on a pair of gloves. At my questioning look, he said, "We've had a couple of cases of fever in the county—it's best to wear protection on your hands in case you have a cut or scratch." He dressed out the two rabbits and flipped the guts to Jack and Sport and said, "You can pluck the bird, since you was so quick on the draw Mr. Dillon."

It was just a real fun job. I strained and pulled until I got everything but the pinfeathers. Cotton opened his knife and gutted it. He had to kick Jack off to keep him from grabbing the whole bird and running off with it. He separated the gizzard and giblets from the rest of the innards and tossed the guts over to Jack, who grabbed the string of them and ran, with Sport chasing after, barking.

Dad and Grandpa heard the yapping as Sport complained about not getting his fair share and came out. Grandpa, said, "Get anything?"

I said, "We got two rabbits and a pheasant."

He looked shocked! "Charley Smoot ain't gonna be real happy about that!"

"That's what Uncle Cotton said."

Dad said, "Well, wash them off and go and give them to your Grandmother."

I washed them and brought one rabbit to Cotton.

He snorted, "One ain't enough for a meal, go on, give them to Mother."

When I went into the kitchen, Mom, Grandmother, and Aunt Gina, Cotton's wife, were all in there talking.

Mom said, "What did you get, Worry Wart?"

"Uncle Cotton, got a rabbit. I got a rabbit and a pheasant."

"Pheasant?" Grandmother said, "Charley Smoot will skin you alive. Killin' one of his tame pheasants."

"Well, it scared me when it went up, and I shot it before I realized what it was."

Dad came in and said, "We'd better be goin', we've still got chores to do."

We all said our, "Good byes." Uncle Cotton was saying, "Goodbye" to Dad when he had a coughing fit that doubled him over. He got red in the face, and it took him a while to get his breath back.

Dad asked, "Those spells coming on more regular, lately?"

Cotton wheezed "Seems like it."

Dad said, "Maybe you should have it looked at."

"Naw, it's just this cold weather. Come Spring, it'll get better."

Dad just shook his head, "Well, we'll be seein' you."

I said, "Thanks for the hunt, Uncle Cotton."

He smiled and said, "My p1easure, Sprout, my pleasure."

CHAPTER TWELVE

Your Fly is Open

My buddy, Gary, had released his girlfriend to date other people. When I asked, "Why?"

He said, "I don't think it is fair for her to be without dates for all the things that happen during her senior year."

I think he was so sure of his charm that he got overconfident. She started dating a guy who came home after two years of college and went to work in his father's business.

When Gary came home and found he didn't have a date, he started taking Barbara Ann out, and that made me so happy I could just spit, except it would probably blown back on me.

I couldn't wait to get back to school—for finals to be over, so there would be new plays to try out for.

The part of college I hated was all the stuff you had to do to get to do what you wanted to do. I wanted to act, but the university insisted that I take math, English, health ed, PE and electives like basket weaving. To further round out my person, there were a dozen or so cultural evenings scheduled each quarter. The university required freshmen to attend at least three of these cultural evenings each quarter. You were given computer punch cards to be turned in at the events you chose to attend. If you went through your college career without turning in all your cards, they wouldn't let you graduate. This program was useful to me in a backhanded way. Most of the cultural evenings taught me what things cultural to avoid. A very few were pleasant surprises. The torture that the culturally ambitious will submit themselves to, to be considered culturally aware is absolutely astounding!

One of the three Anna girls I ever dated was in my biology class in high school. I thought she was a doll, but she was going with a friend of mine. I ran in to her at SIU and asked her out. She said, "No. I have to go to two more cultural evenings and time is running out for the quarter."

I was in the same boat, but I could make them up next quarter, so I said, "I'll attend one and turn in your card, if you'll go out with me next weekend, when we're home for quarter break."

She was desperate, so she said, "Yes."

I attended one of the most boring talks on Fungi of America. The speaker may have known all there was to know about fungi, but knew absolutely nothing about public speaking. Uh's filled the air between every three or four words. The hall was overheated, the chairs were flat-seated-folding-chairs, the sound system was on the fritz, and the speaker went on and on. The evening was a total disaster.

When the folks picked me up for Spring break, it was in a new Dodge Lancer. The Plymouth had given up the ghost. The bearing, I had wound-up too tight trying to avoid a head-on the first week of school, had finally said, "I'm done." I felt bad about that, but I loved the new car.

I had my moves all planned when I went to pick up Janne for the date that I had purchased with my cultural evening. I casually said, "You have your driver' s license don't you?"

She blinked and said, "Yes."

"Would you like to drive our new car? Why don't you drive to the drive-in?" When we pulled up at the ticket window, I handed her the money.

She picked a slot that was not in the notorious twelfth row-makeout alley. When she parked, I got out and hooked up the speaker to the driver's side. She was sitting in the driver's seat, I got in on the driver's side, and she was right over against me. She was rather sulky, and do you know I watched the movie, the whole blasted movie. I kissed her once. I kissed her tightly gritted lips. I knew you could grit teeth, but I found you can also grit lips.

I finally said, "If you felt this way, why did you go out with me?"

She said through gritted lips, "I can't stand those cultural evenings; you seemed like the lesser of two evils."

My self-esteem shrank to where it could fit comfortably into a shirt pocket. The movie was a turkey, too.

My class load for the winter quarter was the maximum a freshman could carry, but all of the units were theatre classes with lots of work to be done in class.

Notices for **Thieves Carnival** tryouts appeared the last week in January. I tried out for the play, not for any particular part, any part would do. I got the part of Du-Pont Du-Fore, Jr. The Du-Pont Du-Fores, were a father-son, idiot team, who thrash around in other people's lives. You know the kind, as they bow to kiss your hand, they sweep the glassware off the table with their coat tails. Well meaning, walking disaster areas who were impossible to hate, but very easy to dislike intensely. When you looked at a group photo, they were the ones standing with one foot in the flowers.

With my limited, country-boy background, I didn't have the sophistication to understand the play. As for my understanding the character, I understood what his surface motives were and let them shape my portrayal, said the lines, and didn't bump into the furniture. This was not a brilliant strategy of performance, but I was cuter than anyone had a right to be, in my straw boater, candy striped blazer and ice cream pants. Cute is always a winner, so I got by without being panned by the critics.

I got my first education in the harsh realities of the theatre world—not all theatre people were as nice as many had been up to now. The man playing one of the villains of the piece was crippled from birth and walked with a cane. Overweight as well, and coarse in speech and manner—vulgar, was the term my Grandmother used about people of this type. The two of us had a common entrance in one scene. Night after night as I was collecting myself to go on stage, at the last second before I was to step out on stage, he would bring that cane of his thumping down on the crown of my straw boater with a growled, "Good luck kid." I would stumble out on stage with my concentration blown and have to play catch-up for the rest of the scene.

Tricks like this are common among the lesser talented hangers on in the theatre. A fellow actor is seen as competition rather than a work-mate, and these shriveled souls will use any kind of oneupmanship to give the illusion that they have talent.

I am slow to anger, but push me far enough, I mean, really work at getting me angry, and this mild mannered country boy will tear your lips off and hand them to you in a sack. Push me far enough, and there is a switch that flips in behind my eyes, and I become a throw back to those Scots-Highlander ancestors of mine; I become what they called berserkers—the ones that Hadrian built a wall to keep them out of Roman England.

Through a week of rehearsals and a week of performances I endured the whack on the hat, but came to the point, that one more time, and I was going to take the cane and break it. I hated to attack a cripple, but I had had it!

His costume was that of a Spanish grandee. A short bolero jacket, its bottom came only to the waist. The tight trousers were stretched to the limit of their endurance by his belly. He whacked me, I turned in anger to take the cane and break it. When I turned, I saw that he had not fastened his fly after his last costume change. The pants were stretched to their limit, his fly gaped grotesquely, and his underwear was on display. I took in the condition of his clothing and instead of grabbing his cane and breaking it, I just smiled and made my entrance as usual. He came on stage at my heels. I played my scene and as I finished, I detoured slightly to pass by him and quietly said, "Your fly is open," and walked off stage. The complete, utter look of panic was far more satisfying than breaking the cane of a cripple.

Usually, I wouldn't see him after he came off stage, but this time, he came to the green room in search of me. "Why did you let me go out there with my fly open?" he roared!

I smiled in my most irritating manner and replied, "Remember those whacks on the head with the cane just before we enter? I don't like that! Tonight was just a sample of the dirty tricks I know. If I get whacked on the head again, that ain't nothin' compared to what I can do—do I make myself clear?"

He had the grace to apologize. "I'm sorry, Bo. I didn't know it bothered you."

We both knew it wasn't true, but what the heck, I had made my point.

Sunday of the last week of the play, Dad called to tell me, "Your Uncle Cotton has been diagnosed with lung cancer. He'll be operated on Tuesday morning at ten AM. Son, I want you to be praying." Cotton was Dad's next older brother.

He called back after the operation, "Bo, they took the lower half of Cotton's right lung. He's resting and appears to be doing well."

Three days later, Dad called again to tell me, "Cotton's dead."

"Dead? I thought he was doing well."

"He seemed to be, he had a coughing fit and broke some stitches loose. They rushed him into surgery, and they said the surgery was a success, they stopped the bleeding, but as they closed him up, a blood clot broke loose and he died of heart failure." Dad asked, "Do you want me to come and get you for the funeral?"

"No. There are too many people who would be hurt by my being gone from the show." That was true, but mainly, I just wanted to remember Uncle Cotton as he had been. That way, he was just not around, and he could show up some time.

Uncle Cotton—that tough, hard Adonis with the hand hewn features. He had no children—a young man's indiscretion in a New Orleans house of the rising-sun had left him with a memento that by the time it had run its course, had left him sterile.

He was a man of many regrets. He took those regrets and made the most of what they left him. He had wasted his way through large sums of money when he was making big money. When age and injuries had pushed those high salaries out of reach, he came home and helped his Dad with the farm. It was quite a comedown, but he swallowed his pride and made his parents' last years better than they might have been.

He had become wise, late—his wisdom earned the hard way. People looked askance at him, but he was what the old timers called, "A man to ride the river with." He would throw every thing he was into the fight to see that his friends didn't come to harm. He was not brilliant, he was not fortunate, but before God, Uncle Cotton was a man!

The joy was gone from the last few performances of **Thieves Carnival.** I walked through my performance, hit my marks, said my lines, and didn't knock over any furniture, I wasn't supposed to knock over. I didn't shine, I didn't stink, and finally it was over.

The double downer—of a play being over, and Uncle Cotton's death, made me less than scintillating company. I went through my days doing what had to be done and only that. After three or four down days, I felt the need to have someone to talk to, other than the internal conversations I had been conducting in the wasteland of my mind. So several evenings in a row, I turned up at my buddy, Gary's room, and talked to him and his two roommates. Both roommates were named Ron—Big Ron and Little Ron. Big Ron was an artist.

My face was drawn down to gauntness by grief. Big Ron said, "Bo, I'd like to sketch your face. Would you pose for me?"

"Fine. As long as I don't have to take my clothes off; I ain't into that."

"No problem!"

That evening, he did several sketches of me to use to paint from in the future. When I saw the first sketch, I couldn't believe that I looked like that. I was a thirty-year younger version of Uncle Cotton. The same hard lines that were so sharp in his face had been padded by baby fat in mine. The honing of grief had turned my face harsh and remote. The eyes held no smile—the face of a young-old warrior. I could not believe the sketch. No, I could not believe that I looked like the sketch, until I took the sketch in their bathroom and compared the face and the sketch side by side. The artist's pen had caught a me I had not known existed.

CHAPTER THIRTEEN

Possums can be Deadly

One of the classes I was taking was theatrical makeup. It seems I have an instinctive understanding of how to create the effect wanted, and was aceing the course.

Marjorie Laurence came as a guest artist in residence to the University to conduct the opera **Aida**. The music department didn't have anyone to do the makeup for the hundreds of people in the cast. They asked Mrs. Harris, the head of costume and makeup, if she had anyone who could take charge of the project—to my surprise she sent me.

These kinds of plum assignments usually went to the grad students; not some pore little, country boy freshman. She helped me to design a simple stylistic makeup that looked Egyptian. From twenty feet—it was great! ! I taught the principals how to do their own makeup, and ran the nearly one hundred extras through an assembly line. They came out darker than they went in and had these funny lines around their eves, but when they put on their headdress you would have sworn you had stumbled into Egypt several hundred years ago.

For several glorious nights, I was the only male in the women's dressing room. The law of supply and demand came into its full potential. I was the total supply, the demand meant I could take

1064-STEW

my pick. I have never been kissed so much in my life, I thought I was going to have to have my lips retreaded. The tread was wearing below the legal limit for road use.

Katy Lee was my seat partner on the bus as we went to the surrounding towns that had requested performances to be held in their civic centers. All this and some of the finest singing voices I, or any human, have ever heard. It was the only time in my life that young ladies were ready to fight over my company. *My, my, don't fight ladies, take numbers—I'll be with you in turn.* I didn't actually say that, but I thought it.

Unfortunately, I am monogamous by nature; I set Katy apart from the herd and began to date her outside of the confines of the harem.

For two months, we were in each other's pockets every free minute. I was in love, at least I was in love with being in love. We were both freshmen, but she was far more mature than I. She wasn't overjoyed that I wanted to be an actor. She had visions of doctor, lawyer, IBM exec, or even school teacher; something that meant a regular paycheck, not the one day chicken, next day feathers cycle of an actor's life.

I called one evening, and she was not at home. When I called back, she said, "Bo, I don't want to see you anymore. We have nothing in common."

"Nothing?"

She paused and then answered, "Nothing lasting," she hung up.

I was crushed or at least I wanted to be. A night's sleep, and it didn't seem so total. I waited two days and called her again.

She came to the phone and said, "Hello, Bo."

"I just called to see if you still feel the same way?"

She hesitated a few seconds, then she said, "Bo I don't think you should call here again." The line was dead; I looked at the receiver as though it was somehow at fault, then slowly hung it up. What is it about me that is so unsatisfying? I limped around mentally for a week. Then I thought, there are far more fish in the sea than I have ever lost. What was the name of that dark eyed girl that almost got into a scratching match with Katy? May Reeder! Yeah, that's it! She lived in Woody Hall, the girls' dorm across the street from Doyle Dorm.

There must be two hundred rooms over there. How can I find out which room? You've got to have the right room number to call over there. I ran into a girl from my hometown that lived there. I asked her, "Does Woody Hall have an internal phone book?"

She said, "Yes."

"Will you get May Reeder's number for me?"

She got the strangest look on her face when I asked her to look up May's number for me. She said, "Are you sure you want May's number?"

"Yeah, why not?" She just shook her head.

That evening Kate called and left a message, "May's number is Room 236."

I looked up Woody Hall's number and dialed. When the switchboard answered, I said, "Room 236, please."

The phone rang four times and a bored voice said, "Hello?"

"May Reeder, please."

"You got her."

"This is Bo Rogers." There was silence. "I'm the guy who did the makeup for **Aida.**"

"Oh! Well hi, Bo."

I thought, well, at least she didn't hang up. I said, "I'm calling to ask if you would care to go out?"

"Sure, when?"

"How about tomorrow, I'll meet you at the door at six."

"Great! I'll see you then."

I hung up and went down the hall to Gary's room. I was bubbling over. He looked up from studying as I came in. I said, "I have a date with a girl from the music department."

He was in the music department. "Oh, who?"

I smiled, "May Reeder." He got this sarcastic look on his face, I asked, "What's wrong?"

"You mean you don't know?"

"Know what?" He looked out the window and didn't say anything. I said, "Come on finish it. You can't say, 'don't you know,' and leave it at that."

Still looking out the window he said. "She, well she's been had by more——She's wilder than a March hare." He looked around at me and then he went on, "The girl's crazy for anything in pants, but they usually aren't in their pants long."

"Well, I've already asked her, I can't back out now."

"Suit yourself, but don't come crying to me when you can't go to the bathroom for the pain."

I left in a blue funk. I thought, Why not? Maybe if I get some experience, it'll make me surer of myself.

It was raining when I met her at her dorm. We shared her umbrella and walked to the pizza place. She had already eaten, so we got milk shakes, and I had a sub.

We talked, or rather, I did. She didn't say much. I told her about our farm and how much I missed not being able to ride my horse. I talked about the theatre and all the plays I'd done. She sat and smiled and nodded in all the right places, so I asked her, "Would you care to go out again tomorrow night?"

She looked intently at me and said, "Yes. My last class finishes at four."

I said, "Four-thirty?"

"That will be fine."

She gave me a chaste little kiss at the door. It was still pouring rain at ten when I left Woody Hall. She seemed totally different than what Gary had described. I thought, people get a reputation for some reason and they're marked. I was feeling smug about uplifting someone who had gotten a bad rep.

Our date was for four-thirty, at four-thirty on the dot, I presented myself at the phone desk at Woody Hall. "Room '236, please."

After three rings, a bored voice said, "Yeah?"

"May Reeder, please."

"She isn't here."

"She's not here?"

"What—have I got an echo?"

"Sorry. Uh, we have a date, it was for four-thirty, do you happen to know where I could find May?"

"Check over at the music building. She said, she was going to be working late this evening."

She hung up. I stood there listening to the hum of the phone. I replaced the receiver and mumbled to myself, "She said she was going to be working late this evening? Well maybe something came up. I didn't check for a message before I left. Well, I'd better go see her and find out what she wants to do."

I knew roughly where the music building was. **Aida** had been in the big auditorium. I ran up the steps into the lobby. The music hall was through the inside door. I could see May as soon as I opened the door; she and five guys were lounging on the steps to the stage. I had seen that attitude before, in a pack of dogs; that should have warned me.

I walked the length of the aisle, at the foot of the steps, I said, "May, could I talk to you?"

She said, "Why?"

"We had a date." That's all I got out.

She turned her head and spoke over her shoulder. "You guys," she said, "This dumb-son-of-a-bitch thinks he has a date with me."

The five guys wore lounging like I had seen hounds do around a bitch coming in heat, one that's almost ready but not quite yet. Their laughter cut me somewhere deep in the soul. They moved to a readiness to take this stray puppy down a few notches. The little switch behind the eyes almost tripped. I was ready to kill. That was what made me turn and walk away, some part of me knew that if I started, I would kill. I had studied some of the dirty tricks the martial arts people don't talk about. I was afraid I would kill May. In my family you don't hit women, except maybe across the bottom if they get owly. The heat that I was feeling made me want to put my hands around her neck, so I turned and walked away. Their laughter kept cadence with the echoes of my footsteps that bounced back from the walls to salute my passing.

My face must have looked like one of the outriders of death and hell. People I met on the sidewalk stopped and turned to watch me pass. When I got back to the dorm, I ran up the four flights to my hall. I repeatedly rammed my fist into a door until the door cracked. Grabbed a towel, ran down to the floor below to take a shower, a long cold shower. When I got out, I felt drained—empty as yesterday's news and just about as useful. What is wrong with me? Not even the bad ones want me! The bathroom had no answers. I dressed and took my towel back to the room, went down to the dining room and ate alone. My hand began to throb, it hurt to touch, but I could move my fingers so I guessed that it wasn't broken. When Howard came in, he wondered how the door got broken. I shrugged as though I didn't know.

I went through the movements of life—I was quiet, soft spoken, but there was nobody home inside. If I had had a car I would have been out running the curves of Hwy 51 as fast as I could go to get the high that adrenaline brings.

I felt that a change in people, place, and activity would do my soul a world of good. I talked JD into lending me his second pistol. Saturday, bright and early, well, it was ten o'clock when I got my body out on the side of Hwy 51 thumb in the air—wouldn't you know it, I got a ride with a highway patrolman.

He said, "Anna, huh?"

Two points for the boy—he can read. My little sign says "College Student—Need Ride Home to Anna."

I sat there hoping he don't read minds, what with me having that pistol of JD's tucked into my dirty underwear in the suitcase.

He was a chatty fellow. "Where do you live, Son?"

"We have a farm seven miles east of Anna."

"The far side of town, huh?" I nodded. "Do you know Bluford Johnson?"

"I've met him, I ran over one of his chickens in the road once."

He grinned. "Is he still letting his chickens run loose on the road?"

"All the time."

He laughed, "He was doing that when I was a kid. He's my Mom's cousin. He always was a weird duck."

"Age hasn't changed him none."

"No. My dad said once, 'He thought Bluford just liked eating road kills.'"

I laughed. "I sold him a magazine subscription when I was in the FFA." I held out my hand to show him the big silver ring with the FFA seal. "Actually, I sold it to his wife, he wasn't home."

He nodded, "If he had been, you wouldn't have made the sale."

I chuckled, "From what I saw the time I took the chicken I'd run over to the house, you're probably right—he didn't strike me as the most friendly fellow I ever met."

We pulled into Anna, and he asked me, "Where would like for me to let you out?"

"The four-way-stop will be fine. I can use the phone booth to call a buddy and get a ride home."

He pulled over, held out his hand and said, "Ralph Tanner."

"Bo Rogers."

"Good luck, Bo," he said as I opened the door.

"Thanks Ralph, and thanks again for the ride."

"Da nadda." At my blank look he said, "That's high school Spanish, it means for nothing."

"Oh, well, uh, Via con dieos. That's a line from a song, I don't know what it means, but it sounds Spanish."

"It is, it means go with God."

I said "Oh! Well, go with God." I closed the door, and he waved as he drove off.

Gene wasn't home when I called, so I called home. The folks weren't home either. I didn't know what schedule they were working. What a dilemma, the choice lay between—were they working or were they simply not home? If they are working, wa l king out and getting the car is the thing to do, but if they are not working, it's walk out-walk back. Finally, it dawned on me, call the duty nurse and ask. I called the hospital, and they put me on hold. The duty nurse was at lunch. After five minutes, someone picked up the phone and said, "She ain't here." and hung up.

Well, I suppose I could hitchhike, but then it's a mile and a half from the highway to the house, and me carrying this suitcase. Heck, stash the suitcase and get something to eat, it's lunchtime.

I walked over to the guy in the Rexall and asked, "Do you mind if I leave my suitcase here till I can get something to eat?"

"Stick it back behind the counter here."

"Thanks, I'll be back as soon as I can."

I went out and started across the street, Gene went by going the other way. I yelled and whistled and waved my arms. He kept on going. "Oh, great!" He turned left at the next corner, so I stood on the sidewalk and watched, sure enough, he came back around and pulled in beside me. He was laughing.

I opened the door and said, "You turkey!"

Through his laughter, he said, "Hello, Bo. You should have seen your face when I drove right on by."

"Pull around one more time, my suitcase is over at the Rexall."

He nodded, I shut the door and ran across the street to the Rexall.

The man looked up in surprise. "Back already?"

"Yeah, the person I was trying to call drove by."

He smiled and said, "Some days are like that."

"Yeah," I said, but to myself I said, "I hope not too many."

Gene said, "Where to?"

"The sporting goods, I need some twenty-twos."

"Right!"

He couldn't find a parking place, so I got out in front of the sports shop. He said, "I'll be back around."

There was a line at the counter. It must have taken ten minutes just to get two boxes of shells. When I finally came out, Gene was just turning the corner. When I got in he grinned, and said, "And around and around and around."

It took me a couple of seconds to catch on, the last thing he had said when I got out was, and "I'll be back around."

I smiled and said very politely, "Thank you."

"Where to?"

"If you've got something to do, I'll just tag along."

He held up his hands and said, "Nada."

I thought, what's with all the Spanish? Out loud I said, "In that case, why don't you run me home, so I can get the truck?"

He said, "Tally-ho, Old Sport."

I said, "Television is rotting your mind." He grinned. "Have you got a date tonight?"

"No, Sandy's Dad has her grounded this week." He reached in the back and got this dumb little pork-pie hat and put it on. He said, "How do you like the hat Uncle Harry got me in Chicago?"

My first thought was, what good is that? He obviously was proud of it, so I said, "That is a hat!" He grinned as though I had admired it.

When we got to the house, the folks weren't home. I changed clothes, left a note, and remembered I hadn't eaten. I yelled out the door at Gene, "You want anything to eat?"

He yelled back, "No!" So I opened a can of soup and ate it cold.

I got JD's pistol, two boxes of shells and as an afterthought, the soup can, too. Gene was out by the barn looking at Smokey. You give Smokey something to eat, and he's your friend for life or till three minutes after the food runs out—which ever comes first. Gene looked around when I came into the barn. When he saw the pistol, his eyes lit up. I tossed him the soup can, and he set it on the fence. I pulled the clip on the Ruger, loaded it, jacked the slide back and put an extra up the spout.

We took turns missing the can. Smokey took off—he didn't care for the sound. We shot a box and a half between us, just goofing around.

I said, "Let's save some for later. What do you want to do tonight?"

Gene thought a minute and said, "Well, I guess we could go to a movie."

"What's on?"

He screwed up his face in thought and said, "I think it is a movie called, 'One Eyed Jack.'"

"No kidding!" I said, "I've been wanting to see that. Marlon Brando is in that."

The movie didn't start until 7:30, so we still had some time to fool around. Just then the folks drove in.

Dad said, "I didn't know you were coming home."

"I didn't either. Last night, I just couldn't stand school anymore, so I threw some dirty clothes in my suitcase and thumbed home. I got a ride with a highway patrolman named Ralph Tanner."

Dad looked at the pistol and asked, "Is that thing loaded?"

"No, I just fired the last shot."

"Check it visually." I jacked the slide and showed him. He said, "Always make sure." He started off, stopped, looked back, and said, "And then treat it as though it still is loaded."

"Yes, sir!" Mom and Dad went into the house.

I said, "Gene, you might as well stay for supper, we've got to eat sometime."

"All right, but I'll have to call Mom and let her know that I won't be home to eat."

When we went in, I told Mom that Gene was staying for supper, while he made his call.

At supper, Dad asked, "Bo, how are you getting back?" I hadn't thought about it. Dad said, "We've got to work tomorrow night, that's why we're off today. The people who usually work Sundays are out of town."

Gene said, "Why don't I go with you. I could leave my car here and drive your truck back."

Dad said, "That's fine with me if you guys want to do that."

"Gene, if we go early, we could see some of Carbondale."

He chuckled, "There ain't much of it to see."

Around six, we left to go to the movie. Gene said, "Let's swing by the house, I want to get some money."

We went in separate rigs, with me following him. When we got to his house, I stayed in the truck. He was back in about five minutes, and I backed out of the drive and took off for Anna. Gene was about fifty yards behind me, when we came over this hill where his road goes steeply down to a tee with the blacktop—on the far side of the blacktop, there is a wide ditch that is over six feet deep. At top of the hill, a possum ran across the road. I slammed on the brakes, shut off the engine and put the gearshift in low—I thought—grabbed the pistol, jacked the slide putting one up the spout, jumped out and ran back to where I had seen the possum. It was getting dark, and I had trouble spotting Mr. Possum. When I did, I flipped the safety off and drew a bead.

Gene leaned out of his car window and yelled, "Bo, your truck is running off!"

I turned around, and my truck was shuddering forward gaining speed with every shudder and headed for that deep ditch. I forgot about the gun in my hand and ran as hard as I could. At the edge of the ditch, I wrenched the door open and leaped as hard as I could. I got one leg in and stomped on the brake. The truck slammed to a stop. I crashed into the steering wheel with my shoulder. The impact made me jerk the trigger. There was a deafening blast in the confines of the truck cab. I thought I had shot myself, and sat there rigid, scared to move, waiting for the pain to start. After a few seconds when there was no pain, I looked at the gun in my hand, slipped the clip out, worked the slide, and removed the shell in the barrel. I put that round in the clip and laid them down separately. Then I started to scan the dash of the truck looking for a bullet hole. I went over the dash inch by inch. No hole! "Thank God for that." I looked at the roof of the cab. No hole! I breathed a prayer "Thank God it went through the floorboards; Dad doesn't have to know." Then the wind hit me in the face. *Wind*? I looked at the windshield, if the shot had come from the outside it would have hit me right between the eyes. There was a spider-web of cracks with the neatest little hole in the center.

"The windshield! Oh no! I do have to tell Dad."

All this had taken two minutes; Gene was sitting in his car. I could see him in my mirror; his hands were white where he was gripping the wheel. I thought, *He's frozen*.

I made sure the truck was in low this time, and got out. The evil thought came to me, to stumble and stagger as I came back to Gene. I thought about it—the actor you know, but I played it straight.

When I walked up to Gene, he was shaking. He said, "Why did you take so long? I thought you had shot yourself."

"No," I said, "Just the windshield."

Gene went on in a shaking voice, "If you had stumbled when you got out, I think I would have had a heart attack."

I grinned and said, "I thought about doing that."

"I'm glad you didn't, I was so scared when you didn't come, I almost threw up."

"You all right?"

"I think so, but I've got to go to the bathroom so bad I can taste it."

"How do you like it?"

"What?"

"Well, you said you had to go to the bathroom so bad you could taste it—I asked how did you like it?" He looked at me blankly. I said, "Never mind. Can you drive?"

"Yeah . . . I think so."

We got to the show early; they were just showing the coming attractions. I was in the center of the row with Gene between me and the aisle. I decided that I wanted some popcorn and a large Coke. "Gene, do you want anything?"

"Just some Milk Duds."

Rather than climb over him, I stepped on the seat arm and dropped into the empty row behind us. When I came back, I had my hands full, and some people had moved into the row behind us, so I moved into the row on the outside of Gene and sat on his new pork-pie hat. He was engrossed in the preview. I stood up again with both hands fu1l and said, "Move your hat."

He fumbled around with one hand, still engrossed in what was on the screen. When he quit fumbling around, I sat down again—on his hat. I said, "Gene, for crying out loud, move your hat!" He fumbled around again, and while I was waiting, I leaned over and lipped a mouthful of popcorn. I sat again—on his hat. I said with my mouth full of popcorn, "Muff yur 'at!"

The lights came up then and he gave it his full attention. "My new hat," he wailed, "you sat on my new hat."

I chewed rapidly and then had to take a sip of my Coke, before I could answer, "Three times, I tried to get you to move it three times. Here, take these Milk Duds." Still moaning about his hat, he held it up to look at it, and that sucker looked like a road kill. It was flatter than a sail rabbit that has been run over, flattened out, and dried until you can pick it up and sail it.

I enjoyed the movie with Marlon Brando. I enjoyed it in a different way than most people did. I was watching Brando for acting tips, he fascinates me. When we came out of the movie, we went to the truck and stood looking at it. Gene said, "We ain't going to be able to drive this thing tomorrow!"

"It sure don't look like it."

"Well, we can take my car," he paused, "if you buy the gas."

"I think that can be done."

He looked at the windshield again and shook his head, "Bo, you scared me half to death, I thought you had killed yourself."

I said, "Once I found out that I wasn't hit, it didn't bother me—except that I have to tell Dad what I did, and that, I ain't lookin' forward to a'tall."

Gene said, "Good night," and went to his car. "I'll see you tomorrow, Bo."

"Thanks, Gene—I'm sorry about the thrill." I decided to wait till tomorrow to tell Dad. Why mess up his sleep?

I told Dad at breakfast. He said, "I want you to take that gun back where ever you got it. You're too careless. A short iron demands that you pay attention all the time. You're just not ready for one yet."

"Yes, sir!"

He looked at me and said, "Make sure you leave all the shells for it at home."

"Yes, sir."

Gene and I left after Sunday lunch. Dad filled Gene's car from our tanks. With Gene driving, it was a nice pleasant trip. No wild skids on the corners, just a nice pleasant trip. All the anger and pain of the last few days were gone. Nearly killing myself had cleaned a lot of rubbage out of my attic. I was ready to go back to school.

I had JD's gun in a sack. He came through my hall at half past nine, I handed him the gun in the sack and thanked him for loaning it.

He asked, "How did it go?"

I chuckled and said, "I got myself into trouble with it."

"Well, Bo, what did you do?"

I told him the story and after I finished he said, "Man-o-man, you were lucky!"

I said, "You're right, possums can be deadly."

CHAPTER FOURTEEN

House of Dreams

Spring term, there were no parts for me in any of the regular productions, but one of the student directors asked me to do a part in his directing class project, a play called, **The Blue Note**. The only audience was to be the instructor and the other student-directors. I was so anxious to act that I would have acted the phone book in a phone booth. The only thing I was to receive for it was experience and a few credits toward joining the Southern Players, a fraternal group made up of theatrical people who had participated in several plays and acquired the credits to join.

The Blue Note production was a rush job; we rehearsed four nights, and Friday afternoon we did our thing for the directing class. After the presentation to the directing class, I was through for the week, so I threw my dirty clothes in my suitcase and was Anna bound. I got a ride with, of all people, my cousin, Dick. He was gear jamming a load of gravel south on Hwy 51. Dick drives like I do, only he does his driving in a 40,000-pound rig. We went through those thirty-five mile curves at fifty-five, with that much weight on—it felt like we were on rails.

Dick drove a stock car on most Saturday nights. He was winning enough to pay for his hobby. One of the first races he drove in was at the Anna Fairgrounds. In the ninth lap Dick was fighting to get the lead from another driver. His wife, Robbin, was in the stands. Dick came around the turn in front of the pits and was trying to power by the other driver as they passed the stands. Dick's car threw a front tire, wheel and all. Dick went from eighty in one direction, to thirty in several others, he fought that car all over the place. Once or twice it looked like he was going to flip. The crowd in the stands was on its feet. A great big fat man stood up right in front of Robbin, while Dick was trying to keep it painted side up. The guy was so tall Robbin couldn't see over his shoulder and so wide she couldn't see around him. The bystanders said later that she took her umbrella in both hands and brought it down right in the fat man's hair part, and screamed, "Sit down, that's my husband. I want to see!"

Dick is a no nonsense straight-ahead type of guy. I asked his big brother, Lee, who is six-foot-four, "If you and Dick were put in a phone booth and Dick was mad at you and you at him, which one of you would walk out?" Lee said, "There's no question in my mind, Dick would." This was from a guy who could pick up three hundred pounds and just play with it. He said, "Dick hates to fight, so when someone is dumb enough to make him fight, he fights to win." He drives the same way, but I think I could give him a run for the money on the track. I've never driven against him, but I'd like to.

He dropped me off at the four-way. Dick didn't say a heck of a lot on the trip. Just, "Hello Bo," when he picked me up. He issued a couple of grunted answers about Robbin and the kids and, "Goodbye, Bo" when he let me out. I said, "Thanks for the ride, Dick." He nodded.

I used the phone booth in the Rexall to call home, and the folks weren't home, so that means they're at work.

I called Gene, and his mother said, "Hold on he's at the barn." I stood there pretending to talk while a fat lady prowled the floor outside the booth giving me looks that could induce cancer in rats and perhaps bad pimples in guys my age, or hemorrhoids if your diet didn't contain enough fiber. She even rattled the door twice, I nodded and waved my hand at her. Gene finally came on the line all out of breath. I said, "can you run in and get me?"

He came back, "I just ran down from the barn, and I'm all out of breath, I can't run anymore."

I said, "Well, use the car when you run in and get me."

"I can't run and drive at the same time. Which do you want, me to run, or do you want me to run in the car?"

The fat lady rattled the door again. I thought about making a face at her, but she was big enough to sit any place the four hundred-pound gorilla didn't want—she got next choosies. I said, "Gene, I've got this big fat lady that's trying to tear the door off the telephone booth—so can you come and get me?"

He said, "Relax, Bo, she just wants your body, you turn them big fat ladies on."

"Very funny! Can you come and get me"

" I can, but I don't know if I will."

"Let me rephrase that, will you come and get me?"

"Say pretty please."

"Pretty please."

"With sugar on it."

I said, "With sugar, corn flakes, potato chips, chili or anything else you can think of! Will you come and get me so I can get off this phone and get this fat hussy off my worried mind." There was a long silence . . . "Gene?"

"Quiet! I'm thinking."

There was another long silence . . . "Gene!"

He laughed and said, "Yeah, I'll be there. Oh," he said, "Where are you?"

I sighed and said, "At the Rexall!"

"I'll see you there."

I hung up, and as I opened the door the fat lady said, "It's about time, Punk!" What she said next isn't printable. She had to squeeze herself to get into the booth. The door wouldn't close with her in there. She squirmed around and banged her elbows on the glass walls digging for change, then she yelled at me, "Hey you!"

"Me?" I asked.

She nodded, "Yeah, you! You got a dime?" Out of fear, I guess, I dug in my pocket and came up with a quarter, two pennies, and a nickel. Her hand came out like a striking snake and took the quarter. She said, "That'll do," and turned and dropped it into the phone and snarled over her shoulder, "Beat it Punk!"

"Right! I'm out of here." I went across and stood on the corner so Gene wouldn't have to park. Gene pulled up, and as I was getting in, the fat lady came out of the Rexall. She caught her dress on one of these curlicue things they put on aluminum screendoors. Her overburdened dress split all the way from hem to neckband right up the back. She had no slip or anything else underneath. When she whirled around to kick at the offending door, she was exposed from the rear. I think that was the ugliest sight I ever saw. Gene almost lost control of the car from laughing. She knew all was not well with her Haut Couture. She whirled back around and put her exposed hindmost parts to the wall, and sidled off down the sidewalk doing a sort of a sideways step-n-glide out of sight. I wonder what she did after the wall ran out?

Gene had to pull over by the bank and stop, he was laughing so hard. As he was trying to get his breath back, he wheezed, "Bo, that experience was worth the price of two movies." He gulped air and said, "Where to?"

"Well, home I guess."

He said, "I don't have time to run you home, I've got a date."

"Oh, right, well, the hospital then. I'll get the car and go home."

He grinned and asked, "You got a date or other plans?"

"No, I'm just going home. Why?"

There was a grin twitching the corners of his mouth, "Sharon Spears wanted me to tell you that she wants another date with you."

"What! You're putting me on! No! No way."

"She told Sandy at school yesterday to tell me to tell you."

"Gene, she's fourteen years old."

Gene shook his head, "She just had a birthday, she's fifteen."

"Wonderful! I don't suppose there's any chance of my getting out of town without her knowing I've been here?"

He shook his head in and exaggerated no. "Nooo." He said grinning.

"You dirty Turk—"

"No, no, Bo. Let us not forget that I'm your ride—your free ride."

"And that's the price of this free ride of yours?"

He nodded in an exaggerated up and down motion. "You got it!"

"I got the shaft, is what I got. All right, let's set this up for six-thirty tomorrow night. I ain't up to the action tonight."

"You got it! I'll set it up on my way home."

"Oh, and thank you so very very much from the bottom of my stomach—Bletch!" I pretended to throw up.

Gene dropped me off at Dad's car. I put my suitcase in the trunk and went to tell Dad that I was home. He was at supper, so I left a note.

I changed clothes, popped some corn, squeezed a lemon into a jug of cider, and settled in to watch TV. At a quarter till eleven, I drove back to Anna to get the folks. Mom got there first, she was surprised to find me there. Dad was about five minutes behind her. He started to get in the driver's side, so I turned the dome light on. He went around and got in on the passenger side.

As we drove out the gates, he asked, "How's school?"

I said, "Fine, things have settled down, it's just the daily grind. Oh, while I think of it I have a date tomorrow night. Could you take the truck to work?"

Mom asked, "Who's the date?"

"The same one as last time, Sharon Spears."

"Spears, is that the same family that had the boy at Sivia when you started?"

"Yeah, that was her older brother."

Mom said, "Huhmnph!"

I didn't ask what 'Huhmnph' meant.

The next afternoon, I was helping Dad with the chores before he left for work. Out of the blue, he said, "I worked with Mrs. Johnston, Kate's mother, last night on the ward."

"I didn't know she had gone to work at the hospital."

He nodded, "Yeah, and they transferred her over from another ward to help fill in. She said something funny last night." I looked at him; he was acting a bit strange, something about his tone of voice. He went on, "She said, 'I thought for a while we were going to be in-laws.'"

My mind was running ninety miles an hour trying to figure out what he was getting at. Dad looked at me and asked, "What have you been up to with Kate?"

"Kate?" I put on my most wide-eyed, surprised, innocent and truthful look. "Why, I haven't had anything to do with Kate in years." I was wondering if Kate had told her mom about me playing seven touches with her. Five years, and it comes back to bite me. "Dad, she's going steady or is engaged to a friend of mine."

He looked disappointed. "Oh, your mother thinks a lot of Kate."

Saturday, Dad and Mom left for work in the truck, and I had a good two and half-hours to kill. *Maybe I could put it to good use sticking pins in Gene's picture for getting me into this mess tonight.*

I put off leaving until I was five minutes late. *I had the feeling it was going to be a long night. As I drove, I thought, if she wears that gardenia stuff in her hair tonight, I think I'm gonna die. I still haven't got the smell of that stuff out of this sport coat.* I sniffed myself. "Whoa! Holy Mackerel, Andy, you still carryin' a load there boy!"

I pulled into the Spears' drive, and Sharon was out the door and into the car before I could shut off the motor and get out and open the door for her—in high heels yet! She was still a little wobbly on them—like she still needed training wheels for those things.

She had changed her perfume though, I don't what it is, but she has enough of it to frighten the horses and make the ducks fly west for the winter, and that stuff was industrial strength, whatever it was. My left sinus creaked shut like there was a hunchback closing up the castle gate against the torch bearing mob. *Yes indeedy, it was going to be a long night.*

"Good evening my dear," I croaked as I wound down my window an inch for air, which was a mistake as that created a draft and pulled more of it by my nose. I asked, "Drive-in OK?"

She hesitated and nodded. I should have picked up the hesitation. She told me later, she had wanted to go to the school for a game. The better to show me off I suppose—to make all those other Anna girls go out of their gourds drooling. If she only knew, the only drooling would have been from laughing helplessly at what she got stuck with.

Maybe we should have gone, the open spaces and the crowds might have spared me the full impact of her eau-de-whatever. It was pretty much a rerun of our last trip here. I put the speaker up, and that was the last time I got to look outside. The movie was a cop show, there was a lot of shooting, grunting and hitting. I could hear that much from the other speakers even though I had turned ours off from the start. There was one part I really wanted to watch; they had a Roadrunner cartoon. I nearly threw an eye out of socket trying to watch over my shoulder.

I will say, she must have been practicing. She was getting nearer to knowing what she was doing, and she threw herself one hundred three percent into her work. I thought, *I'm going to have to send my lips in for their ten thousand-mile rotation and balancing. Have to have them checked for excessive wear on the outside. Have to have my jaw alignment checked, too—it's numb.*

Thank goodness she doesn't wear braces. Man, that would be embarrassing to get a lip caught—I wonder if I could drive like that?

The movie ended. The lights came on, and we had to go home. *What am I saying? We GET to go home!*

I asked her, "Would you like to go somewhere and get something to eat or a coke?"

She said, "No." I'll say one thing for her she was an inexpensive date. If only she was a little older and didn't seem so desperate shout the whole thing. I felt that I was being herded along to wherever she hopes we're headed. I just want to get through college and get on with my life. Whatever that is.

When I took her home; that is, when I drove to her home and parked in the driveway, her folks were home; at least their car was there, but the lights were out. We sat there and looked at each other for about thirty seconds. Then, she slid across and wrapped around me like a honeysuckle vine in springtime. After fifteen minutes of serious Olympic level lip-lock competition, I was beginning to get uncomfortable being aroused so long, my hands started to roam and wound up on the off ramp to Cleveland.

She gasped, came up for air, and said, "I thought you were a good boy." Well, if you don't think that that will make a molehill out of a mountain.

We untangled, and I said, "I think you had better go in Sharon."

She looked like I had slapped her, but she said, "Will you come see me again when you're home?"

I sat for a minute, and then I said, "Sharon you're too young for me. There is just no point for us to keep dating." I got out, walked around, opened the car door, took her to the door, and she reached up and kissed me a little girl's kiss. I said, "Goodbye Sharon." She nodded, went in, and turned—there were tears in her eyes. I said, "Good-night Sharon." She nodded and closed the door. I turned to walk back to the car and heard the door open—I didn't stop, didn't look around, just walked to the car and got in. I could tell that she was watching from the door, and I was feeling lower than mud. I had shoved someone else onto the same path I've learned to love so well. She had built a house of dreams—I just burned it down.

CHAPTER FIFTEEN

The Man with the Shoeshine

The school year ground to an end, and it seemed that all I had was a little pile of dust to show for my year. There's one thing that that I have to look forward to next year, I've been chosen to go on tour for the first quarter. Over the summer I have to memorize two plays for the tour, **The Taming of the Shrew** by William Shakespeare and the **Wicked Wizard of Wobbly Way** by James Lash. Of the two, **Wizard** is my favorite.

James has asked the department heads to allow me to go on tour in the part he wrote for me. He based the character on my personality and speech. "May he be in heaven thirty minutes before the devil knows he's dead."

For the summer I'm just plain Bo. There is no line of jobs waiting for me to apply for. There is as usual, the plowing—although Dad cut back this year, he didn't rent the Mack place again. The college year ends in June, not the third week of May as high school did—we are three weeks behind in the plowing. I read my scripts at noon, and early and late, I p1ow.

***

The First Baptist Church of Anna is celebrating one hundred years as a church this summer. They were going to hold a pageant entitled, Moments In The Anna Church's History. The wise consensus of opinion is Bo Rogers is studying acting, let's make him the director. One rather small problem with the plan—I'm studying acting, not directing, I don't know zip from shineola about directing. The pastor sees that I'm in over my head, so he steps in and takes over in a way that doesn't make me look as hopeless as I am. I do know a great deal about building scenery though, so I'm quietly shifted over to building the scenery.

It was Dad's day off, he was plowing, and I was building scenery. Barbara Ann was assigned to help. I have been avoiding her as much as I can; this new arrangement does not help with my problem. I had been doing fine as long as I don't see her, seeing her is sort of like a self-inflicted wound, and that Texas voice of hers is one of the most dangerous weapons God ever gave a woman. She can say some innocent word, and that southern belle voice can turn it into a lethal thrust that my poor hide is helpless to deflect. To give you a prime example of lethal Texasese, Ray Stevens had just come out with his outrageous song **Ahab the Arab**; there was one line that when Ray sang it, it was funny, but when she sang it, it went through me like a cold wind. (It sounds dumb when I try to describe it, but there ain't no way for me to describe Barbara Ann's voice.) The line was "Rings on her fingers and bells on her toes, ho, ho." We were working away on the scenery, and Barbara Ann started to sing that silly song. When she sang the ho ho, she looked up at me, and it sounded so much like my name, that I went into shock. I was so cold all over it raised such a crop of goose bumps on me—if I could have sold all of them for twenty-nine cents each, I could have retired right then and there. My heartbeat was rapid, my breathing was shallow, and my vision dimmed—I walked into a post. If I could have spoken, I would have been a babbling idiot—as it was I was a quiet idiot, and nobody knew, a few people may have suspected, but they had no proof.

Later, the two of us were sizing some canvas. Sizing is a paste that causes canvas to shrink when it is applied to the canvas. After we finished the job, I was washing sizing out of the brush and flicked most of the water on to the drop cloth. As I went out to set the brush in the sun to dry, I flicked the last few drops of water at Barbara Ann. That red hair should have been a warning to me that said, "Danger—high voltage," or at the very least "Don't bug me, I bites!" She said, "Bo, you know where you can go!" it wasn't so much the words, but the vehemence with which they were said. I was speechless. I had no idea she would take it so badly. I didn't know what to do, so I just stopped, turned to look at her, and then smiled that one sided smile that people seem to think means a lot more than it does. I stood there, it seemed like, forever, just smiling and looking right into her eves, until she dropped hers. Then turned without saying a word and walked out.

I just seem to do the wrong thing when there is someone I desperately want to impress. When she came around the corner in their old Chrysler and pulled in where I was working, I was feeling about as bad as a person could feel. I looked up, as she stopped the car, got out, and came over to me. "Bo, I'm sorry I said that to you."

I didn't rise, I stayed hunkered down and looked at her until she dropped her eyes. I could tell she wanted something from me, but I didn't have a clue what it was. Finally, I said, "Oh, that's alright," and went back to cleaning the brush, my mind twirling like a windmill in a cyclone—*what do I say? What does she want? What would she like for me to say?* I was too scared of saying the wrong thing to say anything.

When it became clear that I wasn't going to say what she needed from me, she said, "See you later Bo," and got into the car and drove off.

For the rest of the afternoon, "Bo, you're dumber than a sack of rocks," ran through my mind on an endless loop.

The pageant was as those things usually are—well received by friends, family, and those too polite to say otherwise.

The plowing, even though it had seemed it would go on forever, with Dad's help, was also over.

It was too early for orchard work, and there weren't too many places eager to hire someone with no experience, who would quit come school time. I had done a halfhearted canvass of' the prospective employers I knew. On Thursday, the Gazette Democrat came out. I went through the help wanted section twice. Almost missed this tiny ad, "Wanted young man to construct computer terminal leads. Two hours per day. Pay is $7.50 per hour. Send resume with name, age, school background, and phone number to Box 19, c/o Gazette Democrat." The pay was fantastic, and only two hours. I thought this has to be a gag. But I sat down and wrote the information requested and posted it off to the listed Box 19.

A week later, I received a card requesting me to come to the third floor of a building on the hospital grounds where my folks worked. The appointment was for 1:00 PM Monday. I kept thinking there has to be a catch.

I had to take the service elevator to the third floor, there was no other way to get there, the stairs were locked. At the third floor, I went to the only door I could see and rang the buzzer. Three minutes later, a little window opened, I told a pair of eyes, "I am, Bo Rogers. I'm here to apply for the job of manufacturing computer leads." The eyes said, "Just a minute." The window closed, and I stood there facing a big plate steel door for five minutes. Then on the other side of the door came the clang, clatter, and jingle of' keys. The three locks were opened one after the other. The door was shoved back into the wall on rollers. A man in a white lab coat looked out at me and said, "Come on in." Then the procedure was reversed. After the last lock was relocked, the man said, "Come with me."

He led me to a small room about the size of a large broom closet. There was a workbench across one wall that contained a large spool of single strand electrical wire on a spindle, a cutting devise, bins filled with hundreds of the female half of a snap, and at the end, was an electric soldering iron with its spools of solder. An eighteen-inch measuring stick was screwed to the back wall.

He crossed to the spool of wire, measured off eighteen inches, cut it, stripped both ends in a notch in the cutter, and soldered a female snap on each end. The man turned to me and said, "Now you do one."

I copied what I had seen him do and handed it to him, and he said, "You've got it! When you've done two hundred of those, I'll have your pay ready. We'll need you five days a week from 1:00 till 3:00 PM. I'll have your money ready when you've finished two hundred of those each day. My name is MacIntosh."

He left, and I sat there not quite sure if I had a job or not, I had filled out no papers, answered no questions, and I didn't I know who or what I was—or was not working for or for how long. I hadn't even given them my social security number. Well, he said two hundred. I unrolled wire and started to cut lengths. When I had two hundred, I started to strip ends. I soldered a snap on each end of each wire. The two hundred were finished in one hour and twenty minutes. They were hung neatly hung on two brackets that I figured were there for that reason. I still had forty minutes to kill. I felt kind of strange just sitting there with nothing to do.

There were still twenty minutes to go when Mr. Macintosh came back. He said "Your name's Bo, right?"

"Yes sir."

He looked at the leads I'd hung up, "Finished?"

"Yes sir."

"Well, bring a book, you have to stay the two hours."

"Yes sir."

MacIntosh reached in his pocket and took out a money clip and gave me fifteen dollars, more money than I could make working a ten-hour shift in an orchard, exactly twice more money. I didn't understand it. It was there; I took it and praised God for it.

When my two hours were up, Mr. MacIntosh came and led me to the big steel door, unlocked the three locks and slid the door open.

"Thank you, Sir."

"You're welcome. See you tomorrow at one."

"Yes, Sir!"

He slid the big steel door closed, and I heard each of the three locks strike home one after another.

I hadn't a clue what this outfit was. I had the impression that it was somehow military. I guess because his hair was short and his highly polished black shoes were just like two pair Dad had brought home from the Navy.

The folks were working swing, and we passed each other on the way home. I would have to wait till tomorrow to tell Dad about this weird job at the hospital. The next morning at breakfast, Dad didn't know what to make or it. He said, "Take the money as long as you don't have to do anything dishonest. I can't imagine the job lasting long, so save your money for school. Don't depend on the money to keep on coming in, it may stop all of a sudden."

The job was in its sixth week, and the people in the white lab coats had gotten used to me being around. I would finish and feel funny about just sitting there; the time I had to just sit there had gotten longer because I kept getting faster at the job. I started to walk around in the big loft—that's what it seemed like to me, a big barn loft. There were hundreds of rats, rabbits, monkeys, and birds in cages. I asked questions until I had pieced together a picture of what they were doing.

One guy told me, "We've got a license from the federal government to run tests on these animals with every hallucinogen known to man. Every time the feds bust a drug setup and get a load of acid, heroin, speed, or whatever, they keep part of the stuff for evidence and give some to us to run our tests."

"What's the purpose of the tests?"

"We're trying to find out as much as possible about each drug—how much resistance a person can put up against this stuff.

Find out if there is something that will neutralize its effect—things like that."

"You're just running tests on birds and rabbits, how do you know what it's going to do to a human?"

"Well, we know how they compare."

"How? You running tests on people, too?"

"Well, Bo, I'm not supposed to be talking about that."

"Oh."

There was somebody that wanted in the big door about then. Mr. MacIntosh went and opened the peephole; then he undid the three locks and slid the door back. In swept a big, tough guy with a crew cut and trench coat, carrying a briefcase. The toes of his shoes had the kind of shine that mommas used to warn daughters against dancing with guys who had that kind of a shine. The guy could look up under their dresses and see their panties.

The big guy came down the aisle with MacIntosh so close behind him, MacIntosh banged into him when the big guy slammed to a halt as he caught sight of me. He spun around, grabbed Mr. MacIntosh and spun him around. As they marched off across the floor, I heard him snarl, "Who the (bleep) is that? He doesn't have a security clearance." The rest of whatever was said was out of my hearing. In a couple of minutes, the big guy came by me like I wasn't there and went into Mr. MacIntosh's office.

Two minutes later, Mr. MacIntosh came and said, "Come with me, Bo." I followed him to the big door, which he unlocked and opened. We stepped through and he closed it behind us. He looked uncomfortable as he said, "I'm sorry, Bo, but I've got to let you go." He pulled out a roll of bills and said, "Here's for today and here's for three more days to finish out your week. Don't come back, you won't be allowed in."

I said, "Thank you, Mr. MacIntosh."

He nodded and went back in closing the big door behind him. I heard the three locks snap, too, one after the other.

I told Dad about it the next morning as we were separating the cream, when I got to the part about the big guy saying, "He doesn't have a clearance!" Dad's head snapped around until he was staring right into my eyes. He lost the rhythm with the crank and the machine stopped. Dad stood there looking strange for several seconds, before he looked away. Quietly, forcefully he said, "Son, forget you ever had that job. Don't talk about it, don't ever bring it up again. It never happened!"

Now that I was back among the unemployed, I had even more time to study my two scripts. I had the dialogue for **Wizard** down, but the iambic-pentameter of Shakespeare was foreign to my country boy's mouth, it was coming, but slower. There was one scene that was worrying me. One of the hardest things for an actor to do on command is to laugh realistically; the other is to cry real tears. My character in **Shrew** comes in laughing hysterically and continues for two minutes. It is hard to do this without it sounding faked. I spent a lot of time this summer in the barn practicing laughing. Even my dog, Sally, could only take so much. After watching me alertly for several minutes, she left. Friday afternoon, Mom came in and caught me alone laughing hysterically. She was watching me when I finally noticed her. One eyebrow was arched skeptically as she said, "Worry Wart, if you can stop your laughing long enough, you're wanted on the phone."

I said, "Hello."

A voice said, "Bo, this is Mark, Can you come in and work in the orchard Monday?"

"Sure."

"It'll just be the two of us this year; most of my crop failed. We won't have pickers or a shed crew, just you and me for about a week."

"What time do you want to start?"

"About eight."

"Fine, I'll be there."

"Thanks, Bo."

Mark hung up, and as I replaced the receiver, I shuddered thinking of working in peach fuzz again, but as much as I hated peach fuzz, no one was paying me for my time. I had enough saved to cover my books and some spending money, but a little more money never hurt a thing. Who knows, I might find a lady to spend it on.

Sunday passed quietly, except that I literally ran into Barbara Ann. I came around from the men's room and bounded up the stairs smack into her. I apologized and backed down so she could come on down. She was cool and watchful, suddenly she seemed to make up her mind and walked off with a purposeful stride. I stood there watching her alluring back disappear, wondering if I should go after her—I didn't. He who dithers, dies in the dust.

As usual, I was five minutes early Monday morning. After five minutes Mark came out of the house. He flipped one of his many cigarettes of the morning into the road as he walked. Since Uncle Cotton's death from lung cancer, I hate for any of my friends to be heavy smokers.

"Hello, Bo."

"Mark, how are you doing?"

"Fine. Letty says, 'Hi.'" I grinned. "Feel like picking peaches?"

I smiled ruefully, "It's one of my least favorite things, but I guess so."

He laughed and said, "It won't be too bad. I don't think that there are more than twenty baskets in the whole orchard. That late freeze we had got most of the blossoms. What peaches there are, are five to a tree, and some trees don't have any at all."

Mark opened the shed and scrounged out two picker bags, and as he threw them on the wagon, said, "Let's force the door back a little farther so we can get at the ladders." It took both of us to move the door so we could worry two ladders out of the tangle of legs. We loaded them, and Mark said, "We'll need a water jug. Run over to the shed and dig one out and wash and fill it at the hose." While I was doing that, Mark started the tractor and swung it around so it was headed toward the orchard. When

I climbed on the wagon with the water, he started for the orchard and parked a third of the way down. We carried a three-legged ladder apiece and worked our way through the orchard looking for peaches. Hauling that ladder would beat a Charles Atlas course any day for wearing you out. I don't know if it built you up, but it shore put a big tired on yours truly.

By noon, we only had fifteen bushels of peaches. We weren't brushing the fuzz off them, but we graded them for culls as we went. Usually over five thousand bushels of peaches went to market from here. A good picker would pick one hundred twenty bushels a day. We took our scant gleanings to the house to load onto the pickup. Letty was going to set out by the road with a sign and sell what she could.

Mark said, "Bring your lunch and come on to the house."

Letty had the coffee pot on when we came in. She said," Bo, do you want any coffee?"

"No thanks, I brought my tea jug."

I was watching them and the difference in the way they were around each other now, and the way they had been a couple of years ago was such a change. There were looks and touches going both ways now. I remembered the hints I'd dropped to Mark the last time I'd worked here. I chuckled to myself and thought, *Bo, you chubby little cherub, you got them both with one arrow—they're acting more like they're dating than the ten years married folks they are.*

After lunch, Letty said, "Bo, I almost forgot, your Mom called; she wants you to call home." She pointed to the phone on the wall. "You can use that one."

I called the operator and gave her the code number for our party line, two longs and three shorts. Mom came on the line, "Hel-lo?" There were seven clicks as parties on our line picked up with their hands over the mouthpiece. Our party line was faster than the radio for keeping up with the local news as it was happening. Mom was one of the worst offenders.

"Mom, Letty said I was to call."

"You had a call this morning from a young lady from Waukegan. She called and asked for you. She said that she was only in town for a couple of days and would like to see you."

"Waukegan?" I thought to myself, *who the Sam Hill do I know from Waukegan*? "Well, did she say how to get in touch with her? First of all, who is it?"

Mom said, "Lacey Vincent was her name. She said she went to high school with you."

"Yeah, she did. How am I suppose to get in touch with her?"

"Just a minute, I wrote the information down, I'll get it." Mom came back on the line and gave me a phone number and a street address in Jonesboro.

Mom hung up, and I called the number she had given me. A woman's voice answered, "Winslow residence."

"Lacey Vincent, please."

"May I say who is calling, please?"

"This is Bo Rogers, returning her call."

Lacey came on, "Hi, Bo!"

"Hello, Lacey, Mom said you called."

"Yes, is there a chance I could see you? I'm only going to be here a couple of days."

"Well, I could come by tonight around seven, if that's all right?"

"That would be wonderful. I'll see you then. Good bye."

I hung up the phone and stood staring at it. Lacey Vincent was one of the girls who turned me down when I asked her out, and now she's asking me out? They must be putting something funny in the water up north. I realized that I was standing staring at the wall. When I turned around, Letty was watching me with an amused smile. "Good news?"

I grinned and said, "I don't know. A girl who turned me down in high school just asked me over."

Letty laughed, "Sounds like the girls are starting to wake up around here."

"Not around here, she moved to Waukegan with her mom when her parents split up. She's just going to be here a couple of days."

"Who is she?"

"Lacey Vincent."

Letty's eyes opened. "You're moving up into the money set."

I nodded, "Yeah. The question is why? She turned me down two years ago."

With a move of her eyes Letty said, "Don't worry about it. Just enjoy it."

"Right!"

Mark said, "Well, Bo, if you're done with your lady killing, let's get back to work."

"Righty ho! Thanks for the use of your phone, Letty."

"You're welcome, Bo."

The afternoon went faster. My mind was on Lacey Vincent. I dragged that blasted ladder to and fro without thinking about it. I dragged the blasted picker bag up and down the ladder without thinking about it—even the blasted peach fuzz didn't bother me.

At four-thirty, Mark said, "I've about had it for today, lets knock off and I'll see you tomorrow at eight."

To me, the sweetest words in the English language are quitting time! We drove to the grader shed and covered the ten baskets that were our total take for the afternoon and left them. "See you tomorrow, Mark."

He stamped out his cigarette, blew out smoke, waved, and said, "Goodnight, Bo."

When I got home, I drove straight down to the pond to wash off. I fed the hogs early and that faked the oinky buggars out, had the trough to myself, but not for long. A hog can hear the pouring of slop at a hundred yards. They came in a running, squealing stream towards the feeding station. Too late! The trough was full and not a single pig got in the way.

On a wax paper covered plate, Mom had left a huge ham and cheese sandwich that had half the garden piled on it. It was piled high with onions, peppers, and lettuce; I opened it and regretfully took the onions out. I hated to do that, I loved them, but on the off chance that the evening might prove delightful in other ways; I felt the occasion warranted the sacrifice.

I left at a quarter to six to allow myself time to go out to the hospital and switch the truck for Dad's car. I caught Dad as he came back to the ward where he worked from the dining hall. "Dad, I came to switch the truck for the car, if that's all right?"

"Why?"

"Well, I got a call from Lacey Vincent, she wants to go out."

His mischievous look was embarrassing to me. "They're calling you now?"

"Well, it doesn't happen often."

"That's three times that I know of."

"I didn't know you'd been keeping score."

"I'm not, but it just seems that you never go out in this town, unless the lady calls you."

"A lot of the local ladies think that farm boys are beneath them. I did take one out, but I regretted it. I wasn't up to her social standards. She was about as friendly as a constipated owl. This one tonight turned me down when we were in school."

Dad chuckled, "That's a lady's right, to change her mind."

"So I've noticed! Well, Pop, I'd better get going, can't keep the lady waiting."

"Be careful, Son."

He was still watching when I got to the car and looked back. As I drove away, he waved and went back inside.

Other than the main drag, I didn't know Jonesboro. It took me fifteen minutes to find the street, and then I went the wrong way and had to turn around in some old lady's yard while she peered at me through the curtains. Finally, at two minutes of seven, I found the house.

When I rang the bell, a voice that sounded as though it had a mouthful of pins said, "Just a minute!"

Three minutes later, a young lady I had never seen before opened the door with a raised hairbrush in one hand. I looked at the raised brush and said, "I'll go peaceably."

"Huh?" She was looking at me blankly.

I said, "You looked like you might throw the brush."

She laughed and said, "You must be, Bo! Come on in, Lacey's almost ready."

"And you are?"

"Diane, Diane Winslow. We just moved here from Waukegan, Lacey was my best friend there, and she came along to see her old home town." Diane said, "I've got to finish getting ready, my date will be here any minute. Could you let him in, Bo? His name is Wallace. Just make yourself comfortable, Lacey'll be right out."

Diane disappeared with the brush going at her hair double time. I sat down and looked around. The place was comfortable, good chairs, nice carpet. I thumbed through a copy of **Life**, and about half way through; the doorbell rang. I thought on my way to the door, *what was that guy's name? Waldo, Ralph, Willy, Pete—whatever*! I opened the door and had to look up, way up, the guy was well over six feet. In my best acting 101 butler's voice I said, "Ye-ss?" He had a handful of roses—I could have killed the sucker.

He said, "I'm Wallace."

Wallace, yeah that was it. "Wallace, I'm Bo. We've been expecting you. The ladies have grown tired of waiting for you to arrive and have gone on ahead."

He blinked rapidly and said with his voice at a rising pitch, "Gone?"

I smiled and said, "Actually, they're almost ready, they'll be out in a minute. Won't you come in and have a seat?" I noticed he kept watching me. I don't think he quite knew what to make of me—it was the flowers, he had given me a complex by his show of couth, my attempted humor was a defensive reaction. He sat, but kept looking at his watch as though he had reservations at the country club. After witnessing his show of couth with the flowers, maybe he did.

The wait for the ladies stretched out, and I felt like tweedle-dumb sitting with Sir Walter Raleigh

The ladies presented themselves together. Odd, the pairing of couples—Diane was short and chesty and perky like a robin, Lacey was long and lean with great dimples, Wallace was long and lean, and I'm short and chesty.

Diane took the proffered roses and said, "I'll just put these in water, won't be a minute."

I said to Lacey, "Shall we go?" I turned to Wallace and said, "You and Diane behave yourselves. We don't want to hear that you've disgraced the family at the country club again. Good night now." I led Lacey out the door as she tried not to laugh out loud.

I got the door closed, before she cut loose. "Poor Wallace," She said between gales of laughter, "he doesn't quite know what to make of you, Bo."

I said, "Serves him right for showing up with roses. Actually, I wish I'd thought of that." She smiled, I opened the door for her and went around and got in. I just sat there looking over at Lacey. "Lacey, I'm curious, two years ago, I asked you out and you turned me down—now you call me. What caused the change of attitude?"

She blushed. "I always wanted to date you, ever since we had biology together."

"I don't understand, if you wanted to date me, why did you turn me down?"

She sat there quietly looking out the window, and I thought she wasn't going to answer, then in a low voice she said, "The reason I turned you down was Meggan Fournier."

"Meggan? What did she have to do with it?"

"Well, you were involved with her."

"I never dated Meggan. I never dated anyone the whole time I was in high school. My senior year, every girl I asked out turned me down."

"That was why! Everybody thought that there was something between you two. She was pretty formidable, the president of several groups, and all those brains, too."

"But why did people think that there was something between Meggan and me?"

"You were in her locker; girls didn't usually let boys share their lockers unless they were going together."

"I never took her out. We were as different as chalk and cheese. She was miss nose to the grindstone, and I didn't give a rip! I was just marking time until I could get out and go do what I wanted."

"We didn't know, we always saw you two at her locker. Well, I was afraid you would find me rather a light weight compared with Meggan."

"But I asked you out."

"Yes, but you were still with her in her locker. I didn't want to go out with you and then be confronted by Meggan."

"She couldn't have cared less who went out with me."

"I wish I'd known!"

"So do I. I was a pretty lonely guy. Although, a lot of it was my own fault, I really wanted out of this town, and I was afraid one of you Anna girls would trap me here."

Lacey was quiet, looking out her window, then still not looking at me, she said, "Bo, I've got a confession."

I grinned at her; "They say that's good for the soul."

"I'm not sure this one will be." She turned to face my raised eyebrow. "I'm engaged to be married."

"Then what are we doing here?"

"I've wanted to date you for a long time, this is my last chance."

"What if you like it?"

"I'm engaged to be married, tonight is all there is Bo."

"What if I like it?"

"Tonight is all there is Bo."

"Well, if that's the case, we better not go too far."

"We'll see." She smiled in a way that I didn't understand.

***

Having gotten home at two-thirty this morning, I was not at my most perky when Dad rolled me out at six-thirty. He seemed to take great pleasure in saying, "If you're going to play, you got to pay." Under that kind and gentle exterior there beats the heart of a sadistic taskmaster.

At eight, when I pulled into Mark's yard, my porch light may have been lit, but there sure wasn't nobody awake inside. Mark watched with quiet amusement the stiff hitch in my get along, finally, he said, "Are you limping this morning, Bo?"

I said, "Yeah, I think I pulled a muscle yesterday."

He nodded, took a last drag on his cigarette, ground it out, and said, "Yeah, I did that once." He chuckled and went up his ladder.

Due to my lack of sleep, during the first two hours, my head felt like a flock of canaries had had a food fight and left the mess where it fell. We were in the part of the orchard that had taken the brunt of the cold wave. On every tree, somewhere in all that foliage, lurked at least two rosy cheeked peaches. We had to move the ladder, look, and move the ladder again. By noon we had picked eight baskets between us—the total produce from fifty trees. We took our eight bushels in for Letty to sell out by the highway. We loaded the truck, and Letty left with her lunch, her, "**FRESH PEACHES**" sign, and a good book.

Mark and I were left to enjoy our own company. I ate my lunch and slumped back in my chair. I wanted nothing more than to sack out for a couple of hours, but there was no way that was going to happen. Trying to nap in a short-backed kitchen chair left me feeling worse than when we came in. Finally, Mark said, "Let's hit it!"

I opened one eye and said, "Hit it gently if you must hit it at all!" I struggled out of my chair to discover that my pulled muscle had stiffened again. I hobbled over to my truck and threw the lunch sack and tea jug in. With a groan I hobbled over to the wagon where Mark was loading a dozen baskets. I stretched out on the wagon. That didn't last long, riding on an unsprung wagon over rough ground will make you sit up if you can manage it at all. Oddly enough, as the afternoon wore on, the better I began to feel. By quitting time I felt good enough to start the day. Not that I wanted to work a double, just by comparison with how I felt this morning, I felt good.

We spent three more days going through the orchard picking widely scattered peaches. The third afternoon we pruned back limbs from the driving lanes as well as the dead wood. We cut limb props from the green limbs and firewood from the dead. As we were stacking the last of the firewood on the back porch, I asked, "Mark, what's Sarah doing?"

"Sarah is going to be a freshman at the University of Illinois at Champagne-Urbana. She's engaged."

"Oh. Well, that figures."

He lit up and asked, "What happened between you two? The first week you worked here, it was Bo this and Bo that—then she cried a lot. Then that next year she was as crabby as a sore-footed duck if anybody accidentally mentioned your name."

"I asked her older sister, Mona out, Mona said, 'No!' but Sarah was standing right behind me. I could tell that I'd hurt her. Letty told me to ask Sarah out, but I felt silly asking a little kid out, so I didn't, and the next summer Sarah was the prettiest thing I've ever seen, and she didn't want anything to do with me."

"Well, I guess that explains why she was so crabby the last week she was here. If your name came up, she stormed out."

"Is she coming here this year?"

"No, we didn't have any work for the girls this summer, so they both got summer jobs at home." Mark grinned and said, "You can't have them all, Bo. Some are going to get away, no matter what."

Yeah, but only the ones I really want get away."

"Well, come in the house, and we'll figure out your time."

Mark dug through the desk and pulled out a yellow tablet. "We've put in forty hours times seventy-five cents, that comes to thirty dollars. That sound right?"

"Yeah, that's right."

He gave me a ten and a twenty. Bo, I'm thinking about getting a Cat in here and pushing the trees out or maybe renting the orchard out to someone else. The way the market's been going and the poor crops we've had the last two years, it just doesn't pay to have an orchard. I'm afraid there won't be any more work for you here."

"I'm sorry to hear that, I've enjoyed working for you, Mark."

He smiled, "I've enjoyed having you, Bo."

CHAPTER SIXTEEN

Here the Bus Come—There the Bus Go

The tour ensemble rehearsed eight hours a day. We all had our lines down, but we had to learn the entrances and exits and all the physical business. The director was shaping our raw grist into capable performers that would not fall apart under the unexpected assaults we would be confronted with as we moved across four states and played in circumstances that would have made a seasoned trooper blanch.

There were a million things to do before we pulled out in our yellow corn-on–the-cob school bus that had the legend, Property of Southern Illinois University, printed along both sides. The director and faculty member who was to den mother us across four states was Dr. Sherwin Abrams. He was qualified in more ways than merely academic; he had served as a lock pilot on the Suez Canal in WWII. He was a man who had seen the scenery fall for real, and he confronted our misapplied enthusiasm with an unflappable, pipe smoking calm. He had the work for the two plays choreographed out like the playbook for the football squad. The chores he assigned to each cast member represented his assessment of the individual strengths of that person. I was assigned to build a table that could stand a hundred-sixty pound actor jumping on and off of it several hundred times during the next three months; it also had to come apart for stowing on the bus, and in under five minutes in the dark, be reassembled. When I had finished, his only comment was an amused, "Mr. Rogers, it looks stout, heavy, but stout." It wasn't long into the tour that I found the reason for his amusement. You carry that thing up three flights of fire escape steps and the reason for his emphasis on heavy became apparent.

We rehearsed **Wizard** in the afternoon and **Shrew** at night, and we were worn to a frazzle most days. My country boy accent did some strange things to Shakespeare's English. I had one line where my character says to another, "Come on!" It came out, "Cum-own." This broke up the cast. We were tired and looking for anything that would relieve the strain. From then on inanimate objects were addressed by, "Cum-own you baby," stretched out as far as you could, "Cummm-owwwwwn you baby!"

At the Baptist dorm, I was ensconced in a much nicer room than my fourth floor hallway of last year. I would only use the room for three weeks at each end of the school quarter, but I had to pay for it the whole time. My roommates were two very civilized young men from somewhere up around Chicago. They looked askance at this uncivilized theatre person whose clothing still emanated essence of horse. One who has a reputation for being out all hours of the night, and his unpredictable and astonishing past behavior has set the dorm on its collective ear on more than one occasion. Like the night I had come staggering into the dorm still wearing makeup that quite creditably reproduced the very nasty bleeding wounds of a mugging victim. My staged collapse had the dorm master trying to do CPR—thank God he didn't do mouth-to-mouth.

My roommates circled their wagons so to speak; they took the beds at the far end of the room and gave me the one by the door. Decent of them, that way I didn't have to stumble over them or their bed as I fumbled in after they were asleep.

We had cast photos taken for a featured article in the "Southern Illinoisian" during dress rehearsal. I got my picture taken on a ladder in Shakespearean costume pretending to be a lighting electrician. On Friday, before we were to pull out on Sunday afternoon, I hitched a ride home—I needed all the clean clothes I could get to start, we were going to be gone several weeks. The folks had to work Sunday afternoon, so Gene Pass got a white-knuckle ride to Carbondale to bring our truck back. On the way up, I was sliding sideways around a curve taking a little more of Hwy 51 than was my rightful share. We met Gary's family on their way home in the middle of the curve, and it took some fast and fancy handling to avoid them and keep the truck shiny side up. Gene was green, and his lunch was trying to decide whether to stay or go. After it was over, I said, "Man, I hate that, of all the people to nearly run off the road, it'll be all over church tonight."

Gene grunted something out the window that I couldn't understand for the wind. And I said, "What?" He just flapped his hand at me and shook his head. At the dorm I got my suitcase out of the back of the truck. Gene came back from some shrubbery he had been very interested in. I said, "I'd invite you up, but I've got to be at the theatre in ten minutes to get on the bus."

Gene was working his mouth as though something didn't taste too good. "See you, Bo. I got to go and get a milkshake." He got in the truck and halfheartedly waved as he drove out of sight.

Being only eighteen I was too young to drive a bus, so the three over twenty-one male cast members had to divvy up the driving between them. Eddy was backing the bus into position at the theatre to load props, costumes, and scenery, the bus had had all but the front ten of its seats removed by the motor pool. After the scenery was secured, our personal luggage was forced into the remaining rear space. At five, we pulled out, singing a song about there being no business like show business, and at midnight, we pulled into the first of many motels we would invade during the next three months.

Rehearsal is one thing, but performance is altogether a different experience. We rehearsed in a theatre designed for the production of plays. On the road we never knew what to expect in the way of stage and dressing rooms. Many places were not stages at all. Sometimes we set up on a gym floor, our pipe and curtains our only cover from the audience.

In a theatre town, you are used to audiences that are theatre trained. In some towns in the hinterlands, the audiences were as ill mannered as one for Live Rasslin'. Some of the audiences looked as though there had been a bit of inbreeding and not as far apart as cousins. The audiences ran the gamut from gracious patrons of the arts through boorish to the absolutely most frustrating to an actor, an audience made up of wheelchair bound geriatrics. That group gave us no response at all. It was as if there was nobody out there. Afterwards, in a conversation with the head attendant, I stuck my foot in my mouth by saying, "We were sorry that your people didn't enjoy our performance."

He answered, "Oh, they enjoyed it, they enjoyed it a lot."

"But there was no response!"

He smiled, "Breathing, just breathing, takes all their energy. They enjoyed it, they just couldn't show it."

The next stage was so shallow that our scenery was up against the back wall. You had to plan your exits, you exited the way you had to come back for the next scene—which made for some very creative coupling of players leaving together—two guys who supposedly were very angry with each other, and were being forcibly restrained by other parties who went off the other side of the stage.

Our schedule included twenty-six towns, and some of those towns were treated to multiple performances of each play.

At the end of our first week on the road, we not only had to set up on a gym floor, the gym was on the third floor and reached by three flights of fire escape. We were exhausted by the time we had carried everything up the three flights of steps. We had arrived behind schedule, so as soon as the set up was finished, we dressed and did the play. When **Wizard** was finished, the cast had to go find someplace to eat because in the small towns off the major highways, the cafe closed early. Before I went to eat, I came back into the empty gym to check on a prop for **Shrew.** Margie, one of the ladies in the cast, was sitting in the front row crying. "What's the matter, Margie?"

"Oh, Bo, my leg muscles are cramped so badly I can't get down the fire-escape. It just hurts so badly that I can't do it." Margie was about five one and weighed about five pounds more than I did.

I asked, "Can you walk on the flat?"

"I'm fine as long as I don't have to climb stairs."

The two of us were the only ones left in the building, so I said, "I'll carry you down."

She looked doubtfully at me and said, "Are you sure, Bo?"

"No problem! Cum—owwwn."

She hobbled across the gym behind me, and we went out the doors to the fire escape. I looked Margie over good for the best way to get a real good hold. There wasn't nooo way I was going to be able to pick her up in my arms Rhett Butler style. So I said, "Margie you stand at the top of the stairs there, and I'll go down two steps and you just fold over my shoulder, then I'll get turned around and carry you down." We went down the three flights in an unelegant combination of a fireman's carry and toting a sack of feed. At the bottom, I set her down on the second step up and helped her lurch down to the ground.

Once on flat ground, she reached up and pecked me on the cheek, and said, "Thanks, Bo."

We walked over to the little cafe and joined the others, Margie told them what had happened. After dinner, (we always called it supper at home, but these folks called it dinner) two of us made chairs of our arms and carried Margie back up the fire escape. Man! It was harder to do that with help than it had been to carry her down alone.

Margie was the costume mistress, so as soon as she got the costumes stowed after the play, two of us made the chair again and got her down the stairs. As we boosted her on the bus, Eddy, who was the other half of the chair grunted, "Cum-owwwwwnnn you baby!" Tired as we were, that seemed like the funniest thing, and the more we thought about it, the funnier it got. We got to laughing so hard we had to lean up against the bus. I guess it was a good thing that no one saw us—that's the way rumors get started.

A school bus is basically a five-ton cattle truck and two or three hundred miles a day of having your bones bounced will give you kinks in places other than your psyche. The others discovered that I had magic fingers—in a few minutes I could have an achy fellow actor purring like a kitten in a sunbeam.

The towns fell behind under the relentless wheels of our yellow corn-on-the-cob, and the litany of towns sounded like a trucker's song—McLeansboro, Eldorado, Harrisburg, Metroplis, Golconda, Carterville, and Effingham.

At Effingham, my aunt and uncle came from Flora to see the show. I received permission to leave with them, as we weren't moving far the next day. It was a welcome change to be among family again.

The cousin my age was off at college. He and I looked like twins; you could tell us apart when we were together, but apart, the family had to ask us which one we were.

The next oldest cousin was off from school. He showed me a sawed-off shotgun. The foot-long barrel had a front grip attached with a plumbing clamp, and the stock had been cut off to just a pistol grip. He called it his snake gun that he carried fishing. I shot the thing a couple of times, shot up the only ammo he had for it. The recoil was so bad; it made you grin to show how tough you were—even though you weren't real sure your hand would ever work right again. He insisted on giving it to me to take home, and I hid the thing in my dirty underwear in my suitcase—actually my clean underwear, my aunt washed all my stuff. I guess she was so used to a college boy coming home with a suitcase that smelled like a collection of old gym socks that she just automatically grabbed every suitcase and washed everything.

I accepted this thing and stowed it in my underwear because I assumed that we would be going straight back to Carbondale, and I could leave it in a safe place there.

My aunt and uncle took me to the next stop on the tour and bought tickets for the children's play. After they saw the play, they hugged me and went on home.

The next morning after all of the luggage was stored and unreachable, I got a look at the schedule, the next stop was Menard State Penitentiary. From movies and TV I had an idea of the security checks of everything going into prison. There I sat with an illegal shotgun in my luggage. I had visions of my coming life behind bars. Who was going to believe that although the gun was cut down to an illegal size and I had smuggled it into prison, I had no more dangerous idea than shooting snakes with it? This kid was sweating bricks. I started to pray that God would get me out of this mess.

When we stopped for lunch, Dr. Abrams called ahead to make sure that the prison was ready for us. The warden said, "Dr. Abrams, we've had a fight in the yard, could you people possibly postpone your visit?"

Dr. Abrams said, "I'll see what can be done." Dr. Abrams called the next town on our list and found they had a severe storm last night, and their auditorium's roof had leaked, they would have to cancel out completely.

Dr. Abrams called the prison back and made arrangements to perform two days from now. We went home to Carbondale for a day off. I was one relieved and grateful fellow. Just a simple prayer of desperation, in answer there was a fight and a rainstorm. God had mercy on His own, even when he didn't deserve it.

My roommates were surprised to see me. I had been there for a short time at the beginning of term; they had not seen me since. I got in around 11:00 PM. They were in their beds with lights out. My flinging open the door had them both in cardiac arrest.

A breaking voice queried, "Wwwho's there?"

"It's, Bo. You mind if I turn the lights on?"

Marshal said, "No, I'm not asleep anymore or likely to be now that you've scared me out of a year and a half's growth."

"Sorry about that. I just got into town."

"You here for long?"

"Just tonight and tomorrow night, I'm going to Menard State Penitentiary."

Without missing a beat, Marshal said, "At their request, I presume?"

I smiled and said, "Yes, as a matter of fact, but just for the evening." I opened the suitcase and took out the shotgun, his eyes bugged out when he saw it. "It might have been longer if I hadn't been able to get rid of this. My cousin gave it to me, and I'd forgotten about our going to perform in Menard, I've been sweating bricks."

"What, pray tell, are you going to do with that?"

"Take it home and shoot some cottonmouths out of our pond."

"When?"

"I don't know, next time I get a chance to go home."

"You're going to leave it here?"

"Yeah!"

"I hope nobody searches the dorm for anything."

"Why, have you done something you haven't told me about? Don't worry about the gun; just tell them it's mine. I'm going to take it home as soon as I can."

"It won't be any too soon for me!"

"Well, look at it this way, if somebody breaks into your room—at least you've got a gun."

From the far end of the room Jerry's voice muffled by the covers he'd pulled over his head, called testily, "Will you two shut up so I can get my beauty sleep?"

"Yes, indeedy, Jerry! If there's one thing the world couldn't stand—the shape it's in, it's facing you without nature having had the time to knit up the raveled sleeve of your face with plenty of beauty sleep." As I turned out the light, I said, "Nighty night! Sleep tight. Don't let the bed bugs bite, but if they do, take your shoe and beat them till they're black and blue."

There came a long rolling, "Phletttttttttuie to you!" out of the dark at Jerry's end of the room.

I ran into the steel side rail of my bed with my shin and had to hunch up while I muttered, "Hesekiah 12:12."

The next day on the way to Menard, we were forced by a traffic delay to buy lunch at a little country store. I got a two-pound bag of the new ruffled potato chips. Potato chips are one thing that Mom won't buy, and I love the things. When I love something, I like a lot of it. I ate the whole two-pound bag. About a half-hour later, the jiggling the bus was giving my innards became a serious problem. I stuck my head out the window and lost the potato chips along with everything but my socks. Now my head hurts and my mouth tastes as though the sanitation engineers responsible for a colony of gerbils are losing the fight for cleaner cages. Then, I had to request a roadside stop; the other end of my alimentary canal was sending code-red warnings of impending emergency evacuation. There was a homey looking stand of trees up ahead on the right. Eddy, who was driving, pulled over as close as he could. I still had about thirty yards to cover double time. Ah! Relief! But using strange leaves made me walk funny.

When I climbed back on the bus, Dr. Abrams dug into his emergency kit and produced a bottle of paregoric. He looked at me wisely and said, "Down the hatch, Bo."

I shook my head at the taste and muttered, "That stuff tastes like mud!"

"Bo, when one attacks life with unheeding gusto, one occasionally eats mud."

I said, "Profound, Sir, that is profound, but, Sir, I really hate it when people are profound at my expense."

The bus was slowly regaining its thumpa, thumpa, thumpa rhythm bouncing across the tar strips as I slid into my seat. The jiggling made my body bearly inhabitable.

Around three we pulled up to the gate at Menard. An armed guard escorted us around to a service gate large enough for simi trucks to pull through. The guards peered at the jumble of stuff and shrugged, they never checked anything—you talk about your Trojan Horse. We didn't have to lift a finger; a line of prisoners unloaded all the equipment. They even set it up for us; all we had to do was direct traffic.

We were doing **Wizard** first; Bill and I traded off playing the wizard's apprentice, but since I was under the weather, he did it. The guys at Menard were the best audience of the tour. They knew how to appreciate—there's just something about a captive audience. **Wizard** was well received.

After the matinee, they served supper. They rolled out the fatted calf or maybe it was road kill. A lot of road-killed deer got sent here. I was still too touchy in the tummy to try and taste anything—just the smell of food was enough to make me queasy. I was allowed to go away from the smell of food and sit in the warden's office waiting room. I soon read the two magazines that were there. I could see out through a glass door to a nice green lawn surrounded by a very high concrete wall. I tried the door and went out and was walking on the grass when one of the trusties came out and politely said, "I'm sorry, Sir, but visitors aren't allowed out here." He chuckled, jerked his thumb at himself and said, "We are, but you aren't."

That evening the best audience I have ever played to caught every pun, double meaning, and laugh that Mr. Will ever wrote into **Shrew**, and I think a few he never thought of himself. **Shrew** ran longer by ten minutes than any other performance, because we had to hold for the laughs, but no actor ever begrudges holding for a laugh.

Afterwards the prisoners loaded and repacked the bus, and guards went through and checked the bus for potential escapees.

We rolled out of there, headed for Carbondale; got in at two AM. I thought my poor roommates, but they had gone home for the weekend.

I awoke at ten-thirty, my long, self-caused fast had my innards yelling, "Check the throat, we think it's cut." I went down to the dining room and overate to the point of being uncomfortable.

I thought, *I've got two whole days, I'm going home.* I went back up to my room and wadded the shotgun into the middle of a ball of dirty clothes, taped my sign, "College Student, Need Ride to Anna, and beat feet to Highway 51 south. I got a ride with a traveling salesman. He drove fast, I didn't mind that, but he was a tailgater. He would pull right up with in eighteen inches of someone doing sixty and ride their bumper until he thought he saw a chance to pass. When he pulled out, I would swear he didn't clear the other car by a good coat of paint. He was an intense gum chewer, not much for talking—thank God! I don't think he could drive like that, chew gum, and talk, too. We did make good time though.

He let me out at the four-way stop. I went over to the Rexall and phoned home, no answer. I phoned Gene, no answer. Oh whoopie!

I walked to the catty-corner and turned my sign away from the road; I didn't want to go to Anna anymore, I wanted to go away from Anna as fast as possible. As soon as I stuck out my thumb, I got a ride to the edge of town where Highways 146 and 51 split. Naturally, I was let out on the 51 side. I crossed to 146 and stuck out my thumb—stood there for an hour, until our neighbor, Mr. Fount came along. Mr. Fount drove an old 1927 bug-eyed Chevy pickup, and he chewed tobacco all the time that he wasn't eating or sleeping. Daddy said one time, "I've never had the nerve to ask Fount about his love life, but I've always wondered, did he or didn't he chew during?"

Mr. Fount had the driver's side window down, and the side of the truck was crusted brown with years and years of spitting out into the wind. The seats had several spots scattered around, too. He wasn't always careful when he spit into the wind, at times there was a lot of blow-back. About half way home was one of those times. He cut loose and a gob got tangled in the wind, curled around and came winging back in—got me right in the left eye. You talk about smarting! That eye watered, and the right one watered in sympathy. I had to sit there wiping at both eyes with the back of my hand, which didn't do a whole lot of good. When he stopped at our road to let me out, I had to stagger out blind. As soon as he pulled back on the road, I dug my shirt tail out and wiped my eyes until I could see again.

The barn where I had kept Smokey while I was in high school was just across from our road. I carried my suitcase over to the barn and left it, I'll get it later when I'm in the car. I started the mile and a half walk home. When I came to Buford Johnson's place, he had a new dog. It came roaring out of his drive and took me by surprise. More by accident than design, I hit it on the nose with my fist when it jumped out at me. It went yipping back to the house, and Buford commenced hollering about leaving his dog alone. Kinda made me want to do the same for Buford as I'd done for his dog.

It was three-fifteen when I got home. I reached in my pocket for my keys and found I'd left them at the dorm. Being gone on tour I had left them in my dresser.

Well, if the folks aren't working nights, I'll get Dad's keys. They aren't due home for an hour and a half. I think I'll catch Smokey and go for a ride. I changed into work clothes and got some grain in a bucket and shook it as I whistled for Smokey. He looked up and began to trot to the barn for the grain. I brushed and saddled him while he ate. When he finished, we went out the gate at a run, down over the bank, and I pointed him at the ditch. He cleared it and came down in a belly to the ground run. Lord God, that feels good—it's been too long.

There's nothing like a running horse to put things right in my world. We made a circuit of the back forty and jumped a couple more ditches. At the far end of the farm, I pulled him down to a walk and headed back to the watering trough. It was running over! I tied Smokey and rolled up my sleeve to fish for the copper ball-float. It was crushed! Smokey! The little bugger! He thinks it's macho to stick his head under water and bite the copper ball, he's done it before. I twisted a piece of wire off the fence and wired the float arm up. Dad'll have to buy a new one. Smokey yawned to show what he thought of the whole thing. I swung up, and he started for the barn at a run. We jumped the same ditch again and pounded up the bank and around the corner of the fence leaning close as though we were cutting barrels in a show.

The folks had gotten home while I was riding. Dad was changing to work clothes as I came in. "Hello, Son. How's the tour?"

"Just fine. Dad, I've left my keys at school, and I had to hitch hike home from Anna, Gene was out somewhere. I left my suitcase in the barn at the highway."

"You going out tonight?"

"No, I'm tired, we got back to the University about two this morning."

"Well, we'll get your suitcase tomorrow, no use making a trip just for that."

"Yeah. I'm gonna sack it early tonight."

He smiled, "It's good to have you home, Son."

"It's good to be home. Oh, I almost forgot—you need to get another copper ball for the float switch on the watering trough. Smokey crushed it again."

Dad shook his head. "The little rascal! He gets bored with you gone. I'll have to build a box around it or something."

Sunday morning, the first thing I saw when I walked into Sunday school was Barbara Ann playing the piano. I had thought that being on tour and all the new experiences would have delivered me from her coils. The first part of the term was rough because she often ate in the dining room of the dorm. But touring had kept me occupied, and I could honestly say I hadn't thought of her more than ten or twelve times in the last few weeks. Now I walk through a door and slam, bam, I'm back on track wanting to run my fingers through that red hair.

Gene came in and sat down next to me. I said, "Where were you yesterday about one-thirty?"

He thought, and then said, "Uncle Harry came down with his new car, we were out trying it out. He bet me five dollars that I couldn't climb over the back of the front seat while he was accelerating from 0 to 60. He put a five in the ashtray and came to a dead stop. He said, 'When I say, go! You try to climb the seat and get this five before I hit sixty.' We tried it three times apiece; Dave almost got it once. That car's something else."

"What model is it?"

"It's a sixty-one Pontiac Bonneville. You coming over after church?"

"I better go home, I've got to go back to school this afternoon. Why don't you come over and ride up with us?"

"Well, Uncle Harry's gonna take Dave and me for a ride in his new Bonneville."

"Well, I'll see you the next time I get to come home."

Dad stopped on the way home so I could get my suitcase. When we got home, I went straight up to my room and hid the shotgun.

We had a quiet lunch and left to go back to Carbondale. Dad drove; the ride was peaceful. I thought as I sat there enjoying the quiet ride; somehow, it seems as though I live in two different worlds. I'm like some young bird that has flown from the nest, but occasionally comes back and sits in the nest. The only thing, his feet don't seem to fit anymore, and all the time he's there, he keeps trying to get comfortable there like he used to be.

Monday morning the yellow corn-on-the-cob rolled out for Murphysboro. The cast was like sailors back from shore leave, trying to get used to the shake, rattle, and bump of the bus after forty eight hours in quieter surroundings.

Harvey Yang, the good wizard in **Wizard,** as opposed to the evil wizard in **Wizard,** was Chinese American. To further confound his persona, he had a beautiful singing voice that was a double of Johnny Mathis' voice. He chuckled and said, "I've got cousins from Mississippi that look just as Chinese as me, but they speak with a southern drawl. It just blows me away to hear these Chinese faces saying, Y'all."

We kept priming Harvey to sing just one more song. It made the trip to Murphysboro bearable; nothing could have made it worthwhile. Harvey and Bill were my roommates on the road. They always put the three bachelors into the largest room with two twin beds and a roll-a-way bed. We took turns sleeping on the roll-a-way.

As the only non-drinker on the tour, I was the—designated—not driver, but what ever it took to keep the others safe in their condition person. In Harvey's case, it was to make sure that his contact lenses were out of his eyes and in the proper ends of the carrying case. Harvey said, "Bo, make sure I don't go to bed with my contacts in, no matter what I say at the time!" One of my greatest thrills was sitting on a drunk Harvey trying to pop his contacts out and into the right end of the container while he was trying to fight me off.

Harvey was a solitary drinker who drank to get drunk. He would get a fifth of Jack Daniels, a glass, a paper bucket of ice, and go into somebody's—you never knew whose closet and sit on the floor and drink the whole thing in the dark. The way I used to find Harvey was, at bedtime I would go from room to room listening outside closed closet doors for the slurred muffled voice of Johnny Mathis. When I heard him, I would open the door, and there he would be among the fallen coat hangers, ice bucket between his knees, singing at the top of his lungs in Johnny Mathis' voice. I would pry him out of the closet whether he wanted to go or not, herd him back to our room, sit on him, and squeeze out his contacts.

After Murphysboro, the next stop on the list was Vienna, (pronounced Vi-Anna). In southern Illinois, some places were more southern than Illinois—some places had their own pronunciations. Cairo, was Karo—like the syrup. Cairo, so verbal history has it, was the place picked to hold the secession convention when the eight southern most counties decided to secede from Illinois and the Union during the Civil War. Somehow they overlooked the fact that Grant was just across the Ohio River. When Grant got wind of the plan, he lined his cannon up, pointed at Cairo, and sent the message, "Go ahead secede!" Somehow, it just didn't seem like the thing to do right then.

Vienna was our last stop on the tour before Thanksgiving. We had four days off for Thanksgiving. The wives, sweethearts, and friends of the cast members decided to caravan the sixty miles between Carbondale and Vienna. Everyone in the cast had someone in the audience except me. The fever of anticipation was hotter than a pepper sprout. Our Petruchio, Will Grant, was married just before the tour began. The cast had agreed to go through the play like the set was on fire. The dialogue was being spoken trippingly on the tongue; until the end of the second act, there we went up. The exit line was missing; no one could remember what it was. We covered beautifully adlibbing like mad, but going nowhere. The rest of the cast was frantic, they wanted out of there, but I was calm and laid-back, after all, all I had waiting for me was a bus ride. As circle after circle of adlibs flowed desperately from cast member to cast member, after several minutes I realized to my horror, the missing exit line that would get us off stage was mine. As the wheel of adlibs spun slowly by, I injected the proper line. The play stopped. Everyone glared daggers at me. Will Grant, leaned over and whispered, "So you're the one!" Everyone thought I had done it intentionally.

My folks had to work Thanksgiving, so I spent the day alone in Carbondale. The dorm was mostly empty. The dining room only served the noon meal, but I was smarter than last year, I bought two meals—one to eat, one to go, so I would have something to eat tonight. Friday morning I didn't have to hitch, I caught a ride with the family of a guy who came back early to work. They let me out at the Rexall, and I phoned Gene. He came and took me back to his place, and we rabbit hunted until dark. He had a date that night so he and Sandy dropped me off at home. I watched TV and went to bed when the folks got home.

Saturday, Dad and I built a box around the float switch on the water tank. The way we built it, even if Smokey pretended he was a moose and went all the way under the water, he couldn't crush the copper ball. That afternoon, Dad took the new car in to the dealer to have it serviced. As we were waiting, Dad was leaning back against a wall with his arms folded across his chest, the sun broke through a tiny hole and lit up his face, and he closed his eyes. The unshakable thought struck me; he'll soon be dead—you've got to finish growing up in a hurry. The sun went back under, but that image stuck in my mind like a cocklebur.

Sunday morning Barbara Ann was home. She walks into a room and takes over my thoughts like she owned them.

Gene drove me back to Carbondale—we were in a nutty mood. Neither one of us could carry a tune in a bucket with a lid on it, but there we were singing at the top of our lungs. We ran through 'Tom Dooley,' 'On Top of old Smokey,' 'Down in the Valley,' and 'Red Wing.' Mile after mile passed by with sounds from two of the worst voices God ever put on this earth. If a cop had heard us, he would have pulled us over for being drunk, and he wouldn't have believed the tests when he ran them. He'd figure that nobody that wasn't drunk could stand to be singing that badly. Sometimes things hurt so bad you just have to do nutty things just to make it through, there ain't no going back or around, you just have to put your head down and plow on through. When Gene brought Sandy home Friday night, for some reason known only to her daddy, Sandy was now off limits to him. I didn't have anyone, but Barbara Ann could just walk through the room I was in, and there went all my good intentions of forgetting her. So we were rolling through the night towards Carbondale singing wretchedly. We had waited till evening church was over—it made the night shorter to get through. Gene let me out at the dorm, and as he took off, I could hear him start 'Tom Dooly' in that terrible voice of his.

As soon as I got to my room, I got my stuff and went to take a shower. School has made me aware of the modern comforts that I'd never known that I needed. As steam filled the shower, I began, 'Tom Dooly.' There was a rapid exodus of the other casual users—all except one old boy caught in the middle of getting relief from his constipation—he left as soon as he could.

Monday morning, we strolling band of players were bouncing along on our way to Highland. Will Grant, our Petruchio upon whose broad shoulders and vast energy our production was balanced, had come down with a cold. He was sipping bourbon, laced with lemon and honey, to keep his voice open. He and Duane traded off the role of the wicked wizard, so **Wizard** was no problem, but there was only one Petruchio. By performance time, the frequent small sips had brought Will to the playful stage. He had not forgiven me for dropping the ball in Vienna. He still thought I had done it as a prank. Will's revenge came in the scene where the introductions are made. My character, Grimeo, has a page-long speech introducing another character. Will knew all of the other speeches by heart. Petruchio has a similar speech just two speeches before mine. Will turned to me just before he began his lines, caught my eye, winked broadly, and gave my introductory speech. The whole cast knew what was being done as soon as he started. Everyone was holding his breath, because we were headed for disaster. I couldn't return the favor and simply give Will's speech because of plot problems, and I couldn't simply repeat the speech he'd just given. Everyone is looking around blinking like owls woke up in daylight. Bill, my roommate, gave his last line and looked longingly at the safety of the wings. I did the only thing I could do, I wrote some new Shakespeare. As I stepped forward to start this new Shakespeare, Will smirked at me as if to say, "Got Ya!" I launched into the page and a half of new Shakespeare I'd just composed, actually I was composing it as I went. Duane is watching me like a hawk because he has the next line and has to be ready to pick up on whatever I give him. Bill is still focused on getting to the wings. Will's eyebrows are pushing his hat up, and Eddy is saying to himself, "I ain't here and this ain't happening!" Harvey is hoping that because he's short, the fruit the audience throws will miss him and hit the tall guys. I got into the flow of the thing, and just for the heck of it, went on and on.

There was a blue-haired, little old English literature teacher in the front row that had been saying the lines under her breath along with the actors, she was going nuts.

When I finally finished, Will gave me a bow, the rest of them were just glad to get off the stage.

As we came off stage, Duane said, "Bo, when Will gave your lines, I thought, we're dead! Where did you get that speech?"

"I made it up!"

"You're kidding!"

"No, I made it up." He went off shaking his head.

Eddy came by and said, "Nice job, Bo!"

Harvey said, "I need a drink!"

Will never mentioned it.

Bill was stretched tighter than a fat go-go dancer's G-string.

Dr. Abrams just lit his pipe and smiled.

If I may quote Shakespeare, "All's well that ends well."

Waterloo is branded across Napoleon's record. It is also a town in Illinois, north of Chester and south of St Louis; it was the next stop on our itinerary. The usual play on word puns flourished and multiplied like rabbits. Some of the cast was singing the Johnny Horton song of that name—there is no depth so low that a bored actor won't sink to it to launch a pun.

The performances were neither great nor bad; we got through the afternoon and evening. I don't remember much about Waterloo except it was close to Belleville. Afterwards, one of our ladies invited the cast to her home in Belleville.

The tree-lined streets wound among the homes of the wealthy, but I was unprepared for her home. It was a genuine stone castle; built, we were told, by the W.P.A. workmen back during the 1930's. The cut stone exterior was impressive. Inside, it was decorated in expensive, understated good taste. For a country boy who came from a two-story frame farmhouse that only has electricity on the first floor, linoleum not carpeting, and no indoor plumbing, it was like something out of the Arabian nights.

They were gracious hosts; the cold buffet had as much food as an indoor church-on-the-grounds picnic. Being a non-drinker, I almost single handedly wiped out their entire supply of mixers; ginger ale just seemed to evaporate in my presence.

After everyone had consumed sufficient quantities of eatables, the Persian rugs were rolled back from the inlaid parquet floors, and the stereo was loaded up with dance music. Being a Baptist, I had never learned to dance—I had a sneaking suspicion that somehow dancing caused babies. I found a comfy corner and was enjoying watching the others. You can't get away with being a nonconformist forever. I was pulled to my feet, over my protests that I didn't know how to dance. The four ladies took turns trying to teach me to dance on the floor, not their feet. Slowly, I began to be able to avoid their feet, and finally, one of them taught me to dip; I was beginning to feel like an Arthur Murray graduate.

We have a travel day tomorrow, no performance, just five hours of thumpity thump here the bus come, thumpity thump there the bus go. At one-thirty in the morning we said our good-byes and trundled off to our motel.

We awoke the next morning to rain. We kept hoping that we could drive out of it, but the rain went before us all the way to Danville, where we have a seven-thirty performance of **Shrew.**

The rain made it hard to see, and the water on the road made it impossible to tell what the surface was like. The drivers switched off every two hours. The rest of us were hunched down hoping the ride would end before our buns died.

There came a tremendous crash and careening bounce as the bus fell into a large water filled hole you could have lost a VW in. Fifty yards further, and the bus quit; the motor still ran, but the wheels quit going around. We shuddered to a halt with the drive train making the howling noise of tortured metal. The driver coasted to the side of the road and put the flashers on.

A discussion led to the consensus that the bus is broken, and we aren't in Danville. The last sign I had seen, read, "Danville, 30 miles."

Dr. Abrams now began to earn the big bucks they pay college professors. He got out into the rain and began to hitchhike. This man of great dignity stood looking like a drowned rat with its thumb in the air. I had the ill-reverent thought, with his legs, rolling up his pants legs ain't gonna help. His face was not one to inspire warm regards. At first glance, it looked like it should be on a post office wall with large sums of money proffered for information leading to . . . etc. The one thing in his favor is the large corn-on-the-cob with its flashers on and several faces pressed up against steamy windows.

Some men look like college professors, but aren't, even if they do have a piece of paper that tells their students that they are. Other men couldn't look like a college professor on their best day, but they can teach. Dr. Abrams was one of the latter. There was an old saying in the theatre, "Those who can do! Those who can't do, teach. Those who can't teach, get another degree and teach teachers." Dr. Abrams was the exception that proves that maxim.

A pickup stopped; there were two people and a large dog in the cab. Dr. Abrams talked to the driver and then clambered into the back. He disappeared, head hunched, nose parting the rain like the figurehead of a ship.

We cranked up Harvey Yang and had a Johnny Mathis concert while we waited.

Two hours later, Dr. Abrams reappeared with another pickup, but this one had stock racks, and there were two station wagons following.

The plan was simple, take everything we needed to do **Shrew** and leave every thing for **Wizard** on the bus. We sorted things and loaded the pickup to the top of the stock rack and dragged over the top a tarp that had suspicious stains that emanated an essence of cow. It looked like a theatrical **Grapes of Wrath.** Our personal belongings went behind the rear seats of the two station wagons. Our bodies went into the seats.

We were twenty minutes past due for our performance when we pulled away from the bus. Dr. Abrams got to wait for the towing company. We were a wet and bedraggled group that looked like a flock of chickens whose roost has sprung a leak.

When we pulled up outside the high school where we were to perform, the sky opened up and dumped. I privately thought it was God's personal message about dancing—Baptist traditions die hard.

We got the stuff inside in spite of the downpour, and when we had enough actors dressed, we started the first act. Then, we discovered that we had left the lyre on the bus. It was the one prop that did not fit in the property trunk—we hauled it with the costumes for **Wizard**. Without the lyre, you can't do a big chunk of the second act. Bill and a couple of others were all ready on stage, and Bill never leaves the stage until the scene where Eddy's character staggers out on stage with the broken lyre around his neck. Kate has rejected his wooing in a most forthright manner.

Will Grant gathered the cast who were free at the moment; we cut Eddy's scene and speeded up our entrance. That meant that Eddy didn't have to appear again. It was muggy because of the rain, so Eddy changed into street clothes to be comfortable. As the actors came off stage, they were appraised of the changes, all except Bill, whose character was on stage until the cut. The first time Bill knew anything was wrong was when we made our entrance, there were more actors than there were supposed to be in that scene. Bill's eyes are switching back and forth, he looked like an out of control pinball machine as his eyes bounced from one person to another. I have never seen such sheer panic as when Bill caught sight of Eddy in street clothes, smoking a cigarette off in the wings. There were only two lines left to be spoken. Bill's face went from panic, to sheer terror, and finally resignation—the clenched cheeks of a schoolboy waiting for the teacher's paddle to fall. In this hopeless state, Bill gave his last line, all the time hoping the last judgement would be announced so he wouldn't have to go through this. He finished his last line with a desperate pleading look at us.

Will Grant smiled and adlibbed, "Sir, I would see your lovely daughter! Will you call her to us," (Will spoke slowly and distinctly) "or will you *go* and *send* her to me?"

Bill knew it was his time to exit; he had no more lines, and he had heard what Will adlibbed, his eyes shot from one to the other of us, we all nodded. Finally, the light dawned. He said so fast, the words ran over each other. "I'll send her to you, that's what I'll do," and he literally ran off the stage.

Bill was just glad to be off stage and leave whatever was going on to those crazy people on stage. Bill was shaking so badly that if he had smoked, he would have had to have someone else light up for him.

Eddy calmed Bill down and filled him in about the missing lyre. We finished this cockamamie performance hoping that there was no one in the audience that knew the play line for line.

It was a starved bunch of players that strolled into a cafe fifteen minutes before closing time and gave the waitress a heart attack. Well, it wasn't quite that bad, but she did get a run in her support hose. When that much flesh is compressed that much, and part of it pops free, it can be quite a thrill. Dr. Abrams showed up and was peeping in the window; the door was locked. She wouldn't let this strange dripping wet man in. She kept waving him away and saying, "We're closed."

Duane said, "Mam, he's the only one who's got the money to pay for this, you'd better let him in."

Dr. Abrams got two cheeseburgers to go and paid our bill. We walked to our motel, Dr. Abrams said, "We will be doing a performance of **Wizard** here tomorrow, since we seem to be stuck here until the bus is repaired." He raised a brown paper sack and said, "I bid you all a pleasant good night, I and Mr. James Beam and my lemons do not wish to be disturbed for ten hours, no matter what. If the world ends tonight, the Lord will find me. Anyone else, stay away!"

Somehow it didn't seem fair to me; I didn't party. Oh I was there, because there was nowhere else to be, but there. We three bachelors always had the biggest room, and the party was always in the biggest room. I never could get to bed until all the others left. Even then I wasn't through, I had to find Harvey, and mug him for his contacts.

The next day the troop straggled over to the cafe for brunch over a period of about three hours. I walked over around ten-thirty. One of the girls came in nursing the worst case of post party pain I have ever seen. She had on shades, when she took them off to rub her eyes, the sun glanced off a passing windshield, and she gave the driver a look of death to you, Sir, that would have made a junk-yard dog run yipping for his home under the tireless, up-on-blocks Oldsmobile.

I said, "Good morning."

She shuddered, and then whispered, "Please, Bo, not so loud! My head hurts, even my hair and teeth hurt."

A passing trucker blew his horn at an old lady in a Caddy, then jammed on his air brakes. There was the screech of tires, and then the piercing sound of air escaping as he released his brakes. Her eyes rolled back in her head, her hands white-knuckled as she gripped the table. She sucked in her lips, moaned, and ran for the ladies room. The ladies room was locked, so she ran into the men's room. A traveling salesman came running out zipping up and looking back. I heard the lock as she locked him out. The salesman still had his comb hanging in his hair, and his shirttail was out. He looked around, blushed, paid his check and left. When she came out ten minutes later, her complexion was three shades lighter with a slight greenish cast to it. She had her shades on so I couldn't see her eyes, but her hands were shaking. She went to the counter and ordered, "Coffee, black!" When she tried to pick up the cup and saucer, they sounded like castanets. She set them down and said, "Bo, could you?" I nodded, went over and carried the coffee back to our table. She came and sat down and carefully sipped from the cup without picking it up, paused and shook two aspirin from a bottle, bent over, sipped again and swallowed them. She sighed, sat back and said, "Bo, there must be a God, I know there's a hell."

I said, "Sheila, your worst day of life is better than your best day in hell."

She turned and looked at me, I couldn't see her eyes for the shades, but her lips were silently moving, so I figured she was trying to get the sense of that. We sat there about ten minutes before the waitress came over and asked, "You want anything?"

To be polite I asked, "Sheila, You want anything?" She gently shook her head. "Will the smell bother your tummy if I eat?" She nodded. I told the waitress, "I'll move over by the window to eat. I'll have the hamburger steak, hash browns, no eggs, cheese and fried onions on the side, and orange juice with rye toast." When I mentioned the fried onions, Sheila's nose got white and her lips curled under. I figured it was time to move.

It was Bill's day to play the Wizard's assistant, so I had a free day. The tractor place called, the bus was fixed, and I went with Dr. Abrams to pick it up. The tractor place had put one of their best men on it. The right rear axle snapped when we fell into that pothole. The tractor mechanic had crawled under the bus in a pouring rain because it was too big to fit inside the shop and removed the broken axle. He had driven a hundred miles in the rain to a junkyard, removed an axle, drove back, installed the replacement parts, and road tested the bus, all without sleep. Some of those good old boys are just that—real good old boys.

The play was over at five. We had the bus loaded by six-thirty. We pulled out to drive through the night to Peoria. It started to rain again and this held our speed down to forty-five. The windshield wipers couldn't clear the water off the windshield, and inside the driver had to run the fans; all those lungs pumping out moisture fogged the inside of the glass. Conversation was impossible over the thunka, thunka of the high-speed wiper setting, the fans, and the gurgle of water hitting the wheel wells. We couldn't use the overhead lights to read, because they blinded the driver's night vision. The dark, the motion of the bus, the whine of the fan, and the thunka, thunka of the wipers had everyone on the bus sound asleep. The driver had his side window cracked open so he could smoke, and he shifted his seating position every few miles as he fought sleep. I sat in the front seat right behind the driver and talked for a while, until I dozed.

It was a quarter of one when we found our motel. It had one of those port-coachery things across the front. Not quite awake, I realized it was three inches too low for us to clear. I tried to come up from my groggy state, but I was too slow. I got out, "It's too"-Crash-"low." Eddy had just streamlined the top of the bus. The port-coachery was slightly horrors de combat.

The clerk came running out in his sock feet, waving his arms. "You've hit the hotel!"

I said, "Hang a sign over that place that says clearance 7' 8", and you won't hardly notice that." He didn't smile.

I told Eddy, "If you'd hit this thing just a little bit harder, we wouldn't have to walk to our rooms." He didn't smile either. Attempted humor ain't what it usta' was. What the heck, I shut up and went in and got my room key.

There is a saying in the theatre world, "Will it play in Peoria?" This refers to the practice of taking new productions to hone and polish them before opening in New York. Peoria audiences are experienced theatergoers. We are doing both plays here, and it is my day to do the wizard's assistant. The man who wrote **Wizard** is a friend, and he wrote the part around my persona copying my speech and mannerisms. James had gotten the department to allow me to do the tour so that I could play this part. He knew that I was a tumbler and wrote a scene where the young would be wizard finds his master's cape that allows the wizard to fly. He dons the cape believing it will enable him to fly as well. He does, like a rock. In the beginning I had used a simple trip, fall, and roll to abort the attempted flight. This sort of worked, but it offended my sense of performance. Early on we had a responsive audience that was letting me know that they were enjoying the play. I pushed myself to give back something extra. When the time came for the attempted flight, I ran across the stage and launched myself as though I thought I really could fly. I did a hands first landing with my back arched to keep my chin and knees from hitting first, and used my arms as shock absorbers. It worked great! It gave the appearance of flight, and the fluttering of the black cape looked like wings trying to fly. The crash to the stage was so realistic that there was a gasp from the audience and the other actors watching from the wings. When I staggered to my feet, the other actors didn't know if I was hurt or not. I could see their wide staring eyes watching me. I turned upstage and winked to the wings to let them know that I was all right. Poor, Bill, once I had done it, he had to learn to do it as well. He was a far better athlete than I was, it didn't take him long to master it, once I had shown him how. A problem I had not foreseen, some of those stages were as prickly with splinters as a porcupine. I soon learned to curl the cape's edges around my hands.

In Peoria, after I did the attempted flight at the end of act one, I made my entrance for act two, and the audience arose en-mass applauding. I looked around bewildered, why were these people doing this; the play's not over? They aren't supposed to applaud until the end. I froze and looked at Duane who was the wicked wizard that day. Under cover of his cape, he whispered," Take a bow!"

I looked at him bewildered, "Why should I take a bow? I haven't done anything I don't usually do." I just stood there.

He whispered again, "Bow, damn it! Or they won't sit down."

I walked to the edge of the stage and bowed. I still didn't know why I was being singled out, why were they doing this? At my bow, the audience sank to their seats. I was lucky to remember the lines for the rest of the scene. Word of what had happened spread like wildfire backstage. I was nearly hugged to death by the rest of the cast. I still didn't know why this extraordinary transaction had taken place between audience and performer.

At dinner, Duane patiently explained, "Bo, there are two kinds of standing ovation. The usual kind is given at the end of a performance, but on rare occasions they give an en-performance-standing ovation. It's rare, but it sometimes happens when a performer has touched the audience with a particular scene."

The combination of a poor dumb country boy playing a poor dumb country boy had rung true, and the audience had responded with an outpouring of generosity, but I couldn't see what all the fuss was about.

I don't remember much about the performance of **Shrew** that night. I didn't fluff any lines, bump into any furniture, forget an entrance, I wasn't ovated, and nobody threw any fruit. As a critic said when asked about a particular actor's performance, "It was a performance!"

The next morning, we strolling band of players headed for Chicago. It had turned off colder than an apprentice witch in a summer weight bra. Eddy drove first and had the heaters cranking out their max BTUs. One of the under-seat heaters had a bent blade. It whanged on the frame about every third revolution. I went from heater to heater until I found the culprit, and Eddy killed the switch. Small problem, it was wired in tandem with three other heaters. We couldn't do without the others. I got a screwdriver and twirled the fan until I found the offending blade and reefed on that sucker until it quit banging on the frame. I told Eddy, "Okay, try her now." No more whang, just a loud roar. Once the heaters overcame the night's chill, people got warm and started to strip. Nothing serious, we had on so many layers of clothing that a person would have to lose fifteen or twenty hands of strip poker before they were in danger of becoming indecent.

We stopped en-route, and Dr. Abrams bought several large bags of cheeseburgers with fries and milkshakes. We ate our noon portion in motion.

Will, who was from Chicago, took over the driving at the city limits.

Our first performance was at North Lake. We arrived around two, and set up, and Bill did **Wizard**.

After the show we went to one of the upscale eateries, and there this country boy was introduced to a culinary delight I had never made the acquaintance of before—the baked potato with sour cream and chives topped off with bacon bits. I had had potatoes fried, boiled, peeled and mashed, hash-browned, baked with butter, au gratin, German French fried, (that is tiny new potatoes boiled in the skins and then deep fat fried,) and raw, but never with sour cream. We had fed sour cream to the hogs. I was so impressed that I ordered it for every meal.

Mom was good cook on most things, but what she did to a piece of cow was a shame; she either boiled it or chicken fried it. I had never had a flame broiled steak in my life. When it came time to order mine, I ordered it well done. The waiter's eyebrows flew up so far it almost undid his hairdo. He had about eighteen hairs left long on one side, that he swirled around across the front of his head like a river levee to hold back the baldness and keep it from running down over his face. My steak came last, the waiter said, "We had to beat the cook to get him to do that to a prime piece of meat. Said he was a Methodist and it was against his religious principles to offer up burnt offerings."

I said, "Mister, some of the steaks I've seen you put in front of people tonight weren't burned bad enough but what they might have recovered if you hadn't gutted them. At least this sucker won't moo when I stick a knife in it."

The waiter came back after the plates were cleared, "Would anyone care for dessert or perhaps an aperitif?" He looked at me.

I said, "What have you got to offer?"

"Vanilla ice made with fresh ground French vanilla beans."

And here I'd always thought that vanilla came out of a Raleigh bottle. Leave it to the French to soak beans in it and then grind them and make ice cream out of the mess.

The waiter beamed at us and said, "You may have it plain, with chocolate sauce or with cream de menthe liqueur," He looked at me and said, "You may have the cream de menthe only if you are over twenty-one! We're not allowed to serve alcohol to minors."

I didn't intend to get into anything with alcohol, so I said, "I'll have mine with chocolate sauce."

Howard said, "If we're over twenty-one, may we have both?"

The waiter gave a flick of disbelief with his eyebrows, "Both? Sir? Surely you jest!"

Eddy said, "I'll have my ice cream with five cream de Menthe, one poured over the ice cream and four on the side."

The waiter's eyebrows went into spasm, and his hair dam came loose on one side of his forehead as he said, "Five, Sir?"

The waiter was back in a few minutes with eight ice creams-cream de menthe, three plain, one with chocolate sauce, and four cream de menthe on the side. He regarded Eddy and said, "For the sake of my conscience, please wait until I have left the area before consuming the four cream de menthe." Eddy smiled innocently. The waiter bowed and left.

The on the side cream de menthe were passed to those whose ice cream was innocent. Three were immediately poured over the ice cream, but I left mine on the tray.

Duane said, "Bo, there isn't enough alcohol in that to matter. It's just for the taste of the mint." I left it sit. "Bo, there's more alcohol in the vanilla extract the ice cream's made of than the cream de menthe. It won't get you drunk, you couldn't stand the taste to drink enough to even get a buzz."

I finally poured the thimbleful of mouthwash colored syrup over my chocolate covered ice cream. "Hmm? Different, but I don't think I'd want six in a row."

That night after the performance, Bill and I were walking around the huge school complex, and two young guys came up and one of them said, "Hey, are you two of them actor people?"

The way he said it, I didn't know if they wanted to fight, mug us or what. I looked at Bill and he shrugged. So I kinda set myself and said, "Yeah!"

He reached into his pocket and pulls out a pen and a piece of paper and said, "Me and my friend here would like to get your autographs."

I said, "But we aren't anybody famous."

He shrugged and said, "Yeah, but who knows, you might be some day, and we'll have them."

The next day, Will Grant's father-in-law hosted a buffet lunch before the performance of **Wizard**. Their tasteful home was decorated with expensive understatement throughout.

I was eating out of my lap over an Oriental rug that probably cost as much as our whole farm. I couldn't relax the whole time, for fear of dropping something butter side down on that rug, or worse, drop a gold rimmed plate and turn a service for twelve into a service for eleven.

I felt like what I was, a gawky country boy come to town. I tried not to expose my ignorance before all these cultured people, but I was totally at sea as they casually threw out topics of conversation that included Picasso's blue period; cultural exchange, Lord Beaverbrook's latest endeavor; limited edition collectibles; the economy of Russia and the implications of their wheat crop shortfall on the futures market. The only things cultural I can speak about are the five plays I've been in, after that I'm down to horses, how to plow, how to make steers out of bulls, and what to do for a case of chiggers.

I heard someone remark to another guest, "That young man with the southern drawl is so quaint."

We left to do **Wizard** around one-thirty. I was relieved to get out of there without breaking anything, spilling my drink, or dropping food on that rug—well, their cat will probably find that little cube of chicken that bounced and rolled under the couch before it starts to smell too bad.

When I came out for the second act, the audience came to their feet again, applauding. This time, even though I had not expected it, at least I knew what to do. I walked to the footlights and bowed. Inside, I was saying, why me, Lord? Why is this happening to me? The first time, the rest of the cast was pleased for me, but this is going to set me apart—I'm not ready to be alone. There are others who know more, and the weight of the production falls on them, why me, and not them?

When I came off stage, there were congratulations, but no hugs, politeness rather than joy.

When I walked by Dr. Abrams, he smiled, nodded, and lit his pipe. There was some secret knowledge involved in his smile, and I wished I knew what, but I knew he wished me well.

At dinner, Duane said, "Bo, why don't you try your steak medium instead of burnt offering style? You're losing half the taste of the meat having it all burnt and dried out."

"I don't like the taste of bloody meat."

"Just try it, you can always send it back to the fire."

I thought, well, why not! When the waiter asked for my order, I said, "I want my steak medium and a baked potato with sour cream and chives. Oh, and some bacon bits if you've got them." I thought to myself, whoa, is the boy gettin' swave or what? Sour cream, and half-raw meat. Whoa!

Eddy's laughter broke in on my self-congratulations. "Bo'll be eating steak tartar next." The laugh went around the table, so I laughed, too, but I wondered, *what is steak tartar?*

This was Will's home ground, he had family and friends in the audience, and he was up, his energy level was fantastic. Will was delivering his dialogue rapid fire and over clearly enunciated. He had a tendency to spray spit when speaking, the footlights lit every drop, they glistened like sparks from a fourth-of-July sparkler. With all this extra energy, Will was a one-man fireworks display. Kate got wooed, tamed, and brought to heel in grand style tonight. The cast wanted the homeboy to shine, and we fed scenes to him. Will was magnificent.

We had booked into a motel that was central to the four big schools we were to play. Each night we got to go back to the same bed, all except Harvey Yang. His folks lived in Elgin, which had been a near-by small town, until Chicago grew out and ate it. His folks came after every performance and got Harvey so he could spend some time with the family. Harvey was the eldest son, or in the parlance of the Charlie Chan Movies, number one son. Harvey's folks ran a Chinese restaurant in Elgin. Harvey's birthday was the day after we were to leave Chicago for Michigan. After the show tonight, the Yangs were hosting a cast party in honor of Number One Son's birthday. We ate a large lunch and raced through both plays. Like the critic said, "It was a performance."

We arrived at the Yang's about the time they would have been closing on a normal night. The huge room was decorated Chinese style, except for a banner. **"Welcome Southern Players To The Celebration Of the Birth of Harvey Yang."**

We were mean to the boy; we made him sing several songs at his own birthday party. Harvey has one of those voices that make people sit back and purr. The little Yang-sters were brought in to meet everyone and then shooed off to bed.

We took our places at the long table and the waiters began to serve large platters of food. I had never been in a Chinese restaurant (they weren't thick on the ground in and around Anna.) It looked like they were serving family style, big platters of everything all at once. I loaded my plate and emptied it. The waiters took it away and brought me another one, and I was all set for dessert. I found out though, that had only been the first course, there were twenty more to come. I had made what I thought was to be my whole meal out of the first course. My momma raised me not to hurt peoples' feelings when I was in their home, so I ate past full, to pain. I ate until I thought they're gonna have to put wheels on me and roll me out of here. I was never so glad to see ice cream in my life; it meant I could quit. If some fool had suggested that we play leapfrog, hopscotch or musical chairs, I think I would have died right there. I had to move easy so my belly didn't get to bouncing.

The ride home at two AM on that bouncing Betty of a bus had me tasting food again, and it wasn't because I was burping, the food was stacked up and the last piece kept flipping up out of the hole. I liked to never got comfortable enough to go to sleep, but you know when I woke up at ten AM, I was hungry again.

Our last gig in Chicago is Orland Park. The day set out to prove why they call Chicago the windy city. The wind had blown the other days we were here, but today it blew in capital letters. I asked the waiter at lunch, "Does the wind ever not blow in Chicago?"

He said, "It quit once when I was a kid, and I fell down three times before I figured out what was wrong."

We had a heck of a time getting the scenery and props for the play into the building. One of the girls was carrying a curtain mounted on a stand, the wind caught her, and she was a block away and still gaining speed when we caught her.

They had some fencing foils in the dressing room, and I was lunging at a door pretending to be Errol Flynn, when Margie walked through, I nearly caused a blowout on the left side of her chest. Was I ever embarrassed?

I was getting ready to do Wizard, and thought, *boy am I glad I didn't have to do Wizard last night right after I ate. I can just see the headlines, "Front row at theatre chowmiened to death as young*

Bo Rogers crash lands while taking off. Thirty-seven second graders drown in tidal wave of chow mien as hundreds watched horror stricken."

That evening, Ol' Bo was cool as he ordered, "Steak medium, baked potato with sour cream and chives, and a side order of bacon bits."

Then the waiter asked me, "What dressing would you like on your salad, Sir?" That was the first time I had been asked that. I always just took what ever it came with, like at home—Mom didn't give any choices. I didn't know what to say and just sat there looking stunned.

Will smiled and said, "Bo, why don't you ask for the blue cheese?"

Blue cheese? That stuff that looks all moldy? Hoping that I hadn't been suckered into something yucky, I said, "All right, I'll have the blue cheese."

The waiter brought me my salad first and everyone was watching to see my reaction, I took a tiny bite, "Hey, not bad!" Now I had a whole new thing to ask for. My repertory is filling out.

After the meal Dr. Abrams gave a little speech. "People, we are getting a little sloppy. We need to have a rehearsal, but we won't have time before we arrive at the University at Ann Arbor. We don't wish to give less than our best at another university, but these people tonight have paid to see us, and they are every bit as deserving of our best. Tighten up the dialogue, project and keep your energy levels up. Now players go out there and break a leg, break both legs!"

I was determined to give it my all!

Grimeo, the rejected suitor, I should be able to play that blindfolded, I've done it so many times in real life, but the part drains me because I have to enter laughing and continue to laugh hysterically for two minutes. To laugh realistically so that the laughter would infect the front row and spread back through the auditorium is draining work. To do this, I have to stand in the wings and tell myself every funny story I've ever heard. I never failed, but it was always a worry until I felt the laughter begin to bubble up through my diaphragm, then it was all right, I knew they were going to laugh. The closest I ever came to failing was that group at the nursing home. I never got them to laugh, but two of them smiled. I left this part of Chicago laughing.

We had a seven o clock wake-up, so we made an early night of it. Ypsilanti, Michigan, is our next stop. Harvey was going home one last night and would meet us on the road in the morning. *I wonder who takes his contacts out at home?*

The next morning, the whole Yang clan met us in their station wagon—looked like the second coming of the Mongol Hordes. By the time Harvey had kissed them all goodbye, we were behind schedule. Will was driving the first leg, since he knew the way out of Chicago, and when he honked the horn as we pulled out, the Yang clan went crazy, I looked back and there were so many Yangs waving goodbye it looked like the station wagon was trying to fly.

The further east and north we drove, the brighter the day got, but there was a bit of a nip in the air. The familiar shake, rattle, and bounce of the bus, and the whirr of the heaters throwing off the chill of the night brought boredom, and the cards came out. Card players and non-players switched seats, a briefcase on a set of knees made a playing surface, and soon their exclamations were just part of the ambiance. Extra wink grabbers curled into the strange positions bus seat sleeping forced them to assume.

We changed drivers at ten. Eddy pulled out of the card game, and Will went from driver's seat to Eddy's seat in the card game and both game and bus rolled on with hardly an interruption.

We cut straight across the top of Indiana. At noon we changed drivers and twenty-four cheeseburgers, twelve sacks of fries, and twelve Cokes came on board as hitchhikers—they didn't make it to the Ohio border. We cut a corner off the top of Ohio.

The sky had cleared. The red in the gadget that hangs on the wall with numbers and hash marks all up and down it, was trying to change its shape from a red dot with a long skinny neck to just a large red dot that was huddled up for warmth at the bottom.

We had to turn all the heaters on. There was a head wind, which cooled the radiator coolant, which cooled the heaters. The heaters were on the high setting and loosing ground. Everyone put on all the coats and sweaters they could reach. The bus driver started to complain of blue feet. He took turns stamping first one foot to try and warm it and using the other foot to work the gas pedal. He switched positions so often he resembled a windsock in a whirlwind. Next we started switching drivers. We did this on the fly, which would have given a driver's education teacher nightmares, but one must do as one must. When we pulled into the University at Ann Arbor, the temperature was zero. We got our stuff unloaded and set up in record time. By the time we finished, everyone was finally warm. It was time to go dine, but it didn't feel like it, we had lost an hour when we crossed the time zone.

The nearest eatery was an Italian place that catered to university students. I have never been big on cooked tomatoes, and noodles are fine in soup, but not as a main dish, the only thing on the menu that appealed to me was the two-pound sub sandwich, but they were only two dollars with drink. Our supper portion of the per diem was four dollars, it was not transferable—we had to use it or lose it. My Scots soul rebelled at that, so I ordered two. When they came, they were enormous. There was enough food there to feed the whole Yang clan. I ate both of them, and felt almost as full as I had after Harvey's party. I thought, *thank goodness I don't have to do the flying scene next*, but I had forgotten about the laughing scene. Trying to laugh hysterically while uncomfortably full—it was a new lesson in theatre craft, eat light or you can't push your lines beyond the second row. **Shrew** was an exercise in mind over body, body won—mind is a blank. After the performance, I left Harvey to get his own contacts out and went to bed.

The next morning a satisfying session with nature put me in a great mood. Those who had spent the night imbibing liquid stimuli found my cheerfulness a drag.

"Harvey? Where is Harvey?" "His bed had not been slept in, and his contacts were not in their proper compartments. "Oh my, oh dear!" I went from room to room peering into closets, no Harvey! I went back to our room, checked the shower, no Harvey. Harvey, also, was not under the beds. I sat down to think. I tried to think like Harvey, no, like Harvey drinking. I noticed a door that I hadn't tried. It was a kitchenette, and there sticking out from under the curtain of the pan storage cupboard under the sink was the toe of a shoe. I pulled the curtain back; Harvey was under the sink. An empty bottle of Southern Comfort lay by his side, and the paper ice bucket lay on its side between his knees, the ice was a puddle, it had run under him. His head was cocked up on the lower shelf. His left hand was hooked through the sink trap, and one leg was shoved in among the pots on another shelf. Asleep like this, he looked about twelve. My first impulse was to get him up and into bed, but to do that I would have to wake him, and then I would have to deal with a very owly Harvey. Either way Harvey was going to be miserable until about two. Leaving him where he is was going to be easier on both of us—for a while.

Dr. Abrams had set up an account for the troop to sign for our meals in the motel's coffee shop. I got the biggest breakfast they had. Sheila came in. Her eyes looked like two cigarette burns in a blanket. She started to come and sit with me, but my large breakfast arrived and the smell of food made her swallow hard with her lips thinned out so they were turning white. She peeled off and went and sat by herself. "Just coffee," she said to the waitress who set a filled cup before her. Sheila shook out two aspirin, chased them down with coffee, lit a cigarette and sat waiting for the aspirin to kick in. She looked as though if the aspirin didn't kick in soon enough, she might try to bite herself to death.

Eddy came in and looked at Sheila and came and sat with me. He nodded over at Sheila and said, "Poor Sheila, if she had to sell herself for what she feels she's worth this morning, she wouldn't get enough to pay for the gas to kick over a piss-ant's motor scooter."

After breakfast, Eddy and I went out to start the bus. Eddy stuck a sheet of cardboard in front of the radiator to keep the cold air off and try to help the heaters. He had plugged the block heater into an extension cord, but I had to spray ether up the air cleaner's nose while Eddy cranked the motor. It finally coughed to life and sat missing for a couple of minutes before it smoothed out. Eddy pulled out the hand throttle, and we left it to warm the heaters before we had to get on board.

When I got back to the room, Harvey's kidneys had forced him out from under the sink. He was in the bathroom checking to see if he was still among the living, or if there really were walking dead. His contacts had floated around on the lid, and he was trying with shaking hands to right their orbit and get the lens back on track. When I said, "Harvey, you better hurry if you want to get anything to eat." He shuddered and then held his head.

I went over and got a large coffee to go. I spooned in six sugars and signed Harvey's name. When I gave Harvey the coffee, he sat and held it in both hands, I said, "You better get ready, we're going to leave for the university in about an hour." He opened one eye, blinked and groaned. I sometimes wonder if there is intelligent life on earth at universities.

The bus pulled out around eleven-thirty, Harvey's body was on board. If he'd been laid out in state somewhere, he would have looked death-like instead of life-like as morticians are fond of saying.

Sheila got on board, she was quiet, her aspirin had kicked in and the desperate look was gone.

We went to the university, and the Theatre Department took us, as guests, to the Student Union for lunch.

It was my day to do **Wizard.** Our audience was made up of children from the area's schools. We had fun; the kids had been to performances before.

After **Wizard,** the Theatre Department hosted us at one of the area's better dining establishments—the food was better than chow, it was cuisine. The meals had been pre-ordered and were all the same: Veal Cordon-Bleu, peas in chicken broth, carrots julienne-en cinnamon glaze, and Pommes-de Tere-frire de Fromage. A nine yard phrase for French fried mashed potatoes with cheese and toasted onions.

The dessert was ice cream with honey and cinnamon coated pecans and brandy sauce flambé, I loved watching the waiter light off the brandy, he did it with such flair. With last night as a warning, I ate moderately, but I asked the waiter for the potato recipe to take home.

We walked out of the warm dining room, and my nose hairs froze together, it was ten below zero. Eddy had gone out and started the bus so it was warm. Dr. Abrams rode in the head of the Theatre Department's car, and we strolling, band of players followed in our yellow corn-on-the-cob. It was a good performance of **Shrew**; the fact that the audience contained our peers had a stimulating effect on us.

The Ann Arbor Theatre Department made up a ten-car caravan and followed us back to our motel. We three bachelors have the largest room, so we were elected to hold a five-minute-till-curfew party. On Friday night curfew was 1:00 AM. We started off with about fifty people in our room, but gradually small groups went to the other cast members' rooms.

I acted as a waiter and did whatever needed to be done. About a quarter to one, a big blond farmer's daughter, big doesn't really do justice to the girl—she was over six feet and weighed three hundred pounds, she reached out and plucked me from where I was standing. She said, "I want this one!" She had me flat on my back and was sitting on my chest before I knew what was happening. Once she was sitting on me, I couldn't move, except to wiggle my toes to see if I could still feel them. She held me with one hand and tossed off her drink with the other. I had no idea what was next; one thing was for sure, I wasn't going anywhere. Whatever she had in mind was probably going to happen unless I got some help from somewhere. She hollered, "Hey, somebody refill this glass!" and held it up.

A guy with a pitcher came and said, "All that's left is Tang. You want Tang?"

She looked at him and said, "Tang? What's Tang?"

"The orange flavored drink the astronauts drink in space."

She screamed with laughter, then she shrieked, "Tang, Tang, I want some Tang." She bounced on my tummy in rhythm to the Tangs. The guys from the curfew sweep up crew came and were shooing people out to the cars. Three of them got her by the arms and tried to lift her off me. She shifted gears, and Tang changed to a chant of, "Poontang, poontang, I want some poontang! Get me some poontang!" The biggest guy in the sweep-up crew grabbed her from behind and lifted for all he was worth, as she chanted, "Poontang, poontang, I want some poontang!"

The guy grunted, "Come on Loretta, you're sitting on the biggest pile of it I ever saw!" It took every guy in the place to lift her off me and get her out the door. After a minute, I sat up and checked to see if everything was still there. If we had been there alone, she would have held me with one hand and peeled me like a grape with the other.

I started to clear the glasses, bottles, and empty cookie cartons off the bed so I could go to sleep. Two ladies walked into the room. One had hair so black it had blue highlights, she was about five four and well endowed. She was wearing a Stuart plaid kilt. The other was a skinny blond with shoes that looked like Minnie Mouse's in the cartoons. I said, The cars are leaving for the university, it's almost curfew time."

The one in the kilt limped over, and I noticed she had her right knee bandaged. She pushed softly against me, and said seductively, "We're not from the university," it was a double meaning that even I could understand. I thought, *what's with these crazy Michigan women?* Other people started coming into the room, I got busy clearing the trash and bottles off the beds, so one could sit or lie down without battering your anatomy.

Bill came in and perked up when he saw the kilt, and Will came in right behind him carrying a blanket and pillow. He said, "I'm bunking in here with you guys."

Bill asked, "What happened to your bed?"

"Sheila's in it."

"Why is Sheila in your bed and not her own?"

"Because her roommate has an old boyfriend from SIU staying over."

I said, "I thought Lynn was engaged?"

Will grunted, "She is—all night." Will caved into Harvey's bed—heaven only knows where Harvey is.

Bill and the kilt had melted into Bill's bed, and the blond Minnie Mouse was circling me with hot beady eyes. Desperately, I sloshed back the dregs from a glass of bourbon, choked and almost swallowed it before I could spit it back out. I just wanted the smell on my breath. I began to play a drunk. She circled closer and closer and the closer she got, the drunker I got. In desperation I started talking about horses, sat down astraddle of the arm of the chair and pretended to spur and fan. "You ought to of seen me ride in the Anna Bronc Bustin' Rodeo."

She sweetly said, "Buck, I know you can ride anything with four legs and hair, but what about two?"

"Two?"

"Two legs!"

In my best drunken cowboy I said, "Naw, not enough hair," and hic-cupped. Somehow, I just didn't want my first time to be with Minnie Mouse, but she walked over and jerked me off the arm of the chair and on to my bed and started kissing me. She may look like Minnie Mouse, but she sure could kiss. I have kissed several girls and one or two were even willing, but I have never been kissed like that. She moved around to my ear and anatomical changes began to become apparent. I rolled over on my stomach to get away from that warm insistent tongue and started to snore like I had passed out. Two more minutes of ear wash, and it would be all over but the guilt. She worked valiantly to revive me, *Lord help me if she finds out what she is doing to me.*

Harvey walked in and turned on the lights and stood blinking, looking from one bed to another looking for a place to lay down. He looked like a stoned owl. The blond got up and went over to Harvey and said, "You're cute! Let's go out to my car and get it on!" Harvey and the blond went out. Bill is moving rhythmically in his bed, and Will is snoring. I heard a car with glass-packs start up outside and settle into a fast idle.

When Harvey and the blond came back thirty minutes later, Bill and the kilt were dressing. The blond told the kilt, "I ain't never had a Chinaman before!"

The kilt said, "Let's go somewhere and get something to eat."

The four of them left, and I got up and took a long hot shower. Other people might think I'm crazy, but I had noticed a white place where a ring had been; other men's wives—the Bible says that they are a snare for a young man's soul—I'm glad I passed.

The four happy campers came back around six. There were long passionate good-byes just inside the room. Then Bill and Harvey went out with the girls, and the car with the glass-packs started. Bill came back and got into his bed, and Harvey went to his and found Will in it—the turkey came and got in with me. He was so cold his shivering was shaking the bed—oh well, I'm not sleeping anyway. I got up and packed my suitcase and went to breakfast. I had just ordered the big breakfast when Duane came in. He laughed when he saw me, "How did it go with the girls?"

"What girls?"

"The ones I saw go into your room."

"You'll have to ask Bill and Harvey about that." He raised an eyebrow—somehow, even though I'd done the right thing, I felt guilty. I fumblingly said, “I didn’t have any protection, I didn’t want to catch some disease.”

Duane smiled and said, “Bo, you don’t have to make excuses. If you didn’t want to, you don’t have to explain, that’s your business and nobody else’s.”

At eight, we pulled out of Ypsilanti and headed for Vandalia, Illinois.

We had lunch at a catfish place on the Ohio River, outside of Cincinnati. We had all the catfish and hushpuppies we could handle, then we mounted Old Yeller and trundled across Indiana to Terre Haute, where we dined for supper. We remounted the Old Cobb and trucked on through the evening, arriving at Vandalia around 10:00 PM. All of us were so tired that we willingly donned our Winnie-the-pooh jammies with the feet and went night-night. Harvey even took out his own contacts.

The next day was Sunday, an open day for us. At breakfast, Will said, “Bo, your hair is getting so long you’re going to have to swing from a tree limb to go to the bathroom.”

“Well just when have I had a chance to get a haircut?”

Lynn said, “Bo, I cut hair. Come over tonight, and I’ll cut your hair.”

The weather was so cruddy I stayed in the room and watched TV. At noon, Harvey came in the middle of a movie I was watching and without a by your leave he went over and started switching the channels, and then went into the bathroom and started to shave. He had about a half a load on, I think he’d tried to drown a hangover. I got up and changed back to the movie, and he came boiling out of the bathroom half shaved and took a swing at me. I ducked and came back up with Harvey in a crotch lift ready to pile-drive his head into the mattress. The door opened just then, Sheila was bringing our forwarded mail to each room. Sheila shrieked and threw mail all over the room. “You guys are fighting!”

I said, “That is true.”

We both helped Sheila pick up the scattered mail. Sheila waved an envelope that emanated perfume. "Harvey, after the other night in Ypsilanti, I don't know if I should give this to you, it's from Elaine, she thinks you're being faithful."

Harvey was just drunk enough to be maudlin, he started blubbering and sat down and read it through twice and then wrote a long (five pages) letter to Elaine.

After supper, Harvey was drinking ginger ale as he joined the whole cast in Eddy's room to play cards. Lynn and I were the only non-card players and I told her, "Lynn I'll take you up on your offer to cut my hair."

She said, "Shower and leave it damp so the curl is out of it and come over to my room."

When I got out of the shower, I just pulled on my jeans, stepped into my shoes, grabbed a fresh towel, and trotted on over. Lynn had spread newspapers on the floor and set the vanity bench in the middle of the papers. As she moved around, I became aware that she had on a cashmere sweater with nothing under it. The movement of the sweater was driving me nuts. When she moved around behind me, the 'sinsation' of soft caressing warmth waggling against my bare back heightened by the sensual texture of cashmere put my system into overload. Then she said, "Turn around so I can clip the front." I know that a young gentleman is supposed to look into a young lady's eyes, but at that range her eyes didn't stand a chance. That much feminine pulchritude at that close proximity—it would have taken a bolt of lightning to bring my eyes back to her eyes. As she worked, the fascination became overwhelming; I slipped my arms around her waist. She looked at me and smiled and asked, "What do you think you're doing?"

I smiled back, "Putting my arms around you."

"Why?"

I gave her a candid answer; I had not yet learned to tell them what they want to hear. "Because I want to make love to you."

"Why?"

"Because I'm horny!"

"That's not a very flattering reason."

"You're beautiful, and I want to make love to you."

She laughed and said, "Let me finish cutting your hair first." When she finished cutting, she turned the mirror so I could see what she'd done. Then she told me, "Go into the bathroom and shower off that loose hair."

When I finished showering, the papers were gone, and she was standing with her back to me. There was something pensive about her. Without turning she said, "I think you'd better go now."

"I don't want to."

"Well, I want you to."

"Do you?"

She nodded. I slipped my arms around her and reached up and turned her face so that I could kiss her. She shook her head until I kissed her, and then suddenly she started to kiss me back. I picked her up, and still holding the kiss, carried her to the bed. As I eased her down, the door burst open and Sheila came in blind to the world. We rolled apart to the edges of the bed, and Sheila walked straight to the bed and flopped face down between us and began to snore.

I looked at Lynn, she laughed and said, "Better luck next time, Bo," and threw the towel at me; I went back to the bachelor quarters and took a long hot shower.

I was paired off with Will playing the wicked wizard. Duane usually did it when it was my turn. Dr. Abrams felt it would give us all a boost to have to play against different styles. Will was far more razzle-dazzle than Duane. He was unpredictable and kept me on my toes. Working with Will was like dropping your chewing gum in the chicken yard—made you examine everything very closely before you picked it up.

We were back in the area of small towns. The kids only came to watch Shakespeare because it got them out of school, and most of the men came because their wives dragged them off their tractor seats early. Why the wives came, well I guess it was a hangover from high school literature classes where Shakespeare was held up to be the ultimate—you may not like the stuff, but it's the best there ever was. I say that because I regarded Shakespeare that way until I saw Marlon Brando as Mark Anthony. Brando, in contrast with the gifted English stage actors who were renowned for their handling of the English language, was a human being living out the pain of having a friend murdered. When he gave the, "Friends, Romans, countrymen, lend me your ears," speech, for the first time I understood the humanity of Shakespeare. It was a lesson in how to act—if people can't relate to you as a fellow human being, I don't care how great your command of the English language, you will never touch their souls, and if you can't touch the soul, you will never take them with you to feel what it is like to be the character. Soul is the ability to communicate so that others can empathize.

The towns left on our itinerary were like the last verse of a trucker's song, Taylorsville, Shelbyville, Newton, Carmi, Marion, Sparta, and last and perhaps least, Wolf Lake. After the performance of **Wizard** at Wolf Lake, one of the guys I had met in the FFA came backstage to see me. We said, Hello," and I noticed that he was looking at me in a speculative way. He finally, said, "Bo, I thought you were bigger. When I was watching you up there on stage you seemed bigger."

"Carl, when I'm on stage I act bigger, and people think I am bigger."

"Oh, I see!" He went away happy with that answer.

We had the weekend off. After the corn-on-the-cob deposited us at the theatre in Carbondale, we unloaded the sets, props, and set up ready for performance, grabbed our personals and fled. We had five more performances of both plays, but that was next week, now all we wanted was space from each other.

I went to the dorm and made my roommates so happy they could just spit. They had gotten used to me being gone and having more space.

Saturday morning found yours truly with suitcase in hand with a sign taped to the side, "Help Me Get to Anna!"

A fat, cigar smoker who thought he was macho picked me up. His condescending conversation irked me. "You a college kid?"

"Yeah!"

"You college kids got it knocked! You don't have to work for a living like me!" I thought, *Buddy, I'd like to have your fat butt on the other end of a stand of lights going up three flights of fire escape in five above zero weather, except I'd probably have to drag you back down by the heels when you passed out.* He started to brag about how quick his sexual conquests were, then he asked me, "You getting any kid?"

"Well, I consider anything under an hour a quickie, if you can't last that long you're just wasting the lady's time."

He never said another word until he let me out at the Rexall in Anna.

I called home from the Rexall. Mom answered, "Hel-lo?"

"Hi, Mom, it's me." I figured since I'm an only child she can tell which one I am.

"Hel-lo Worry Wart!"

"I'm in town at the Rexall; any chance of a ride home?"

"Well, your dad's picking corn, and I've got a cake in the oven."

"Is that a yes or a no?"

"Well, Smarty-pants, that's a maybe."

"Is that a firm maybe?"

"It's getting more iffy the longer you talk." She laughed and said, "I'll be there in a little over an hour."

"Thanks, Mom!"

I had an hour to kill. It was noon, I could eat, but I didn't want to spend the money. Being on tour had spoiled me; I'd gotten used to someone else picking up the tab. There was a gas station on Main that sold a cheap chocolate candy bar for just three cents. They tasted like chocolate flavored wax, but they were filling. When I had consumed three of the imitation candy bars, I went back to the Rexall to wait. The druggist was bored, when he saw me come in, he called, "Hey, Bo. You hear the about the guy who came in here the other day with the hiccups?" I shook my head no. "He walked in and I was busy restocking, and my helper said, 'Yes, Sir?' The guy is hiccuping between every other word and he says, 'Can you give me something for my hiccups?' and my helper says, 'Sure!' He threw a dab of this and a pinch of that into a Coke cup and mixed it up and gave it to the guy, and said, 'That'll be fifty cents.' The guy paid and drank it and left. When I came back up to the front he told me about it, and I said, 'There ain't no cure for hiccups that I know of; what in the world did you give him?' 'He said, 'I gave him oil of wintergreen, one ex-lax cube, caster oil, cod-liver oil, and some bran-fiber.' 'You what? That won't cure hiccups!' My helper said,' You want to bet? Go look out front, the guy's out there hanging on to a parking meter; he's afraid to hiccup!" The druggist is turning red from laughing at his own joke. When he got his breath back he started again, "There's this hearse going up Main. Some old lady pulled out in front of him, and he swerves and runs up on the sidewalk to avoid hitting her. The door pops open when he hits the curb and the gurney flies out with a body in a casket on it. The gurney rolls back down the street, jumps the curb, and the gurney legs collapse when they hit the step. The coffin flies off and slides down the aisle, hits my counter here, and the lid flies open, and the body sits up and the guy says, 'Doc, can you give me something to stop this coffin, it's killin' me!"

He is doubled over and red in the face. I chuckled twice to be polite. I guess every profession has its own jokes.

Mom pulled up outside and saved me from dying of attempted apothecary humor. When I got in, she said, "Well, Worry Wart, to what do we owe the pleasure of your unannounced company?"

"We finished the road trip, and I have the whole weekend off. Next week, we're going to do both plays in Carbondale."

"Well, it's good to have you home!"

"It's good to be here, but I thought you would be working today."

"We traded days with another couple so they could see their daughter, we have to work tomorrow."

"Maybe I should have called, well, I'll call Gene tonight and maybe he can run me back."

Dad was picking corn in a small creek bottom, as we drove by on the way to the house, he was down at the far end. He had the team trained to pull down a row without any driver. He just yelled, "Git up Jack," and they would start. He walked along side the wagon picking and shucking corn and throwing the ears in the wagon. When they had pulled ahead far enough, he'd yell, "Whoa, Daisy," and they would stop. He only had to grab the lines on the turn around. I changed into work clothes and dug out a pair of work gloves. Shucking corn was murder on your hands.

When I joined Dad, he smiled and said, "Well, you made it! How's your tour going?"

"The road trip is over, we're back in Carbondale. We're doing both plays for five days there."

"You gonna be out of school early?"

"No, we have to write a paper about what we did; that's the final exam. Any time we have left, we'll be assigned things to do around the theatre."

"Your trip go well?"

"Well, the bus broke an axle outside of Danville. The professor had to hitchhike in the rain in the back of a pickup. And in Michigan it got down below zero, and we couldn't keep warm on the bus. Eddy put cardboard in front of the radiator and got us warm. But all in all, it was a good trip, but I'm glad to be back home."

When we reached the end of the last row, we both got on, and Dad drove up and backed around to the grain room, and we took turns scooping the corn out of the wagon. I pulled Daisy's harness and hung it while Dad unharnessed Jack. We rubbed them down with sacks, and as soon as we turned them out, they rolled and undid our work.

I called Gene, and his mother said, "Gene is somewhere with his Uncle Harry and won't be back until late tomorrow night." It was looking like I might have to drive the truck to school and hide it.

Something was missing at Sunday school. It took me quite a while to figure out what it was. Barbara Ann wasn't playing the piano. The lady who took her place wasn't nearly as good. I hadn't thought of Barbara Ann in weeks; who knows, maybe there's hope for me yet.

My buddy, Gary, was home, and if I could go home and get back by one o'clock, I could ride to Carbondale with them. I dashed home and threw some clothes in the suitcase, ate a cheese sandwich, and dashed back. I called Dad from the church and told him, "I'm leaving the truck in the church parking lot."

On the ride back, Gary said, "I've met a new girl and next week I'm bringing her home to meet my folks and visit our church."

I had seen them eating in the dining room at the dorm. She was really pretty, some guys have all the luck.

Marshal and Jerry are saddened that I really am back and they are going to lose all that extra space. Oh well, into each life a little rain must fall.

The theatre was dark Monday, we spent the day rehearsing both plays. We couldn't do a less than perfect performance in our home theatre. We opened Tuesday with **Wizard**. Bill and I flipped for the extra performance, Bill won, I had to do it. I didn't mind, I'd just as soon be working. Both plays went well all week. Word of the two 'en-performance standing ovations went through the theatre, we tour people were treated like favored children. People were wishing us well, and we were invited to two parties—I was sick of parties, but I went to be polite. I made an appearance and ducked out.

Saturday night was the end; I was sad to lose contact with these people in whose pockets I had lived so long. I went to Saturday's party to say goodbye.

Bill had brought his car up, his girlfriend, a cheerleader from Anna, had brought a friend for me. My date smoked, and her breath turned me off. The party was a bittersweet time of saying goodbye.

It took me four days to write an essay answering the questions Dr. Abrams posted. I got a C+ on the essay, and an A for the tour. I was assigned to the scenery shop, where I built flats and risers until Christmas break.

The folks had to work Christmas Day. I spent the day riding Smokey; took a pack of hotdogs and rode to the sinkhole spring where Gene and I had thrown the belt of machine gun ammo into the fire without counting them. Smokey got some Christmas, too; I'd hauled along a sack with hay and a couple of ears of corn. "Merry Christmas, Smokey old buddy!" I built a fire in the same place to roast hotdogs and have my own Christmas celebration. *What am I going to do with my life? I would like to be a professional actor, but I don't know how one goes about doing that.*

CHAPTER SEVENTEEN

You Could'da Heard an Ant Pee on Cotton

A notice went up on the theatre bulletin board:

A NITE OF STUDENT PRODUCTION!
WRITTEN, DIRECTED, ACTED, AND
SETS DESIGNED AND BUILT BY STU-
DENTS, AN ALL STUDENT NITE!
THREE ONE ACT PLAYS
OPEN CASTING! COME ONE, COME ALL!

The student directors had heard about the standing ovations, they let me know that any part in their productions I wanted was mine. Nineteen is too young to have people start to fill your head with the idea that you are something out of the ordinary. I felt personally that what had happened was an accident, and I would never be able to live up to what had happened.

I had a ball reading for several parts. I had picked the part of a wisecracking basketball coach in a play about a bond drive to build a sports center at the expense of the educational departments. As I finished reading for this part, I was sure I had the part because the people had been in stitches as I read with my sarcastic deadpan delivery.

As I came off stage, a foreign grad student spoke to me in an accent so thick you could cut it with a knife. "Mistare Ro-jares, I would lik' for you to reedt for my play."

I was dismayed to be trapped like this, but Momma had taught me to treat all people with respect, never to mock the foreigners or anyone less fortunate. So I said, "All right, Sir." He handed me a script, and I glanced through it. It was a deadly, talky play, grim, stark with only small amounts of humor splashed around like mud. I thought, *This is a turkey*! I tossed off a reading and handed the script back.

He said, "Thank you, Mistare Ro-jares. My name is Soby Kalman." I had heard about Soby, he had been a student at Budapest when the Russians invaded, he had fought tanks with rocks, and got out of Hungary two steps ahead of a firing squad.

"Bo Rogers, goodnight Mr. Kalman." I thought*, that throwaway reading of mine would discourage him from wanting me.*

The next night, somebody banged on my door and yelled, "Rogers, you're wanted on the phone." I ran down to the phone in the first floor hall, thinking it would be Paul, the director of the play I wanted to do. "Hello?"

My stomach did a flip-flop as the broken English of Soby Kalman came over the phone like the croak of Poe's raven bringing bad news. "Mistare Ro-jares, ze othair directors haf agreed since I haf only two characters to allow me to choosh first. I haf chosen you to play ze part of ze derelict in my play. Vill you do it?" My stomach felt like a bar of lead lay in the pit of it; I was being trapped into doing this deadly play, but if I turn him down, he'll think it's because he doesn't speak good English. He'll think I'm prejudiced, I've got to do it. Grimly I said, "Alright, sir, I'll do it."

"Mistare Ro-jares, ve vill rehearse in Room 120 at ze speech building beginning tomorrow night at six-thirty."

"I'll see you there, sir." I hung up and gave vent to my frustration with several "Blast-dang and cruds." Just what I did not want to spend the next four weeks doing. "Well, I gave my word; I'll have to keep it."

I went into Room 120 and found Allen Mathews waiting there. Allen was to play the banker in this grim gem.

Soby came in right at six-thirty, and asked, "Do you know each othair?"

"Yes, we do!"

Soby gave us scripts, and the three of us sat at a table and dissected the lines for meaning. This was the first time I had worked this way. Usually I was on my feet stumbling my way through the lines discovering the meaning by accident as time wore on. It became obvious to me that I did not understand the play; I was nineteen and knew nothing of the failures that so desperately drive a man in his fifties. As Soby walked us line by line through the play, the more I found out about the play, the more I hated it. The play was not fun!

Soby took tape and marked the outline of a jewelry store: the alcove here, the windows, and the door here. Soby built the performance he would have played, through me. When I asked, "Why aren't we rehearsing on stage?"

He replied, "I don't vant anyvon to see it yet*!*" I thought, *I don't think I ever want anyone to see this thing.*

The lines were committed to memory, and Soby began to add business and movements to flesh out the characters. I still didn't understand it. No, that's not true, I still couldn't relate, this character was as foreign to me as a chimpanzee.

Dress rehearsal forced us out of Room 120 to flaunt our sins before an audience—our little piece of hell was the third play of three. *Oh great*! I thought, *send them home with a bad taste in their mouths.*

I watched the part I had wanted to play being done in a way that if anyone had asked me what I thought, I would have answered "That was a performance!"

Our set was wheeled out. It was the first time I had seen it, much less worked on it. We didn't do makeup for dress rehearsal just costumes. The casts and crews from the other two plays were our audience. I spoke the lines the way Soby had taught me and made the moves he had directed, and when we finished the play, the applause was deafening. I looked at Allen, and he shrugged. The curtain opened for us to take our bows, and the other casts and crews kept on applauding. I thought, *all right you guys, enough is enough, don't put us on, knock it off already!* People started coming up on stage and saying, "You guys did a fantastic job!"

They were all so positive about the performance that I thought, *maybe there is something to this turkey that I don't see—maybe I won't be embarrassed by it tomorrow night.*

The grand night came upon us and the house was packed—they even had folding chairs in the aisles—the fire laws were being stretched. The front row was filled with newspaper people, and photographers and the heavyweights of local society. If Carbondale had had a king, he would have been there. My only comp ticket I had given to Tom, my dorm father. You couldn't get a ticket for love or money, well, maybe love, but definitely not money.

The first two plays received thunderous applause. The play right before us got a lot of laughs, and then it was our turn. The audience was so enthusiastic I was hopeful that we would get away with this turkey.

TIME HONORED is a play about a loser who has failed at everything. He is the sweeper in a bar supper club where they feed him leftovers and allow him to sleep in the storeroom. His one friend in the world was a cat. The bartender fed his cat fish-bones, and the cat choked and died. He beat the bartender severely about the face and lips and was fired. He is now homeless and is walking in the rain checking for cans to turn in, when he chances upon a banker huddled in the alcove of a jewelry store to protect his custom-made suit.

My character assures the banker that he means him no harm, just wants someone to talk to. The banker listens to the man reminisce about his life on a farm before he was injured and had to come to the city to survive. Once assured the man means him no harm, the banker listens with sympathy and talks to the man. The man is hoping for a friend, someone who cares about him. Once the rain stops and the banker is no longer a prisoner to the salvation of his suit, he leaves, giving the man ten dollars. The man had read too much into the banker's willingness to talk, and as he realizes that he hasn't really made a connection, that no one cares one way or the other about him, he breaks the jewelry store window, waits until the police arrive and then runs—they shoot him.

As the lights go to black and the curtain fell, there was absolute silence—no applause, no weeping, no laughter, no nothing! As a friend from Texas was fond of saying, "It was so quiet in there, that you could hear an ant piss on cotton."

I stood behind the curtain stunned—they had been generous with their applause for the other two plays. Then I got *mad—I knew it! This thing is a turkey! I never should have done it—I knew from the beginning that I shouldn't have anything to do with it.* I turned and ran to the dressing room and tore off my costume and dressed to leave. I was putting on my shoes when the stage manager burst in—"Bo, get out there, they're tearing the place apart!"

"I don't blame them, I'd be mad, too, if I'd had to sit through this turkey!"

He gaped at me, "What do you mean?"

"They never applauded at the end. The curtain came down and there wasn't a sound."

His mouth snapped shut, "Bo, get out there, they're on their feet giving you a standing ovation!"

"But there wasn't a sound?"

"Damn it! They were too stunned to make a sound, but now they're on their feet applauding you. Get out there, now!"

I ran with my shoe strings flapping. Allen was standing there waiting for me. The stage manager opened the curtain, the house lights came up, and it was true they were on their feet. When we walked through the curtain the applause rose to a roar. Allen stepped back behind the curtain, and I turned to bring him back, but the crowd said, "No. We want you!"

I was bewildered, what on earth was happening? They stood and applauded for fifteen minutes. I tried to bring Allen back again, but he wouldn't come.

Finally, the critic from the Southern Illinoisian held up his hands and asked the crowd, "Please sit so we can interview the young man." When they were seated, he turned to me and asked, "Young man, would you sit on the apron? What is your full name?"

"Beaulieu Rogers, Sir."

"Your age?"

"Nineteen, Sir."

He went into grandiose flights of hyperbole, and threw around words like genius, brilliant performance. I couldn't grasp what was happening—I mean, I hadn't even understood the play. They ought to be giving Soby this ovation—this was his performance.

For forty-five minutes the audience savored the afterglow of the performance as though, if they let go of it, it was gone from the earth. Something had happened here, something that they had been apart of—something that only happens a few times in a lifetime—they knew that most likely they would never experience its like again. I was left feeling as though I had stolen something, something priceless.

Tom, my dorm Father, was waiting in the hall of the dorm for me to come in. He thanked me for the ticket and invitation, asked me to sign his program, then pinned it to the dorm bulletin board, and wrote across it, "A perfect performance!"

I went to bed, but sleep never came, I relived the evening over and over all night.

A full page spread came out in Saturday's Southern Illinoisian; there were pictures of me. Again, I felt as though I had stolen something.

People brought that paper to Dad at work and asked, "Now that you've got a famous son, are you going to quit work and live off the fat of the land?" Dad just smiled, and Mom snorted something under her breath that no one caught.

I saw Dr. Abrams as I was walking to class. He gave me a thumbs-up and his smile almost split his face.

Dr. Moe brought me back to earth. He said, "I don't know why people liked your performance, I don't think it was as good as all that!"

I raised an eyebrow and replied, "Neither did I!"

He had the grace to look shocked.

CHAPTER EIGHTEEN

Rubber Doesn't Twinkle

Barbara Ann cut across my bow like a clipper ship—an odd simile for a southern belle, but she was neat, crisp, and coolly collected. Then there was all that red hair. She was as easy for me to ignore as a blooded horse at full gallop, mane and tail afloat. More and more I was seeing her in the company of a tall geek who had a mouthful of teeth like crooked fence posts—they leaned every which way, and he was so skinny he had to stand twice to throw a good shadow. I will give him one thing—he was funny—I mean that sincerely, he had a great sense of humor, and his timing wasn't bad either. I had hoped the tour had cured me, but seeing her under full sail every day had brought on a relapse. I had the virus again.

The Baptist Student Union was having a get over the mid-winter-blues party. I came up with the theory that women seem to want what they couldn't stand when they see another woman take it, ala the dog in the manger. What I needed was a drop dead gorgeous date, but one who couldn't care less. I saw Lynn at class, and she seemed to fill the bill perfectly—she was engaged, she was drop dead gorgeous, and she was a friend, but if I dropped out of her life tomorrow neither one of us would shed any tears.

I asked Lynn if she would have lunch with me. Over lunch I explained my plan and asked, "Lynn, would you go to a party with me?"

Her peals of laughter drew looks from the other diners and she lowered her voice and said, "Bo, that is such a hoot! Yes, I will, quote, be your date for the party."

The party was on Saturday, so bright and early I hitched home and brought the car back. I arrived dressed in the sport coat that the smell of gardenias was still embedded in from a year ago. It wasn't strong, but occasionally the sent wafted out. I timed my arrival at Lynn's to be ten minutes early. When I pulled up, I noticed a Fifty-four Ford that had been chopped, channeled, Frenched, and everything on it was chromed. The paint job was seven coats of lacquer over metal-flake—a veritable rolling fortune. The big chrome wheels and chrome lake-pipes gave it a macho look. I sat in my car admiring it, not that I would want it, but when someone puts that much time and money into something, it should be looked at. I had one foot out of my car, when the door to the house flew open, and Lynn shot out of the house and around my car in curlers and housecoat. She gasped, "Go get me some cigarettes and come back in fifteen minutes." I opened my mouth to ask questions. She said, "Don't ask. I'll explain later." She ran back into the house.

The license plate holder said Belleville. The light dawned! I muttered, "Oh ye of slow perceptions hasten thee from here post haste, before you get your hindmost quadrant in the grinder," and drove away wondering if my date was a lost cause. I found a gas station, bought cigarettes and used the bathroom. I've found that one faces pucker factor situations better with an empty bladder.

I gave it a good half hour before I presented myself at the front door. Just to be safe, I had parked two blocks away only after I had driven around each block within three blocks in every direction—even went up the alleys looking for the Belleville tricked-up Ford. If by some chance he was still there, I would ask for her roommate.

Her roommate answered the door and said, "Oh, hello, Bo. Come on in, Lynn's getting ready."

I handed Jo, her roommate the cigarettes, and said, "She might need one of these about now."

When Lynn came in, she looked gorgeous, just what I had in mind. She said, "Let's go, I'll tell you about it on the way." I opened the car door for her, and she slid over by me when I got in. She said, "That was Roger, my now ex-fiancée. He came down to get things straightened out—I gave him his ring back."

"I'm sorry."

"It's okay, I haven't worn the ring since Ypsilanti. I didn't feel I had the right after what happened with Walter. Well, I realized that I didn't want to marry Roger when I feel the way I do about Walter."

"If you'd rather not go out tonight, I'll understand."

"No! I want to be with someone or I'll just drink, and I don't want to start that."

"Does Walter care about you, too?" She nodded. "Then why don't the two of you get married?"

"Walter won't marry me, because he's dying—he knows he only has a short time. The specialist can't say how long, but not more than a couple of years. Walter has had open heart surgery, and there is nothing more they can do." We drove to the party in silence.

Barbara Ann never even looked in my direction—she had eyes only for her tall friend. We ate the too sweet cake and drank the too sweet punch. Baptists seem to make up for their lack of alcohol with sugar. It's no wonder that a lot of Baptist girls grow up to be ladies of size. There are two sins Baptists haven't been able to beat into submission with their list of don'ts—gluttony and gossip.

"I have enjoyed all of this situation I can stand, Lynn, we could still catch the movie at the drive-in, would you care to go?"

"Why not!"

The movie was **The Alamo** with John Wayne. I had been to it before, but I had never seen the movie—I didn't see it this time either—Lynn needed to be held. Things never went as far as they might have—because there were just too many people in that car—Barbara Ann was there, along with Roger, and Walter, and I kept seeing Walter dead. The evening ground to an end by mutual consent around 1:00 AM. She didn't have to be in, but old habits die hard—besides the movie was over—the drive-in people wanted us to leave.

I walked Lynn to her door and kissed her goodnight—she asked, "Bo, you want to come in?" I shook my head—I just couldn't bring myself to add to the sack of emotional rocks she was carrying. Lynn went home at the end of the quarter—she never came back. I heard later that she had a nervous breakdown.

***

Barry Stavis had written a new play called **Banners of Steel**. He came to SIU to see it in production before attempting Broadway. Dr. Moe is directing, I wondered how we would get along, as he seems to have developed a dislike for me or my work or both. He selected me to play two separate small parts. The play concerns the acts of the pre-Civil War murderer, John Brown. It focuses on his raid on Harper's Ferry, his capture, trial, and execution. I played one of his merry band of murderers in the first act and his executioner in the third act.

Dr. Abrams is teaching my acting class; the man is one of the greatest scene-stealers I have ever had the privilege of watching. His face was as mobile as silly putty. Just by moving his eyes, and always in character, never anything unrelated, he could steal the scene from anyone. I watched and learned to take a scene at will—to make an audience watch me. In class I was assigned the role of the young rejected lover in Checkov's **The Seagull**. The scene is where the young man has crudely killed a seagull and brings it to his intended and is refused. The part fit me like a glove—I played it many times in real life. I knew what the character is thinking, because I have thought it myself. On the afternoon that my scene is to be performed, I prepared by using sense-memory, where you relive in your mind an episode similar to the one you are to play. You use the emotions dredged up from the storage vaults of your soul to play the current scene. When I finished, the class was stunned, and then they burst into applause. Marjorie summed up the class's reaction when she said, "Oh, my God!, that's Checkov!"

Between puffs on his pipe, Dr. Abrams said, "No, my dear, that's Bo—he plays everything the same way!" His timing was impeccable. He built up the ego to the bursting point, paused, waited until the ego was at its fullest, and then deftly pricked it to deflation.

That evening, Dr. Moe changed my costume twice, trying to keep my minor character from overpowering the principals. He changed my blocking three times. The final blocking had me with my back to the audience most of the time. He still wasn't satisfied, but there wasn't anything more he could do. Soby watched in amusement. During a break when we were sitting together, he said, "Bo, you are one of the best physical actors I've ever seen, if you develop your speaking voice to match," he didn't finish, just shook his head.

After a while, I asked, "What is wrong with my speaking voice?"

"It's untrained, and you have a heavy accent—people can't understand you. You don't always project and sometime you don't speak clearly, listen to yourself on a tape recorder." This came as a shock, I had never heard my voice on tape. We don't know how we sound to other people. When I first got to hear myself, I couldn't believe that that was my voice.

The publicity started to bring sharks to circle me. Ladies who once wouldn't have given me the time of day were suddenly there—the bored daughters of wealthy fathers who had shipped them out of Chicago to get them out of town so that past deeds could be, if not forgotten, at least not currently worried about. I met one such young woman, who let me know that she was available if I wanted her. We had three or four dates and things were progressing to the point that the Saturday before I opened in **Banners of Steel** on Tuesday evening, I was going to get the car, and we were going to a motel. Friday night was a lighting rehearsal. In the scene where I am among the last of John Brown's party at Harper's Ferry, I'm running from window to window firing my gun, at one point I exit and dive back in through a window. The marines break in and bayonet me and a couple of others, and then beat Brown senseless and capture him alive.

Eddy, my buddy from tour, is playing the marine who charges screaming across the stage and bayonets me. As Eddy's bayonet crosses a baby spotlight that has been left on by mistake, it twinkles. I thought, *rubber doesn't twinkle. Naw, couldn't be . . .* We were using an eighteen-inch, civil War, rod bayonet reproduced in rubber that would bend against my body—I always took it straight on. I stood facing a screaming Eddy as he lunged at my guts with an eighteen-inch bayonet. Inside, a little voice said, "Move!" I twisted to one side, the bayonet slit my shirt in two places, put a scratch across my stomach, and pinned me like a bug to the theatre wall. The tip of the bayonet was sticking out into the hall on the other side of the wall, if anybody had been leaning there it would have killed them, and actors often awaited their entrances there. When Eddy saw what had happened, he threw up.

Dr. Moe starts yelling for lights. His investigation shows that all the rubber bayonets have been replaced with steel ones. We assume that it is a simple accident.

Saturday evening, when I got back from home with the car, I went to pick up my date, but she's not at the dorm, her roommate says, "Cathy is at the library."

When I walked up and said, "Hello, Cathy," she got up and ran. I followed, she turned wild-eyed and said, "Please, get away from me, don't you know I'm engaged to Jack Washington?" Jack Washington is, I realized, one of the prop-men. She gave me a terror stricken look before she turned and ran out of the library.

I heard later that she married that murderous gentleman—she was warm-blooded, and he could be cold blooded. I hope they enjoy each other to the fullest.

CHAPTER NINETEEN

The End of the Twine

Since I don't have a date, I headed down Hwy 51 just fast enough for the adrenaline to chase the poor-me blues away. At Anna, I drove out to the hospital and switched the car for the truck. The speed limit from the hospital gate to the city limits is thirty-five, and I'm doing forty; a long black limo comes roaring up behind me at high speed and runs me off the road. A guy as big as the side of a house gets out, so I took the jack handle with me as I got out. He eyes the jack handle and mumbles something about hospital security.

I said, "Mister, you mess with me, and you'll never walk right again. Get back in the car and leave me alone." He tried to stare me down and gave it up and got back in the car, and left at high speed with his headlights out. When I told Dad, he shook his head and said, "They probably saw my name on the side of the truck and thought it was me."

He left it like that and wouldn't explain.

Sunday, as the folks drove me back to Carbondale, we stopped at the Dixie Burger and got lunch to go. While we were waiting for our order, Dad said, "Son, you're getting your picture in the papers quite a bit, and people are starting to make a fuss over you. Keep your head and don't believe all they say—if you believe it all, it'll set you up for a fall. Son, give God the glory, everything you have is a gift from him."

At the dorm, I kissed Mom and she said, "Be good, Worry Wart!"

I said, "I'm always good, but sometimes I'm better than others." She made a face at me. "Thanks, Dad!"

"All right, Son, we'll see you." He pulled away, and I stood and waved until they turned the corner.

I put my stuff in my room and went up to JD Hardy's room. I knocked and at his "Come in," stuck my head around the door. "JD, you going shooting anytime soon?"

He said, "What are you doing now?"

"Let me change my jeans, and I'm ready to go."

"Bo, I'll be by your room in fifteen minutes."

JD pulled his car in by the sandpit. We set up targets at twenty-five yards, fifty yards, and one hundred yards. We shot twenty rounds apiece at twenty-five yards, twenty rounds apiece at fifty yards, and ten rounds apiece at one hundred yards. JD scored 95 at twenty-five yards, and I scored 65. He scored 85 at fifty yards, and I scored 40. At a hundred yards JD, scored 65 and I scored 50. It seems I can see better at that distance than I can at fifty, but JD has the best hunter's eyes I have ever seen. We were walking side by side as we went back to the car, JD put out his hand and stopped me in mid stride. He pointed, "See the rabbit?"

"What rabbit?"

"Look down my arm!"

I peered along his arm. "I still don't see anything!"

"Look for the eye to blink." I waited for something to twitch, the little black orb winked, and then I could see it, but JD had seen it at a fast walk.

JD and I went to a smorgasbord for supper; his having a car opened up opportunities that were out of reach to me on foot.

Banners of Steel opened to a packed house. The cast in this play was so big they had added an epic projection to the stage. It stuck out beyond the procienum and replaced the four center seats of the first two rows.

The scene where the marines storm John Brown's stronghold seems to have a puckish muse—opening night, the actor playing the lieutenant of marines had not received his jackboots until just before his entrance. He had only worn them from the dressing room to the stage. The leather soles and heels were slick. In the fight scene he and John Brown are engaged in personal combat, the encounter takes place as far down stage as the epic projection will allow. The two men were surrounded by the audience. The lieutenant lunges with his sword, and Brown counters with the butt of his musket, and the lieutenant's foot slips. The actor breaks wind in the most uproarious fashion—the poor man's face turned so red he glowed.

One of the other actors was a printer on the Egyptian (the student paper) he set up a dummy front page to the next day's paper:

> LIEUTENANT FARTS JOHN BROWN TO DEATH!
>
> Last night on the stage of the Southern Players Playhouse, a new and deadly armament was used with devastating effect. The lieutenant of marines, played by Jed Hunter, used an unfair tactic while engaged in mortal combat with John Brown. During the exchange of thrust and counter thrust, the before mentioned lieutenant took unfair advantage with the use of a deadly fart. John Brown was so confused by the unorthodox tactic that he was easily overcome. Continued on page 8.

This outrageous gem of practical joking was propped up at Jed's dressing table. It was authentic in every detail, except it wasn't real. When Jed walked in and saw this paper, he almost cried. We had to show Jed a real paper to convince him to even appear.

Jed made sure the soles of his boots were well rosined before the performance—now he squeaks with every step, and each boot is in a different key.

When the offending sound occurred, I was laying on stage dead. I suppose people wondered why a corpse was shaking with laughter. Two nights later, the same scene, but at the end, there is a grandiloquent speech by the lieutenant that is delivered as the lieutenant, John Brown, and a marine are marching in lock-step sideways toward the stage right wings. They are to exit via a set of removable steps. Those steps are removed when not in use, because they block backstage traffic. The two marines have John Brown at arms length between them. The lieutenant is at mid stage when the first marine steps off into space, because the steps aren't in place. The first marine fell pulling John Brown after him. The lieutenant made an airborne exit from mid stage. The lieutenant's last line ended with, "This great land." He had started to say the word land, when he flew to his exit. It became, "lan-n-n-d!" There was a loud crash, the lights flickered, and a single loud, "Shit!" came floating from the wings.

I was lying with my face upstage facing these actors when they disappeared. I almost strangled trying to hold in my laughter. The light booth brought the stage to a sudden black rather than the usual slow fade.

In my second part, as captain Avis, John Brown's executioner, I was leading John Brown to his death, and the baby spot that had saved my life was left on. When I hit my marks for the scene, the spot picked out my face and turned me from stage prop to a man of sympathy as I observed Brown prepare for death. Dr. Moe and the lighting people had some unkind things to say after the show—thus further enhancing my reputation as a scene-stealer.

Dr. Moe saw me one morning and called, "Bo, would you step in to my office?"

"Yes, Sir?"

He seemed agitated. "Bo, do you still have your script for **Time Honored**?"

"Yes, Sir."

"Don't get rid of it yet." That's all he said, and mystified, I went off to my next class.

Two days later, he stepped to his door as he saw me pass and called, "Bo, would you come in?"

"Yes, Sir?"

"The theater department and the University have decided to send you to Lawrence, Kansas, to represent the University at the National Drama Festival. I might add, over my objections. I don't feel that you're good enough to represent us, but I was overridden, and you are to go." I stood there with my mouth open, blinking. "See Mr. Kalman for the schedule of rehearsals. The Festival is one month from Friday. Any questions?"

"No, Sir."

"That's all then."

Thank you, Sir."

"Don't thank me, I had nothing to do with it."

I left not knowing whether to whistle, go blind or wind my watch. The last time I did this play was a fluke—I don't know if I can do it again.

Soby left a note to meet him at five. We began rehearsals in a small room again. It took a week to get the lines back. They put the set back together under Marjorie's supervision, and trucked it to Kansas, a week in advance. We were assigned a lighting and sound technician to go with us and take care of the lights and sound.

Allen and I buckled down and the same feelings were coming back—it began to seem that there was a chance to pull this turkey off.

Three days before we were to leave, I was in the library to study, Meggan the girl I had shared a locker with in high school, walked in and sat down beside me. My heart almost stopped. Over two years since I had seen her—I had thought that I had forgotten her, but my guts are strung tighter than a cheap guitar. "Hello, Meggan."

"Hi, Bo."

"When did you start school?"

"Just this term, my baby is old enough that I can leave him with my husband."

"What are you studying?"

"Home economics education."

"How have you been?"

She looked at me and said, "Just fine! How about you?"

Lying like a dog, I smiled and said, "Just fine. I'm going to Lawrence, Kansas three days from now to represent the University at the National Drama Festival."

"Good luck, Bo."

"Thanks." I got up. "I've a rehearsal, but I'll probably see you from time to time."

"Perhaps."

"Well, goodbye, Meggan."

"Good night, Bo."

I went to another part of the library to study, I still had a half-hour before rehearsal. I couldn't study, Meggan crowded in. A mother! She's a mother! Oh, God! Why now? This was the one place I thought I was safe from those memories—seeing her will keep reminding me that she's gone forever. Rhyming lines kept intruding, so I started writing them down.

She has the kind of a face
Time can't erase
From my mind.
She comes back
Time after time
To haunt my mind
Though many times
I've left her behind.
She tugs at a thread

Unravels my head
Brings the dread
I've come to the end
Of the twine.
She has the kind of a face
Time can't erase
From my mind.

Beaulieu Rogers 1962

The five of us left for Kansas in a University-owned Mercury stretch limo. Everyone was older than I, so I was left out of the driving, We drove through St. Louis, across Missouri and Kansas to Lawrence. The University of Kansas at Lawrence is like Rome—it's built on hills. Each building was perched on a hill. The students weren't allowed cars—on campus you walked. There were no fat people at Lawrence.

Marjorie had friends she could stay with. Our sound tech was black and a member of a black fraternity. He assured us, "My fraternity brothers will put us up." Since we were representing the university, I couldn't understand why the university wasn't springing for motels, but they weren't. Thank God, the fraternity was gracious to us.

The Drama Festival was a one-day affair. Twelve universities were entered. The university at Lawrence had a large auditorium with a stage designed for band practice built across one end. A total of five hundred people from the competing universities were scattered around an auditorium built to accommodate several thousand.

This was the rudest audience I have ever seen in a theatre. They were playing cards, talking at the top of their lungs, running and chasing each other, whistling, and laughing out loud at their own jokes, often aimed at the people performing at the time.

I got some idea how the early Christians must have felt while kneeling in the arena to pray, hearing the roars of the wild animals before they were loosed to rend and tear.

We broke at noon to eat a cafeteria lunch, it was no better than ours, school food is school food. We resumed at 1:00 PM, at three it was our turn. I looked out from behind the curtain at the rabble we were to play to, and bowed my head and prayed: "Lord, help me do my best, and give us a chance to be heard. Amen."

Soby and Marjorie oversaw the placement of our set while Ed, our sound tech set the lights and plugged our sound system into their board.

The curtain opened with Allen in place in the storefront. Thunder rolled and the lightning flashed, and the sound of a downpour started—the audience was as noisy as ever. I made my entrance and played with a trashcan lid under a downspout while I searched for cans. Then I saw the banker and started toward him. The sound in the auditorium began to die off. By the time I gave my second line, the audience was still—my prayer was answered. The whole auditorium got still for the first time today. When I was shot at the end, there was absolute silence, no moving, no coughing, no laughing, no nothing . . . Then the place exploded in applause!

Paul Baker, head of the Drama Department of the University of Texas at Baylor, climbed the steps to the stage and spoke to the audience, "Ladies and gentlemen, I believe that there is no question that this is the finest acting we have seen here today." The audience applauded wildly.

I changed into street clothes and went out into the lobby. Soby followed me out, and we stood quietly trying to absorb what has happened. A gentleman came up and offered his card. He was from A.C.T. in San Francisco. He offered me a contract, but I had two more years in school. I turned him down, but when he found that Soby had directed this production, he offered it to him as well. Soby took the contract, which meant he was going out of my life, but he had taught me how to touch people's souls, make them care, even when they didn't want you to.

I had wondered the first time I had done this play if I had stolen Soby's performance; but today had taught me that the interpretation might be borrowed, but the power that shut that rowdy audience down and made them applaud, was a gift from God.

THE END

BVG